I was looking for Bart. They told me he was dead, but I knew it wasn't true. He was alive, but I could not find him. I pursued shadows down the dark streets of dreaming, shadows that sometimes paused long enough to give me a glimpse of shining gray eyes, or let me hear an echo of mocking laughter.

The dream that night was one of the worst. He was so close I could have reached out and touched him when my feet went out from under me and I fell, down, down, through thick fog into infinite depths, lit far below by a ruddy glow of fire.

The Grey Beginning

Look for these TOR books by Barbara Michaels

THE GREY BEGINNING
HERE I STAY

The Grey Beginning

BARBARA MICHAELS

TOR

A TOM DOHERTY ASSOCIATES BOOK

THE GREY BEGINNING

Copyright © 1984 by Barbara Michaels

Reprinted by arrangement with Congdon & Weed, Inc.

First Tor printing: October 1985

A TOR Book

Published by Tom Doherty Associates
49 West 24 Street
New York, N.Y. 10010

ISBN: 0-812-52252-4
CAN. ED.: 0-812-52253-2

Printed in the United States of America

0 9 8 7 6 5 4 3 2 1

To Linda, without whom this book and a number of others might not have been completed on time

I know my own way back.
Don't fear me! There's the grey beginning.

—Robert Browning, "Fra Lippo Lippi"

Chapter One

FROM THE Piazzale Michelangelo you can see all of Florence. In the sunlight of late afternoon it looked like one of the *pietra dura* inlays at which Florentine craftsmen excelled—a picture shaped from antique gold and semiprecious stones, amber and carnelian, topaz, heliodor, and chrysoberyl. Few cities are as beautiful; few can boast such a heritage. The names ring in the mind like trumpets—Michelangelo, Leonardo, Brunelleschi, Fra Angelico.

I sat sullenly in the car with my back turned to the spectacular view. I didn't want to be there. I had done my damnedest to avoid the place, and Florence itself. On the map the route looked simple. Leave the Autostrada del Sole at Firenze Est, cross the Arno by the first possible bridge, and head north toward Fiesole, skirting the inner city. I never even made it across the river. The map didn't show the

1

sprawling suburbs with their mystifying mazes of streets and their inadequate signs. At least when I reached the Piazzale Michelangelo I knew where I was. I stopped there because I had a feeling that if I turned the steering wheel one more time I would keep on turning it, around and around, in circles, till I ran into another car or a tree or somebody's front door.

Finger by finger I unglued my sticky hands from the wheel. The weather wasn't hot. It was early spring in Tuscany, crisp and cool despite the brilliant sun. My hands were slippery with perspiration and stiff with cramp. I had held that wheel in a death grip all the way from Rome. But I had made it—so far. If someone had told me three months ago that I would be in the hills above Florence, Italy, after driving a rental car all those miles from Rome, I would have laughed—and laughed, and gone on laughing till a nurse came and gave me a shot.

It had happened, more times than I cared to remember. Even now I wasn't sure what had shaken me up and out of what Aunt Mary called "Kathy's high-priced crazy house." Dear, tactful Aunt Mary. Nobody in our family had ever had a nervous breakdown. Only weaklings had nervous breakdowns. That was how Aunt Mary referred to it; the newfangled jargon of psychiatry was not for her. Call it a crazy house or a nursing home or a psychiatric institution; call it a nervous breakdown or severe depression—or melancholia, as the Victorians did; it hurt just as much by any name.

Aunt Mary was smugly sure that it was her "down-to-earth, no-nonsense" lecture that had shamed me into getting my act together, after weeks of lolling around feeling sorry for myself. Dr. Hochstein took the credit for "curing" me with his new, advanced methods. Dr. Baldwin didn't think I was cured. "We haven't reached the root of the problem, Kathy. Four or five years of intensive psychotherapy...." Baldwin and Hochstein belonged to opposing schools—

Baldwin the traditionalist, Hochstein a firm believer in encounter therapy: Never mind what caused the problem, face it and learn to deal with it. Theoretically I've nothing against that approach, but the application of it in my case almost killed me. The first time Hochstein got me into a car I just sat there behind the wheel and sobbed till he let me get out. The second and third times weren't much better. I hated Dr. Hochstein, but it worked for me. I had just proved that it worked. Even in my carefree pre-breakdown driving career I'd have had qualms about driving on an Italian autostrada in a rented car.

I picked up the car at the airport outside Rome, avoiding the city traffic. But it had not been an easy drive. I had to concentrate fiercely on every movement I made and keep a close eye on the movements of other cars, all of which appeared to be driven by people even crazier than I was. I concentrated so hard I was able to forget, for minutes on end, the memory that haunted me—the bright-red Torino looking like a child's toy in the distance, spinning off the road, lifting in dreamlike, impossible flight before it dropped, down into the trees below. Then the sound, splitting the winter stillness, and the leaping column of flame and smoke.

I reached for my cigarettes. I'd quit smoking years ago, started again after. . . . Baldwin protested. Baldwin didn't believe in crutches. When he lectured me about emphysema, heart trouble, lung cancer, I laughed and quoted Alfred P. Newman. What, me worry? Why should I worry, Dr. Baldwin? Who cares about heart trouble thirty years from now? The young lives are snuffed out too soon, mangled and crushed and burned. I saw it happen, Dr. Baldwin.

I moved so fast I bruised my knuckles getting out of the car. It was the only way I knew to stop that train of thought. Do something, anything, and do it fast.

I knew what I would see. I had read the brochures and seen the photographs. The view from the Piazzale is *the* view of Florence. But I didn't know it would be so beautiful. I couldn't see crumbling mortar or flaking paint. I didn't know the soft mist in which the city floated like the fairy land of Lyonnesse was auto exhaust. I wouldn't have believed it if someone had told me. It was not a real city, it was a legend suspended above the earth; Avalon, swathed in veils of cloud.

I hung over the parapet for a while playing tourist with the other tourists, trying to see how many landmarks I could identify. Brunelleschi's great dome, with Giotto's bell tower beside it; the slender crenellated tower of the Palazzo Vecchio and the spires of Santa Croce and the Bargello. The gentle curves of the Arno, gilded by sunlight, and the Ponte Vecchio.

The sinking sun furnished me with the excuse I had been unconsciously seeking. I couldn't walk into a house of strangers so late in the day—not on an errand like mine, at any rate. Given my obviously inadequate sense of direction, and the fact that I had only the vaguest idea where I was going, I was bound to get lost again—and again. It had been a wild idea anyway, to plunge in without some preliminary reconnaissance. I'd never have considered doing it if I had not been driven and possessed. Get it over with, get it done— a childish approach to a dreaded but necessary task. I wasn't a child. I was twenty-three, independent, self-supporting, and—relatively—sane. No matter what you say, Dr. Baldwin.

The city became more bewitching with every change of light. Shadows of mauve and lavender and opalescent gray dimmed the rooflines, and I reluctantly turned from the parapet and bade farewell to the two amiable Danish ladies with whom I had been playing "identify the monument."

"I have to find a place to stay," I explained.

The ladies were scandalized. "But, my dear, don't you have reservations?" one asked. "You should have made them in advance. Never travel without reservations."

If they weren't somebody's aunts, they should have been. Their lecture had the familiar ring, but I couldn't resent it. Their concern was too genuine. After they had done fussing at me they admitted that the less time I wasted discussing the problem the sooner I could get to work on it. They insisted on giving me the name and address of the *pensione* where they were staying. It was filled by the tour group of which they were members, but if I found myself in a bind I must come to them, they would think of something.

I had forgotten strangers could be so kind. "Strangers" was the key word; I'd had too much concentrated solicitude from my family, from my doctors—smothering me, imprisoning me in a muffling featherbed of concern. It's easier to accept favors from people you will never see again. Hello, good-bye, it's been nice knowing you. I thanked the Danish ladies and drove away, ready to face the horrors of Florentine traffic at what would have been rush hour back home and probably was here, too.

There is no such thing as rush hour. The traffic in Italian cities is horrendous all the time. I didn't exactly lose my way. I kept seeing things I recognized; it was like a family reunion where there are all those people you've encountered in old photograph albums—"Good Lord, that must be Cousin Jack!" "Good God, that's the Medici Palace!" But I didn't want the Medici Palace, I wanted a hotel. The first two I checked were full up. I was beginning to think I would have to sleep in the car or cast myself on the generous (in every sense of the word) bosoms of the Danish ladies when I got lost again, and this time lost was lucky. I had wandered away from the city center, past the University and San Marco, when I spotted the Grande Albergo San Marco e Stella di Firenze. It wasn't as big as its name—a narrow slit of a building squashed in between two massive piles of stone that might have been medieval palazzi or modern banks. In Florence it's hard to tell one from the other. As soon as I walked in the front door

I knew it was my kind of place. Everything was red and white. Red walls and white trim in the lobby, white walls and red trim in the dining room visible through an arch to the right.

I rushed to the desk. "I'm doubled-parked," I gasped. "Have you got a room?"

The man behind the desk looked up from the magazine he was reading. Its cover depicted a mostly unclad female in the hot embrace of a masked man with a knife.

"For you, signorina, there is a room. All the rooms are yours. For one person or..." He paused. "For two?"

"I'll take anything. I'm double-parked—"

A delicate flick of his fingers dismissed the problem as unworthy of consideration. "If you expect a friend, you will want a room for two."

I was about to say I was not expecting a friend when I caught the dark eyes fixed on mine. He was barely a man— seventeen or eighteen at a guess, though his expression of weary cynicism would not have been out of place on an old roué. I hesitated.

Why did I hesitate? I wish I knew. There were several theories. Aunt Mary's is the simplest: "That girl is the worst liar I've ever met." Sister Ursula took a more charitable view, which was rather nice of Sister Ursula, since she had been fighting for twenty-some years to combat the varied vices of the tenth graders of Our Lady of Sorrows High School. It was an uphill fight, and might well have soured her outlook on life. A frown of perplexity wrinkling her smooth, pale brow, she would say, "I'm sure you don't intend to lie, Kathleen. You simply tell people what you think they expect, or want, to hear. But you must overcome this weakness—you really must. One of these days it will get you in serious trouble."

I tried. I really did, and I would like to believe that Sister Ursula's interpretation, not Aunt Mary's, was correct. Sometimes, though, I lied out of cowardice instead of kindness.

My reply to the young man behind the desk was compounded of both elements. He so wanted me to have a lover. He expected me to have a lover. And I was afraid that if I said I didn't have one, he would take it upon himself to supply the missing necessity. It was so much easier to say, "My friend has been delayed. For tonight, a single room."

"Delayed? Not coming?"

"Not till later."

"He is a foolish man."

"Thank you," I said, trying not to laugh. "You are very kind. Are you the manager, Mr.—?"

"Angelo. To you, signorina—Angelo. I am everything. I do all things, to learn the business of the hotel. Someday I will own my own hotel. Very fine, very expensive hotel."

After I had registered he carried my suitcase upstairs. The Grande Albergo had no lift, which may have accounted in part for my success in finding a room. Then he asked for my car keys, saying confidently but rather vaguely that he "knew a place." As I unpacked I wondered what other hats Angelo wore besides those of bellboy, desk clerk and car-park attendant.

He was also the waiter—the only waiter. The dining room was small, only six tables, but he was kept busy whizzing back and forth with aperitifs and the endless courses that constituted an Italian dinner. I guess the food wasn't particularly good—in fact I was soon to learn that it was not—but it was all new to me and I enjoyed it. After I had devoured spaghetti alla bolognese, scaloppine, salad, and crème caramel, and finished half a carafe of wine, I began to realize how tired I was. When I looked out my window and saw silver tinsel streaks of rain against the pane, my vague intention of taking a walk was forgotten. I fumbled out of my clothes and fell into bed, confident that tonight at least I would sleep.

I dreamed, of course, but this time I was lucky. I didn't remember the dream.

IT WAS still raining next morning. The streaks on the window weren't silvery tinsel now, they were just rain tracing paths through the dirt on the panes. I was worn out from dreaming and in no mood to face the crowd of twelve in the dining room, so I took advantage of the "service of the room" Angelo had proudly mentioned. "Press the bell, signorina," he had said, indicating the topmost of a row of buzzers next to the door. "And *ecco—la colazione*."

The buzzers must have dated from an earlier era when hotels had larger staffs. There was one for a chambermaid, one for a porter, and one bafflingly designated "*tutti lavori*." I pressed the top button as directed, and *ecco*, breakfast duly arrived. Angelo, of course. He probably answered all the bells, including the one marked "*tutti lavori*." He gave my wash-and-wear robe a hurried and conventional leer— obviously part of the service. "What hours do you work?" I asked, genuinely curious, as he deposited the napkin-covered tray on a table.

Angelo came to a dead halt. He didn't do any of the obvious things that betoken surprise—roll his eyes or purse his lips or wrinkle his brow—but I could see he was stunned by the question. "Hours?" he said.

"Thank you, Angelo."

"*Prego, signorina.*"

The food was foreign enough to tempt my appetite. Two steaming pots, one of coffee and one of milk; rolls hard as a rock on the outside, but silky soft within; strawberry jam thick as glue, and excellent sweet butter. There was also a glass of canned orange juice, as a concession to American tastes. I enjoyed it, even the canned juice, but I was impatient to be on my way. If the sun had been shining I might have been tempted to put off my errand a little longer and play tourist, see some of the sights I had looked forward to seeing under far different circumstances. But if matters went as I expected, I would have plenty of time for sightseeing later. She might refuse to speak to me. I had not been able to reach her by phone. Extracting an unlisted number from Information in a foreign city may not be literally impossible, but it was a complication I had not been able to cope with. She hadn't answered my letters. That in itself suggested that she was unable to face the truth, or that she preferred to have no dealings with a lunatic American. Admittedly, the letters had not been very coherent. Yet I could not dismiss the possibility, however remote, that the mail had gone astray. That she didn't know. I had to make one last effort, for my sake as well as hers.

It was Angelo the omniscient and indispensable who gave me the directions. If I'd stopped to think sensibly I would have realized I could never find the place on my own. I had not been thinking. I had been reacting to stimuli like an animal whose brain is wired to electrical probes.

When Angelo finally replaced the telephone after a long and unintelligible conversation, he appeared slightly perturbed. "Why do you go there, signorina? Is it to look for your friend?"

This time I was not tempted to slake Angelo's thirst for romance. I said wryly, "I don't expect to find a friend, no. It's something I have to do."

"It is very far, signorina. Very hard to find. Stay here. See the beautiful city. I give you a better room, a cheap rate, not expensive. And if you are lonely—"

"That's kind of you. Later, perhaps. You understand, Angelo. It's a job I must do—like all the work you are doing now so that someday you can own your own hotel. How do I get there?"

It wasn't so very far. It might indeed prove difficult to

find—I was dismally aware of the fact that maps don't show the complications of actual landscape—but Angelo's directions were clear and concise. I didn't ask him why he had tried to dissuade me. Perhaps if I had . . . But it wouldn't have made any difference, in the end.

I told him to hold my room, that I'd be back. I left my suitcase. If, against all my expectations, she asked me to stay, I would politely decline. This was not a sentimental journey or an attempt to forge lasting ties. It was a dirty job that had to be done before I could get on with my life.

I made one detour before I left Florence. It had stopped raining, but the skies were still a muddy gray, and in the dull light the building looked more like a prison than a palazzo. It presented a frowning face to the passerby; the stones of the wall were rough-hewn rectangles, the windows on the street level were barred by iron grilles. Hard to imagine anyone actually living there—eating and drinking, sweeping floors, playing. . . . It was now a bank. I wasn't tempted to go in. I double-parked for a few minutes, ignoring the infuriated bleats of cars trying to get around me in the narrow street, remembering what Bart had said.

"The palazzo was sold years ago, along with practically everything else that could be turned into cash. If you married me for my money, *cara*, you made a bad mistake. The only thing my profligate grandfather managed to hang on to was the villa. That's where I grew up—an innocent little nobleman in the hills of Tuscany."

And that is where I was going now—to the Villa Morandini in the Tuscan hills where Bart had spent his childhood, to tell his grandmother he was dead.

AFTER MY pilgrimage to the former Palazzo Morandini I headed out of town. I made several wrong turns, not because Angelo's directions were faulty, but because I kept finding myself in situations where I couldn't follow them, blocked into the wrong lane by streaming traffic. It took a long time to get out of the city, whose ancient boundaries had now stretched far out into the valley and up the surrounding hills. The outskirts were as unsightly as those of any American city—rows of drab little houses and cheap shops, industrial areas, garages and warehouses. Even after I passed Fiesole and headed north toward the mountains the view was less than inspiring. Patchy fog blurred the higher peaks, and the slopes were bleak and bare. It was a far cry from the sunny, pastoral landscape described in the guidebooks. No teams of white oxen moving in slow dignity across the plowed fields, no vines spreading green ribbons along the curve of the hills, not even a castle crowning a ridge. Bart had warned me; I remembered his snort of contemptuous laughter when I read one of the more fulsome passages aloud. "Better rid yourself of those romantic illusions. You'll see more television antennas than medieval towers and more cheap houses than castles."

The weather matched my state of mind, and my state of mind reflected the weather: gray, all gray, without a ray of light. On the seat beside me was my purse, a brown plastic shoulder bag, shabby and worn like everything else I owned, including my thoughts. Under my raincoat I was wearing the only new outfit I had bought in months—a tailored brown suit whose only virtue was the fact that it didn't hang as loosely on me as my other clothes. The color was all wrong—not the soft, warm russet that matched my eyes, but a drab, dead gray-brown that stripped the color from my face. It was my grudging version of mourning, my halfhearted concession to what she would consider proper. Unsatisfactory, like most compromises; I might as well have bought black and been done with it.

In my purse was a magic potion that could brighten the clouds, and cast a rosy glow of false serenity over the dullness of my thoughts. I had sworn I wasn't going to take any more tranquilizers. Better cigarettes than Valium, I told Baldwin. If cigarettes kill me, at least I'll know I'm dying. I had brought the medication with me, though. If the interview was as painful as I expected, I might succumb. Cheer up, I told myself. It can't be any worse than you expect. Forewarned is forearmed.

I have a sizable collection of tired old clichés. I should have remembered another one: The worst is yet to come.

When I reached the little village of Sanseverino I stopped to ask directions, as Angelo had suggested. The villa was only a few miles away, but he had not been certain of its precise location. The village was very small. It was the first place I had seen since leaving Florence that resembled my idea of a picturesque Italian town. Small stone houses, a central plaza with a sculptured fountain, now dry except for the drizzling rain—and those inevitable signs of modern life, a red sign admonishing the reader to "*bevete Coca-Cola,*" and a garage with two gas pumps.

There must have been someone in Sanseverino who spoke English but he wasn't working at the garage. The young man who filled my gas tank and tried to tell me where I was going was dressed like an American teenager, in tight jeans and a crumpled khaki shirt. A combination of vigorous gestures, sketches on the back of my map, and a miscellaneous assortment of unconnected words finally got the idea across—at least I thought so, until I drove off and he began yelling and waving his arms, pointing in the opposite direction.

That difficulty having been overcome and the village hav-ing been left behind, I looked for the side road the young man had mentioned. *Tre chilometri* past the last house. . . . I almost missed it. The road hardly looked wide enough for two cars, even Fiats, and the entrance was overhung by an enormous oak. The branches scraped taloned twigs across the top of the car as I made a sharp right turn into the lane.

Trees and shrubs on either side cut off my view, but I could tell I was climbing at a steep angle, with abrupt curves to complicate steering. After a while the roads surface dropped, with steep banks on either side. Through the tangle of vines and brush I caught occasional glimpses of brick walls, barriers no more impenetrable than the thorny tangle that had almost enveloped them. If these were the walls of the grounds be-longing to the villa the estate was more extensive than I had supposed from Bart's casual references to the declining family fortunes.

The road was paved, but the surface had deteriorated badly and I was forced to shift down. After a while the steep slope leveled out and the brush on the right-hand side of the road became sparser. The wall was so high I could see nothing above it except clouds and fog, but I thought I must be ap-proaching the entrance. Before long a gatepost emerged from the mist. It was surmounted by a lump of stone that might once have been a sculptured heraldic figure. Beyond it was a pair of ornate wrought-iron gates.

There was enough space in front of the gates for me to pull off the road. The small building beyond them must be the porter's lodge; half hidden by overgrown rhododendron and the branches of overhanging trees, it resembled the witch's cottage in a German fairy tale. The witch did not appear to be at home. A graveled drive curved away from the gates and to all intents and purposes disappeared ten feet away; it was closely lined on both sides by the tall, elegant spires of cypresses, alternating with a lower, shrubbier deciduous tree.

13

I got out of the car. The gates were immovable. They didn't even creak when I pushed at them. The only visible means of communication with the regions beyond was a rusted button which, when pressed, gave off no sound whatever. I tried yelling. "Hey! Anybody home?" I sounded the horn. I banged on the smaller gate, designed for pedestrians.

There was no response, no sound at all except the drip of water from the branches and the muted chirping of a bird high in one of the cypresses. I got back in the car and lit a cigarette while I considered my next move. I couldn't go through this again. It was now or never, and I wanted it to be now.

It might be never, though, if the villa was as empty of occupation as it appeared to be. Just because it still belonged to the Morandinis didn't mean any of the family were in residence. Bart had not mentioned brothers or sisters, cousins, aunts or uncles; my impression was that he and his grandmother were the last of the family. An old woman might not want to stay in such a remote place. She might be in a nursing home or a hospital. That would explain why she had never answered my letters.

I was on the verge of abandoning the quest when I heard someone coming. Footsteps crunched on gravel beyond the point where the drive curved out of sight. The humid, hushed air distorted the sound in a peculiar fashion, suggesting the approach of something extraordinarily large and heavy, a wild animal rather than a human being. Which was nonsense, of course. I got out of the car and went to the gate.

A man came into view between the trees. He was big enough, over six feet tall and built like a fullback—thick-bodied and muscular, with shoulders like matching boulders and a bullet head sitting squarely on them, with no sign of a neck. He wore dark, shabby clothing and a cap pulled down over his forehead; he carried a thick stick, with which he slashed at branches and weeds as he walked. It was not until he came out from under the trees, into the open space beyond the gates, that I could see his features clearly. They only increased the impression of brutal, formidable strength. His nose looked as if it had been broken and improperly set; it sprawled sideways, overshadowing his coarse lips.

When he saw me, the scowl that had darkened his face changed to an expression I liked even less. He tossed the stick aside. I stepped back as he came toward me, his walk now a slow, sensual swagger. His eyes moved from my face to my feet and back again. I didn't understand what he said. The words might have been in another language than Italian, a harsher, more guttural tongue.

I had prepared a few phrases. *"La contessa Morandini—è a casa?"*

"Sì." I knew that word. It was accompanied by the universal affirmative nod and by a grimace that might have been a smile. But instead of moving to open the gate he just stood there staring at me.

I tried again, with phrase number two. *"Io desidererei vederla."*

The sentence came out of an old Italian phrase book, and I'm sure my pronunciation was all wrong; but he knew what I wanted. His smile became even more offensive. He shook his head, and his lifted forefinger, slowly from side to side. *"No, signorina. La contessa—no.* Would you like to see me? Would you like..."

He spoke slowly and simply, as if to a child, using the same words I had used. The only word whose meaning I didn't know was the verb of the last sentence; but his gesture made it perfectly clear.

Every woman, young or old, homely or pretty, who has lived in a large city for any length of time has heard suggestions of that nature. You never really get used to them. You never get over wishing you could reply by heaving a rock at the appropriate part of the speaker's anatomy. But you soon

15

learn that an indignant response only invites more of the same, as in an obscene phone call, and you cultivate an appearance, at least, of cold indifference.

I had not expected it here. The man was a servant in the contessa's employ. What sort of household was this, where the porter felt free to insult his mistress's visitors? I felt the hot color rising to my cheeks. The man laughed hoarsely and embellished his invitation with graphic gestures.

When he started toward the small side gate, I retreated with more haste than dignity and got into the car. I couldn't believe he would actually do anything—but he had already behaved in a way I wouldn't have believed possible, and it was a lonely spot. As I backed out, I saw he was leaning against the gate, convulsed with laughter.

I was so furious and so anxious to get away that I drove blindly on, in the direction in which I'd been going. Another half mile or so brought me to the top of the hill or ridge I had ascended, and, as my temper cooled, I realized I should have gone back the way I came. I had seen no houses or driveways. If this was a private road, leading to a dead end, I would have to turn around.

Before long, however, the road began to descend and a series of tight curves brought me out of the trees. Below lay a valley dotted with houses and farms. It was a through road. I could get directions in the village a few miles ahead.

But I didn't. As soon as I reached a place where I could turn I went back.

I had to give it one more try. Surely the contessa was unaware of her servant's behavior. He had said she was there. Was she alone, with only that animal to care for her? I had heard of old people, friendless and neglected, who were victimized by unscrupulous servants. Could that be the case here?

Over the months a picture of Bart's grandmother had taken shape in my imagination. From his comments about her I got the impression of a dignified aristocrat who commanded his respect as well as his love. She thought of herself as a strict disciplinarian, but as Bart had laughingly admitted, she spoiled him badly. He could always wheedle her out of the punishments she devised.

Another part of my mental picture was created by the word itself. My grandmother had a passion for aerobic dancing and for pizza (the correlation should be obvious), and her hair ranged from bright orange to jet-black, depending on her mood and her hairdresser; yet the Whistlerian image persisted when I thought of the Contessa Morandini. Recent developments had done nothing to dispel that image—a frail, white-haired old woman, swathed in black bombazine and widow's veils. I could see her sitting in her lonely room, rocking, while the slow, senile tears of old age dripped down on the knitting in her gnarled hands.

As I drove back along the rutted road I could feel it coming over me—the impulse my father described, with awful sarcasm, as "Saint Kathleen's holy mission of the week." He was a fine one to criticize, always handing out money to drunks and beggars, bringing home strays, both animal and human, if he thought they looked hungry....All right, Pa, all right, I thought. But I can't just leave her there, until I'm sure she's safe.

I didn't want to approach the gates again. There must be another entrance. I thought I remembered seeing a gap in the brush, at the point where the wall ended or turned. When I reached it I saw a rough, weedy track leading away from the road, paralleling another section of the wall.

I pulled into the track and parked. It might have been meant for service or farm vehicles, but it hadn't been used recently; the sections that weren't covered by weeds were solid mud. It struck off across a stretch of pasture studded with rocks like raisins in a pudding. A sharp wind rattled the dried stalks of last year's weeds. I slung my purse over my shoulder and put my hands in my pockets. Who brings mittens to sunny Italy? Not me. Apparently yesterday's lovely weather had been an unseasonable fluke.

I started slogging down the track. Before I had gone far my feet were soaking wet. Over the wall I could see the tops of trees, but there was no sound and no sign of life. I made a right-angle turn, still following the wall, before I found what I wanted—not a gate, but a section where the bricks had crumbled and fallen. They had fallen outward, forming a rough ramp, up which I scrambled.

At first all I could see was a jungle of tangled branches. I made more noise than I would have liked pushing through them, but in a way I was glad to hear some sound except my own breathing. The place felt like a cemetery. When I got out of the trees I found myself in an enclosed space that had once been a formal garden. I had a hard time finding the way out; if there had been paths or walks, they were buried under the sod. The next ex-garden was larger, and just as disheveled. The next—and the next....

I had only the vaguest idea of what the grounds of a big estate were supposed to look like; this wasn't anything like any of my ideas. There were no sweeping terraces or pools or stretches of lawn, only a maze of enclosed spaces like ceilingless rooms. One had been a topiary garden, its shrubs clipped into the shapes of animals or mythological creatures. They had not been trimmed for a long time. Sometimes it was possible to guess at the original form; the distortions created by new growth made them appear even more monstrous than they had been at first.

At long last I located a gate leading to a space that was comparatively open. The graveled walks were weedy and the shrubs were overgrown, but compared to the jungles I had traversed this area showed signs of recent tending. The shrubs were azaleas and rhododendron; the fresh green of the new leaves pushed impatiently at the old, winter-browned foliage.

I started down one of the paths and then froze as a voice cried out in sharp tones. Something whizzed through the air straight at me. Instinctively I put up my hands.

iv

WHAT DO you do when you see a big, brown, roughly spherical object hurtling toward you? There is only one sensible answer, especially if you are trespassing. You duck. But if you had two older brothers, both of whom aspired to be quarterbacks, you hear words echoing down the corridors of time—"Get out for that pass, Kathy!"—and you catch the thing.

It *was* a football. My old instincts had recognized it, even before my hands cradled it. It wasn't until I actually held it that the full, Alice-in-Wonderland unlikelihood of the event struck me. I sat down with a thud, hugging the ball to my stomach. ("Don't let go till you hear the whistle, dummy, the other guy's gonna try and strip the ball....")

A child emerged from behind a bush and trotted toward me. He could not have been more than ten, and he looked younger. He was trying not to grin, and not succeeding. "That was a hard one! If I saw you were only a girl I would not have throwed it so hard."

I gaped at him. He wasn't American, despite that semi-spiral pass. His English was stilted and accented, his clothes not just European but old-style European. The ubiquitous blue jeans have conquered the world; but this youngster wore gray flannel shorts, knee socks, and a gray pullover. He needed to wear brighter colors. His skin was sallow. He was too thin. But that wasn't why I stared. He had tumbled dark hair, a thin, sensitive mouth—and eyes of pale silver-gray, the pupils theatrically dark against the irises—eyes fringed with lashes

19

so long and thick and black he looked made up.

Bart's eyes.

His smile faded. "Did I hurt you? You catched it good, for a girl."

I got my breath back. "It was a hard throw. Wow!"

He squatted down beside me. "You have the good hands," he said graciously, and then, with sudden anxiety, "It is right? The good hands?"

"It's the right phrase," I said, laughing. "But my brothers wouldn't agree with you. Butterfingers Malone, they called me. I guess it was a lucky catch."

"Will you catch another?" he asked hopefully.

"Sure. Just wait a minute, I'm a little out of breath."

"Sit on the bench and rest." He helped me up with an old-fashioned courtesy that matched his clothes. He sat down beside me. "I am Pete," he said with an air of defiance.

I gave him my hand, and the football. "I'm Kathy. Pete? That's a good name, but I'd have thought it would be Pietro, for an Italian gentleman."

"I am only half Italian. The other half is American."

"Which half?" I asked, smiling.

"My mother."

I'm not sure how I knew. Maybe it was the way he avoided using a verb—past or present. Maybe it was the way his thick lashes dropped, veiling his eyes.

"And your father?" I asked after a moment. I didn't use a verb either.

"I lived in America for a year," he said evasively.

"Was that where you learned to play football?"

"Yes. Where did you learn? I thought girls did not play."

I told him about Jim and Michael. "They spent all their spare time practicing, from August to December, and when they couldn't get anybody else, they made me play receiver. I was only too happy to oblige; usually they complained when

I tagged along. Luckily for me, neither of them wanted to be a linebacker."

He had to think about that one. Then his lips parted in a tentative smile. "To tackle you, you mean. That would hurt, yes."

"Yes."

"I knew you were American," the boy said, swinging his legs. "From the way you caught the ball. No Italian girl could do it."

Feeling it necessary to defend my sex, I said, "Football is an American game. I'll bet a lot of Italian girls can play soccer."

His eyes lit up. "I'll bet. I'll bet...I had forgot that. It is a good word. Like 'right on' and 'baad, man.'"

Last year's slang. I didn't want to ask him outright how long ago he had been in America. There was something wrong about his parents—his mother certainly, perhaps his father too. I thought I was safe when I said, "Your English is very good. You must speak it often."

But I made a mistake there, too. His lashes again veiled his eyes. "They do not let me talk English. '*Sempre Italiano, Pietro; non parlare inglese.*'" He slid down from the bench, the football extended invitingly. "Will you catch it again? Are you rested now?"

I had actually forgotten how I got there and why I was there. I said with a sigh, "Pete, I wish I could. But I have no right to be here. I climbed the wall. I'm trespassing."

"I thought so," he said coolly. "It is lucky you came here. They do not let the dog here because it is my place."

"The dog? What kind of dog?" I asked apprehensively.

He didn't know the breed, but he measured the dog with his hands. *This* long—*this* high—black, all black, with teeth *this* big....He was right, it was lucky for me I had not met the dog. I got to my feet.

21

"Well, I'd better go and make my apologies. I came to see the contessa. Is she at home, do you know?"

"I think yes. If you go there—" He pointed to a gate at the far end of the garden. "It leads to the door of the kitchen. You don't mind, to go to the door of the kitchen?"

"Not at all," I said, smiling at the apologetic face looking up at me. "Any door is fine so long as it doesn't lead to the dog's run."

"It is the way I come, so the dog is not there. I would go with you, but I must play for one hour. That is the rule." He glanced at his wristwatch. "It will be twenty minutes more."

I reassured him, resisting the urge to give him a hug or call him honey, or any of the other awful things a boy his age would bitterly resent. He was a darling; those odd, old-fashioned manners in a frustrated football player. . . . I looked back when I reached the gate and saw him standing watching me, the ball cradled in his arms. I smiled and waved before I closed the gate.

Every house, no matter how grand, needs certain humble adjuncts. Garbage is garbage and mops and brooms have to stand somewhere. The path I followed between rows of green sprouts that would one day be peas and carrots, onions and lettuce, led to a paved courtyard with a variety of homely objects scattered around—buckets, rakes, mops, and empty boxes. This wing of the house was humble enough—low-roofed and sprawling, its walls a mosaic of peeling stucco and rough brick. The sun broke through the clouds as I stood there, trying to summon the courage to proceed.

I knocked on the door. My hand was still lifted when the door was flung open by a stout gray-haired woman wearing an apron. Finding my knuckles six inches from her nose unnerved her for a moment; then her alarmed expression turned to a broad, amused grin. My halting apologies only increased her amusement. She replied, but of course I didn't understand a word; I only noticed that her accent sounded softer and more musical than that of the man at the gate.

I produced my memorized sentence. "*La contessa Morandini—io desidererei vederla.*" Then I presented my card.

Heaven only knows what I had had in mind when I ordered those cards. They were five years old if they were a day, the product of some long-forgotten adolescent whimsy. I had found the dusty, dog-eared packet a few days before I left for Italy and had put it in my purse. I suppose I had some vague idea that a calling card would increase my aura of respectability. When you call upon a countess—an elderly, European countess—a countess who has never so much as acknowledged the fact of your existence—every little bit helps.

Naturally I had anticipated handing the card to the proper servant at the front door. If I had not been so rattled I'd have revised my plan; for a trespasser who has climbed over a wall to present a visiting card to the cook was nothing less than ludicrous.

The cook wasn't amused. She was flabbergasted. She finally took the card, holding it by the edge as if it might explode any second, and gestured at me to come in.

The kitchen was big and low-ceilinged, with a floor of red tile. The world's fussiest housekeeper (my mother) couldn't have found fault with it—spotlessly clean, filled with delectable odors from the pots bubbling on the stove. Yet it had an indefinable air of desolation, perhaps because there were only two people occupying a space designed for many times that number. A young girl, slim and black-haired, stood at the sink scrubbing vegetables. She stared at me over her shoulder, her eyes wide with curiosity. The cook turned my card over and over in her fingers; this was a situation she had never encountered, and she didn't know the proper procedure. Finally she shrugged and indicated one of the chairs at a long wooden table. I shook my head, smiling. Again she

23

shrugged, studied the card, and plodded out of the room.

The minutes stretched on. I wished I had had the sense to sit down. I felt like a fool standing there, my hands primly clasped, my feet primly together. The girl at the sink kept glancing at me and giggling. She'd have been the scullery maid in the days when houses like this had dozens of servants. Instead of a uniform she wore a tight skirt that hugged her rounded bottom and a knit blouse that was even tighter. I smiled at her and said, "*Buon giorno*," and her giggles expanded into a high-pitched laugh.

On the back of the card I had written, "I must see you. It is about your grandson." Eloquent it was not, but it was brief and to the point. By the time the cook returned, I rather hoped she would open the back door and show me out. Instead she beckoned me to follow her.

My heels clicked on bare boards and then were muffled by carpeting before they clicked again, more sharply, on marble. That was all I remembered afterward—the sound of my footsteps, like drumbeats tapping. I could not have described the rooms or corridors or furniture; my heart was pounding and my stomach wasn't too steady either. I expected the cook would hand me over to a butler or footman or parlormaid, but she led me across the marble floor—acres of it—to a door, and threw it open.

I walked into a blaze of sunlight. It filled the room, with its gilded woodwork and white walls, like champagne in a crystal glass. I was too nervous to take in the details then; I saw only the woman seated at a desk near the French doors. She did not rise.

The mental picture I had formed shattered like a window hit by a stone. It isn't easy to guess people's ages these days, but I would have sworn she wasn't a day over forty. That most unflatteringly truthful of spotlights, the sun, fell full on her face. It was exquisitely made-up, but it takes more than makeup to hide the lines carved by years of living. There

24

were no lines visible on her smooth forehead. Her hair was a marvelous shade of silvery copper and her eyes were gray—not silvery bright like Bart's, but darker, tarnished, like old mirrors.

I'm sure I looked as gauche and uncomfortable as I felt. Her lips curled slightly and she said, "You don't speak Italian, I suppose."

"No—I'm sorry. . . ."

"Then I must speak English, much as I dislike doing so. You wrote to me, not once but several times. You might have assumed, when you received no reply, that I had not the desire nor the intention of communicating with you."

I started to answer. She cut me off with a quick movement of her hand. "I did not suppose you would have the effrontery to appear in person. If you came here hoping for money, you will be disappointed. I don't intend to give you a penny. Have I made myself clear?"

"Very clear."

"Good." She turned and touched a bell sitting on the desk. "No more need be said. Good-bye, Miss"—she glanced at the card she was holding—"Miss Malone."

My father used to say, "Us Malones take no lip from no-body." My father is six foot three. I'm ten inches shorter and a hundred pounds lighter, but so far as my father was concerned, size had nothing to do with it. I said, slowly and deliberately, "Not Miss Malone. Mrs. Morandini. I was your grandson's wife, Contessa."

She leaned back in her chair, fingertips together, face calm. There was no way of telling what effect, if any, my speech had had. Before I could elaborate, the door opened, in response to her ring. It was not the cook, but another woman, heavy-set and swarthy, with a perceptible mustache and dead black hair. She glanced quickly, avidly, at me and then looked away.

The contessa spoke to her in Italian. She bowed her head

25

respectfully and went out, giving me another of those quick, unsmiling stares. For some reason I had the impression that the contessa had changed her mind—that the order she had given the servant was not the one she had originally intended to give.

She said nothing to me. I didn't speak either. It was up to her to respond to my challenge. Indignation still boiled in me. I wanted to do something rude—delicately, aristocratically rude, to match her rotten manners. So I sat down, without being invited to do so, on a love seat covered in yellow brocade. It was horribly uncomfortable.

I think the gesture amused her. One arched eyebrow lifted just a trifle. I stared defiantly back at her and we sat like a pair of waxen images until the servant returned.

Pete was with her. I'd not have known him. His thin face was a sullen mask. When he saw me, his eyes lit up and the corners of his mouth quirked, the way Bart's did when he was trying not to smile.

The contessa didn't miss much. "I wondered how you had got in," she said conversationally. "I imagine, however, that you two have not been formally introduced. This is *il conte* Pietro Francesco Morandini. My grandson. My *only* grandson."

Chapter Two

THE WEARY contempt in her voice was not directed at me. Her meaning was as plain as if she had spoken the words aloud: This weakling, this half-barbarian, this insignificant thing is all I have. And he isn't much, is he?

She was cruel, but not sadistic. She let the boy go, dismissing him with a flick of her fingers. Another, deliberately more gracious gesture, sent the servant out of the room after him.

"Well?" she said.

I stood up. "You needn't worry. You'll never see me or hear from me again. I'm glad I came, if only to find out what kind of family I have the pleasure of *not* belonging to. I don't know why you are lying to me, and I don't care. I married Bart—Bartolommeo Morandini—and we were together for six months before he was killed in a car accident. He told me his grandmother was the Contessa Morandini. And," I added, "you have a photograph of him on your desk. There. That's my husband. I don't think much of your manners, or your morals, or your methods of raising children, but thank God none of those things are my concern. Good-bye."

"Wait." I was almost at the door when that one word cut the air like a whip. "I am beginning to believe you," she went on.

"Thanks so much."

"You do not wear a wedding ring."

"I put it in . . . in with Bart."

"Were you married in the Church?"

"In the . . . No. In a registry office in New Hampshire."

The wry twist of her lips dismissed this as unsuitable, almost illegal. "But you are Catholic?"

It was a reasonable guess, given the good old Irish name of Malone. It was also an impertinent question, by my standards. I said stiffly, "I was raised in the Church."

She studied me thoughtfully. Then she said, "Bartolommeo's mother was my sister-in-law. My husband's sister."

That was when I realized that my increasing queasiness was not caused solely by emotional factors. Change of water, change of air, the milk at breakfast, maybe . . . I must have turned a shade greener, for she said quickly, "You had better sit down."

I had to fumble for the chair. "I'm sorry," I said, swallowing. "I don't feel very . . . Your nephew. Then why did he tell me—"

"He often used the Morandini name. It was not his own, of course. His father was a commoner—a Milanese physician. He was incapable of understanding a child like Bartolommeo. The boy came to me after his mother died. I raised him."

There was no sign of softening in her face or voice when she said that. I wondered why, if she had served as his foster mother, Bart had not claimed to be her son instead of her grandson. Her statement—which, oddly, it never occurred to me to doubt—raised a number of other questions, but I was in no condition to wonder about them. I felt horribly sick. I stood up, hoping I could get outside the house before I threw up.

"Thank you, I'm sorry to have bothered you. Good-bye."

All at once she was beside me, holding me with hard, cold hands that did not so much support as confine me. "Wait," she said again. "Wait. A civil ceremony, but...Is it possible? Did you come here because....Tell me the truth. Are you enceinte?"

I could claim the question dealt my reeling brain the final blow that toppled it over into catatonia. But the answer did not require profound thought or elaborate explanations. It required one single, two-letter word. I didn't say it. Something had awakened in the contessa's gray eyes, like an image dimly seen in a dusty mirror. But that wasn't why I let her believe a lie. To respond to that shadowy awakening as I did was not kindness, it was wanton cruelty. If I were superstitious....But I'm not.

Ten minutes later I was lying in a bed the size of a football field in a room the size of a grand ballroom. I was wearing one of the contessa's silk nightgowns, and she was holding my head while I was thoroughly and disgustingly sick.

ii

SOME KINDS of illness are romantic—consumption, for example. All the best tragic heroines have consumption. Some ailments have at least the dignity of being deadly. Others are regarded as essentially comic. People always make jokes about seasickness. If I had sprained my ankle or been attacked by the dog; if I had been carried, pale and limp, to that elegant

29

bedchamber—it would have been a fitting episode in one of the romance novels that are all the rage. Even if I had really suffered from what is loosely called morning sickness, as the contessa believed, my "interesting condition" would have glamorized the unpleasant effects. There was nothing glamorous, or romantic, or dignified about my affliction. I had been warned about it, and I knew what it was, and it wasn't one bit funny. I forgot about minor matters like dignity and good manners; I just wanted them to leave me alone so I could die in peace.

They finally did, after making me swallow some revolting stuff that looked and tasted like chalk, and may have been. I didn't die, but I fell asleep; and when I woke I felt much better.

The room wasn't quite as large as a ballroom, but it was big—about four times the size of the Malone living room. Heavy forest-green draperies shrouded the windows, and hangings of the same gloomy shade enclosed the head of the bed. A single lamp burned by the bed. Otherwise the room was as dark as midnight, but a thin finger of light stretching across the floor suggested that I had not slept very long.

For a while I lay still, enjoying the simple pleasure of not feeling sick. Then the full enormity of what I had done struck me. I owed my present position, swathed in silk and occupying what appeared to be the best bedroom in the house, to a lie. The contessa had not played Good Samaritan because I was ill. I had seen enough of her to feel sure she'd have pushed me ruthlessly out the door if she had not misinterpreted the cause of my illness. There was no excuse for what I had done—or rather, had refrained from doing. Even Sister Ursula's boundless charity could not excuse this.

I groaned. "Oh, God," I said aloud.

The dagger-slim streak of light widened. It came, not from the window, as I had supposed, but from the door. A voice said timidly, "Are you going to die?"

It was the first indication I had had that anybody was interested in me, sans embryo. I knew the voice. "Come in," I croaked.

He slid in like an eel, closed the door, and trotted to the bed. "I listened," he whispered. "They sent me to my room, but I listened. Did you throw out?"

"Up," I said automatically. "I'm afraid I did, Pete."

"Up."

"Sorry, I didn't mean to correct you."

"No. You tell me when I say it wrong. I must not forget." His voice rose. "I will not forget!"

I had heard that note in a child's voice before. I said casually, "I hope you won't, because it's great to be able to speak two languages. I wish I could. Tell you what; you teach me Italian, and I'll correct you when you go wrong with English. It'll be harder for you than for me."

His face lit up like a candle. "Are you not going away?"

"Well . . . I'll be here for a while, I guess. Till I stop throwing out."

He could laugh at himself; I suspected it was a rare quality in a Morandini. Then he sobered. "Is it in here"—he pointed— "that you hurt?"

"Right."

"Was it—it is that—I hit you there."

"The football?" I managed to laugh. "Oh, no, Pete, it wasn't that. What kind of receiver would I be if a ball in the midsection made me sick? My brothers would have kicked me off the team if I let a little thing like that bother me."

"Tell me about the brothers. Where do they play the football?"

I had to admit they weren't with the Raiders or the Redskins or even the Pats. It was a blow, but Pete took it bravely. We were deep in a discussion of last year's play-offs when the door opened, without a knock of warning. He flinched, literally and actually, one hand lifting as if to ward off a blow.

31

Standing in the doorway was the woman who had brought him to the sitting room. She had also helped put me to bed. The contessa had addressed her as Emilia.

She touched a switch and a light went on, somewhere in the galactic reaches of the ceiling. The boy had been sitting on the side of the bed. Now he shrank back into the shadow of the curtains, but the woman saw him and spoke to him in the same harshly accented Italian the man at the gate had used.

"She says for me to get off the bed," Pete whispered. "She says I should not be here."

"Tell her I want you to stay."

When he did so, the woman's scowl darkened. Her eyebrows had not been plucked within recorded history. Some of the hairs were so long they curled back on themselves, and others stood out like the antennae of an insect. She turned on her heel and marched out, leaving the door open.

The boy hastily got down off the bed. "She will bring the contessa. I go now."

I didn't try to detain him. I was feeling queasy again. "Come back and see me later, will you, Pete?"

"You want me?"

"I want you very much. Please."

"O-kay." As he spoke he was edging toward the door. "If I don't come, it is that they lock me in."

He heard the approaching footsteps before I did, and was out the door like a flash.

I lay back against the pillow, trying to control the rising tides of nausea and indignation. It would be foolish of me to overreact. Any boy that age needs discipline, and locking him in his room was a comparatively mild punishment. No doubt the contessa favored good, old-fashioned methods of child-rearing. I might not agree with those methods, but they did not constitute child abuse.

I had been teaching for three years. Not long—but long

enough. If, in that length of time, a teacher hasn't caught on to the tricks of her students, she had better find another profession. I knew all the devious wiles the young devise to win sympathy. I knew there were usually—not always, usually—two sides to every question. So why did this situation bother me?

When the contessa appeared and I pleaded the culprit's case, she confounded me by agreeing that he should not be punished for disobedience. "I did not actually forbid him to see you," she said. "I did not suppose you would want him here."

I could believe that. She didn't want him. As she stood there by the bed, she looked as calm and perfect as a wax mannequin in the window of an expensive shop. The folds of her soft wool crepe dress fell in perfect symmetry around her perfect size-six body.

However, when I began making polite noises about getting out of her bed, her house, and her life, she responded with unexpected warmth. "We will discuss that tomorrow. Now you must rest. Call Emilia if you want anything. She understands English, though she speaks it poorly. You are better, I think, but you must not take unnecessary risks."

That was my second chance to set the matter straight. I could have done it then with a minimum of awkwardness—a casual reference to the hazards of travel. I smiled wanly and told her she was very kind.

Pete didn't come back. I spent the rest of the day dozing, in between trips to the neatly appointed bathroom adjoining my room. Not surprisingly, I did not sleep soundly that night. I woke several times, thinking I had heard voices talking or laughing. But when I went to the door and opened it, there was no sound at all.

MY MALADY turned out to be one of those twenty-four-hour bugs. It lasted just long enough to encourage the contessa's delusion, and then cleared up as rapidly as it had begun. By noon the next day I felt fine. I wondered what she would think when the "morning sickness" didn't appear on schedule. Ah, well, these things are unpredictable.

To say that I had reached a conscious, considered decision about how to resolve the dilemma in which I found myself would not be strictly accurate. At some point I simply knew what I was going to do.

Nothing.

It wasn't my fault if the woman had jumped to the wrong conclusions. The purpose for which I had come to Italy was now accomplished, and if it had raised more questions than it had resolved, that was another problem—my problem. I only lie to other people; I'm reasonably honest with myself. I knew my real reason for visiting Bart's childhood home had nothing to do with his aunt's needs.

I had known him such a short time. He was already fading, slipping back into a limbo of nonexistence. For weeks after he died I couldn't close my eyes without seeing his face, sharp-cut as a colored photograph. Now the image was only a featureless blur. I had never really accepted his death. That, said Dr. Baldwin pontifically, was one of my problems.

So I knew that. I knew what the other problems were. Unlike the patients in those super-psychology books, I had not solved the problem by identifying it. How I envied those patients, and their moment of truth: "Hey, that's right, Doc, my dad hit me on the head at nine-fourteen on the morning of December 10, 1965." Click, snap, crack, all the pieces whiz into place, and the patient is whole. I knew what had hit me;

but there had been no click, snap, crack. Maybe here, in Bart's world, the pieces would start to fit together. That was why I had come—not to console a bereaved old woman, but to heal myself. Whether the visit had done any good remained to be seen. It would be a long time before I knew. But I had made the gesture, and now I could go. Once I got home, I would write the contessa and tell her about my miscarriage. I might even have the courage to tell her the truth.

One thing psychologists tell you is true—any decision, even a wrong decision, is better than none. I stood at the window of my palatial room that bright noontime, feeling an incredible surge of relief.

As if in approval the spring weather presented me with a seductive picture of what Italy had to offer. The sky was the soft, clear blue Fra Angelico used for the robes of his Madonnas, with a few plump clouds hovering like fluffy-winged cherubs. The surrounding hills, decked in young green, resembled one of those dreamy Tuscan landscapes that form the setting for so many paintings of the Cinquecento. Cutting across the foreground was the wall enclosing the villa and its gardens. It should not have been there; nothing straight and geometric should have marred that scene of soft color and gentle rolling curves. In the garden below my window I could make out the pattern of formal beds and walks. Shrubs heavy with rose-pink and scarlet blossoms flung their boughs across the weedy, graveled paths. My windows were closed; Emilia probably had antiquated ideas about the dangers of fresh air. I wrestled with the catch, opened the windows, and stepped out onto a small, iron-railed balcony.

Immediately below was a flagstoned terrace with a fountain at one end. The fountain was dry; in its center a winged figure, streaked with verdigris and bird droppings, stood on tiptoe, offering a bowl to some dead god.

I left the windows open and was about to turn back into the room when the shrubs at the far end of the garden shivered and shook. Through them came the man I had seen at the gate. He thrust the branches aside with a careless sweep of the stick he was carrying; petals dropped, covering the ground with a silky pink carpet.

Dark clothes, black scowl on his face, gray cap pulled low over his brow, he was as unseemly in that gentle pastel garden as an ink stain on a Chinese water color. He seemed to be pulling something heavy and resistant; his left arm was stretched out behind him, and when I looked more closely I saw he was holding a heavy chain. He gave it a jerk and snapped out a word that sounded like an epithet rather than a command.

I had forgotten about the dog. It emerged from the low-hanging branches in a sudden rush, snarling. It was as big as a calf, all black except for a white patch on the chest. The man struck it over the head with his stick. The dog stopped, cringing. Another blow; a harsh command; slowly, grudgingly, the animal dropped down and sat still. The handler's thick lips stretched in a smile. The next command must have been "Heel." He walked off, swinging his stick, and the dog fell in behind him. They crossed the garden, treading indiscriminately on gravel and on budding flowers, and passed out of sight.

I let my breath out. It had been a nasty little scene. The dog wasn't a Doberman, it was even bigger, with a massive chest and huge jaws. Had I but known such a creature lurked behind the wall I wouldn't have been so quick to climb over it.

But the man was worse than the dog. I had known a lot of dogs in my time; every stray in the neighborhood gravitated to our house, with or without assistance from Mike and Jim. "Hey, look, Ma, he followed me home." Many had been abandoned, some had been mistreated, a few nurtured a deep and justified suspicion of human beings, but after a few days of good food and kindness they had been slobbering all over us and trying to climb on our laps. I suppose there are some psychotic dogs, just as there are some psychotic people, but in general dogs (and people) aren't vicious unless they are consistently, thoroughly abused, over a long period of time. No doubt the human brute justified his behavior under the pretense of "training" the dog. It wasn't training, it was sadism, ugly and inexcusable.

I had been invited to lunch with the contessa—a formal invitation, written in a delicate, precise hand on notepaper bearing a gilt crest and delivered on a silver tray by Emilia. I'd have dressed up for the occasion if I had had anything appropriate, but I didn't—only the suit I had worn the day before. It had been sponged and pressed; my lingerie and blouse had been neatly laundered. Even my shoes had been shined—and they needed it. The nightgown I had been wearing obviously belonged to the contessa. She was about my size, but a few inches taller; I had to lift the trailing silken skirts when I walked. I had never seen clothes like hers except in windows of fancy shops in New York and Boston. According to Bart, the Morandinis were as poor as church mice, but I was beginning to suspect that "poor" was a relative term. Yet the grounds were untended, the staff inadequate for a place of this size. . . . It was an anomaly, and not the least of the ones that puzzled me.

After I got dressed I stood around waiting for someone to come and escort me to the presence. Nobody came, and after a while I got very bored. I had already inspected the room. It was interesting, like something in a museum. The bed was a magnificent piece of furniture, every inch of its surface carved into intricate patterns, including the posts. For all its splendor it was not very comfortable. The mattress was thin and hard, and a musty smell pervaded it. The dark-green hangings had been looped back, but the effect was rather like lying in a cave whose entrance was fringed with thick grass, a cave in which something had died long ago, leaving a ghostly aroma of decay. This might be the state bedroom, where a long line of counts had breathed their last. I wasn't sure of that, though. Villas and palaces were not my ambience; for all I knew, this could be a minor guest chamber reserved for spinster aunts and unmarried daughters.

The room appeared scantily furnished, but that may have been because it was so big. A huge armoire of heavy dark wood, summoning up Poesian images of hidden corpses— it was large enough to hold half a dozen unwanted wives; a couple of straight chairs with cushioned seats and backs carved so vigorously a person couldn't lean back in them; a single overstuffed chair, covered in faded chintz; a Persian rug or two; a few tables; and a desk-secretary inlaid in ivory—that was about it. The bookcase section of the secretary actually contained books. The glass doors were locked.

I was extremely bored by that time, or I wouldn't have tried to open the glass doors. It was not polite to investigate cupboards and drawers in other people's houses. My mother had drilled that into me at an early age, after she took me to visit Aunt Mary and found me removing that lady's long underwear from a drawer and festooning it over the furniture. "Look but don't touch...." No wonder I had not been an outstanding student. My juvenile mind had been so stuffed with aphorisms and admonitions, by a variety of mentors, there was no room left in it for facts.

Finally I opened the door and looked timidly out. The corridor was completely unfamiliar. I hadn't paid much attention to my surroundings the day before, as I was towed up the stairs and thrust into bed. I saw closed doors and a few odds and ends of furniture, but no stairs. I went looking for them.

I was lost before I had gone fifty feet. I'm good at getting lost, but in this case there was some excuse. That house was big. One door looked as if it might lead to a landing and the stairs I wanted. But I had not gone far into the regions beyond when I knew I was on the wrong track. This part of the house seemed older than the rest; the ceiling was lower, the windows were shuttered. It was very quiet. I was about to turn back when I heard something that stirred the hairs on the back of my neck—the sound of someone laughing.

Impulsively I started forward. A door opened and closed, and a moment later Emilia came around a turn in the corridor. She was carrying a tray covered with a white cloth. When she saw me, it shifted in her hands with a clash of china and silver. She recovered herself and hurried toward me, almost running.

She did know some English. She had not bothered using it before, but in that moment she found the words she wanted. "Go back—out from here! Go—now—quick, quick."

She kept on walking as she hissed the words, the tray held out in front of her like a weapon. I could have stood my ground, or tried to get past her, but either would have been awkward—and of course I had no business being there in the first place. I let her nudge me away. I must have imagined that laughter. It had only been an echo down the corridors of time. . . .

She was careful to close the door after we left the empty wing. Another gesture indicated the direction I was to follow. She stayed behind me, prodding me with the tray when I hesitated.

The route took us back to the corridor on which my room was located. A few feet farther on, beyond my door, was a wide landing flooded with light, and the stairs. I had gone in the wrong direction.

At this point Emilia decided it was safe to stop herding me away from the forbidden regions. She preceded me down the stairs. The surroundings began to look vaguely familiar. I had crossed that vast expanse of white marble the day before. This must be the entrance hall, and the door opposite the foot of the stairs, flanked by windows, must be the main entrance. The hall was shell-shaped, with fluted niches where plump nymphs cowered, trying to draw their scanty draperies around their nakedness. The effect was more pathetic than erotic. They looked cold. The temperature in the vast unheated room was arctic, and the icy whiteness of floor and walls made it feel even lower.

Then I saw something I had not noticed the other day on my trek from the kitchen across the back of the hall. Between the stairs and the front door an inlaid pattern had been set into the floor—the only color in the room, shockingly, vividly brilliant against the ice-white marble. In my proletarian ignorance I assumed the colored shapes were also of marble, natural or tinted, but as I was to learn, they were semiprecious stones. The deep blood-red of jasper, malachite green as summer, pink and yellow agate formed a spray of roses growing from a central stem. Each petal and leaf had been cut separately; the shading, from soft rose-pink to dark amethyst, created a stunningly realistic bouquet. Bart had given me red roses. . . . They must have had a meaning for him, beyond the conventional language of flowers—red roses for passion, for consummated love.

The door to the left of the stairs was the one I did remember; it led into the room where the contessa had received me. Emilia paused only long enough to deposit the tray on a carved chest before she opened the door and indicated I should enter.

A small table had been opened out and set with crystal and china. I decided I wasn't high-class enough to rate the dining room, or baronial hall, or whatever it was called, but in this I did my hostess an injustice. This was her favorite room, where she spent most of her time. After I had seen the rest of the house I sympathized with her choice. The huge formal *salones* were cold and dismal; most had been closed up, to save money and labor.

The contessa was seated on the brocade love seat leafing

through a magazine. On the table before her were a decanter and two wineglasses. She greeted me with a cool smile that quickly changed to a look of concern. "Perhaps you should not have come downstairs. You are quite pale."

"Thank you, I feel fine." I had no intention of telling her what had upset me. It had been nothing more than an auditory hallucination—and not the first one, either. But, said a voice deep down in my mind: If there was no one there, why was Emilia carrying a tray of food?

"I'm afraid I got lost," I went on, squelching the inner voice. "I hope I haven't kept you waiting."

"Lost? Why didn't you ring? One of the servants would have come for you. They were waiting until you were ready."

The gulf between us was never more apparent than when it was illumined by a casual comment like that one. I had never thought of using the bellpull to summon a servant. It had not been too many generations since the Malones had been the ones who answered the bell. Instead of making me feel small and kind of humble, like Tigger, the thought amused me.

"Sorry," I said breezily.

Emilia poured wine like chilled winter sunlight into the glasses and offered them. I took one, with a gracious nod of thanks. The contessa might intimidate me, but I was damned if I was going to be bullied by the maid.

After Emilia had gone we exchanged polite pleasantries for a while. Then the conversation turned to a monologue, as the contessa described the vast antiquity, enormous nobility, and distinguished history of the house of Morandini. As I listened I began to get a feeling that I was missing something—some underlying assumption that colored all her remarks—but I didn't identify it until she said, "If you would prefer another room, that can of course be arranged. Or if there is anything you would like changed..."

Fortunately I had finished my wine. The glass slipped; I

caught it just in time. "But you mustn't go to so much trouble," I blurted. "I have a room—at the Grande Albergo—"

"Alberto will bring your luggage."

"But—but I—"

"Naturally you will stay here. Bartolommeo's wife cannot stay at a hotel, even one called the Grande Albergo."

A smile touched her mouth as she pronounced the name. It was the first sign of genuine humor she had displayed, and I found it attractive. She added, "You must allow me to make amends for my rudeness. I was under a misapprehension."

I thought guiltily, you don't know the half of it, lady. But less than ever was I moved to confess the truth. The blunt, cruel words would have shattered the porcelain facade of her dignity like a rock tossed through a shop window. Call me coward, call me craven—I couldn't do it.

Without waiting for me to reply she pressed the bell. Emilia promptly appeared carrying a tray and began arranging dishes on the table. The tray was not the one she had been carrying when I first encountered her. It couldn't have been. The soup was still steaming hot.

Emilia served every dish, though the table was so small I could have reached across it. The contessa talked about the beauty of spring and the loveliness of the Tuscan countryside. She quoted Dante—I guess it was Dante. Not until Emilia had collected the dirty dishes and gone out with her tray did the contessa relax. She leaned back, crossed her legs, and lit a cigarette. I was surprised to see such a fastidious woman smoking, and I noticed, as her hands dealt neatly with a gold lighter and gold cigarette box, that those members at least showed signs of age. Veins squirmed like little blue worms across the backs of her hands.

Then she got down to practical matters. We started from the fact that I would be staying at the villa. I never got a chance to protest that basic theorem because I was too busy protesting the corollaries that followed it. Alberto would collect my luggage. . . . No, he wouldn't; thanks very much but I would rather do my own collecting. Alberto would pick me up after I had returned my car to the rental agency. . . . No, he wouldn't; thanks very much, but I preferred to keep the car. She didn't argue; instead she launched into a description of the villa's domestic arrangements. Apparently it had finally dawned on her that I was a barbarian who would have to be instructed in the proper behavior toward servants and other conveniences.

The staff consisted of six people. No wonder the house was closed up and the grounds untended; six people to do the work of forty! Emilia had the impressive title of house-keeper; she also acted as the contessa's personal maid, and I suspected this latter job took most of her time. Emilia's husband Alberto was chauffeur and "head" gardener. A local "half-wit"—the engaging term was the contessa's—was his assistant. The cook was Rosa, the *tuttofare* a local girl named Anna. The contessa didn't translate the second title. I knew just enough Italian to understand; the two words meant "to do everything," and it was an accurate description of a maid of all work. Except for a woman who came in periodically to do heavy cleaning, that was it.

My chief reaction was sympathy for the *tuttofare*. My ignorance of high living kept me from noticing one singular omission in that list. No one for the boy. No nurserymaid, governess, tutor or nanny. It was some time before I thought of that. I assumed he attended the local school, and that he was too old to need a nurse.

Alberto and Emilia were not local people. They had come from Rome with the contessa when she married. That explained the strange harsh accent I had noticed. Florentine Italian is musical and beautiful; the Roman dialect is considered crude. Maybe so, but I imagined the unpleasant personalities of the pair did not improve the charm of their speech.

The scene I had viewed from my window came back to me, and I said, "I take it Alberto is the man in charge of the dog?"

My hostess glanced unobtrusively at her watch. "Thank you for reminding me. I have an appointment at my hairdresser and must leave shortly; but first you must meet the dog."

The dog got more respect than the servants—she hadn't suggested that I be introduced to them. I was not keen on meeting that dog, but if I had to meet him, I preferred to do so under formal conditions.

A tinkle of the bell brought Emilia, who received her mistress's instructions with a respectful nod and went out. After a few minutes the contessa took her gloves and bag from the desk and we went to the front door.

It was odd to go out a door I had never come in, and see the front of the house for the first time. It was big enough, but compared with the grim palaces of Florence it looked almost homey—if one may use such a word to describe a house that contained twenty or thirty bedrooms, not to mention innumerable reception rooms and *salones*. The facade was a simple rectangle of whitewashed stucco, accented by window frames and piers of the dark-gray stone called *pietra serena*. There were three stories above a high terrace reached by an ornate double staircase. Open arches in the platform supporting the terrace gave access to a lower, ground-level floor that presumably contained the domestic offices. The huge red-brown pots lining the terrace held small shrubs and trees that might, when the season was farther advanced, put out leaves and flowers and fruit; but they didn't look especially healthy. Small statues alternated with the pots. At the foot of the stairs the drive widened into a semi-circular expanse of gravel, with a fountain in the center and a statuary group in the center of the fountain. Bronze muscle-men blew soundlessly into verdigrised shells and conches, or clutched coy mermaids to their metal chests. The fountain was dry. The sweep of grass that stretched down to a belt of trees in the far distance was in reasonably good condition and the flower beds had been weeded. I could see why Alberto and his assistant had no time for the rest of the estate. Keeping that four-acre stretch of turf mowed and the flowers weeded and watered was a full-time job in itself.

The car—a Mercedes, what else?—was waiting at the foot of the steps. Alberto had changed into a regular chauffeur's uniform. It didn't do much for his looks. The collar squeezed his bull neck and the buttons strained across his chest. In his polished boots and military jacket he looked like a retired storm trooper.

He held the dog's chain. When the animal saw me, it lunged forward. Alberto let it go the full length of the chain, grinning when I jumped back. The contessa snapped out an order, like a row of ice cubes. Alberto's smile disappeared. He practically genuflected, his manner as servile as that of the dog. He gathered up the chain and brought the animal to heel.

"Walk slowly toward him," the contessa directed me. "Hold out your hand and let him smell it."

I knew the procedure, but I had never seen a dog I was less anxious to try it on. When it was sitting, its head was on a level with my chest. The dog rumbled low in its throat as I sidled toward it. Alberto struck it across the face with the slack of the chain.

"Stop that!" I yelled

The dog and Alberto appeared equally surprised. I crossed the remaining space in a few strides and thrust my hand at the dog's muzzle. "There, good boy, you're a nice dog. . . . You don't want to hurt anybody. . . ." In the same crooning voice I went on, "Alberto, old boy, I don't know how much English you understand, but I'll bet you know a little, and I am telling you right now to stop beating the dog. *Stupido, cretino,* don't *battere* the *cane.*"

I did not turn to observe the effect of this high-handed behavior on the contessa, but I thought I heard a murmur of musical laughter. Alberto looked black. He understood the insults, at any rate. The dog was not impressed. I let him have a good long smell—his sniffs sounded like an old train engine getting up steam—and dared to run my fingers gently under his jaw before I retreated.

"That man has no more idea how to train a dog than how to solve a differential equation," I said angrily. "Why do you let him—"

"He has his methods," the contessa said calmly. She gestured at Alberto, and he dragged the dog away. The contessa drew on her gloves. "I dine at eight," she said. "I hope you will join me at seven for a cocktail."

She strolled slowly down the stairs. As she reached the car, Alberto appeared out of nowhere in time to open the door for her. It reminded me of the old saying about Queen Victoria—that she never looked over her shoulder when she sat down, because she knew someone would always make sure she had a chair under her.

I watched the car glide smoothly down the drive and vanish into the trees. I felt exhausted, as if I had been trying to walk against a strong wind. I fancied the contessa usually got her way. Or had I yielded, not because she outfought me and won, but because I had not fought very hard?

I got my purse from my room—*my* room—and went in search of my car. Somewhat to my surprise, it was still where I had left it. I got in and headed for Florence.

The drive took almost an hour, long enough for me to think about what I was doing, and decide that what I was doing probably wasn't very nice. My parents would not approve. Sister Ursula certainly would not approve. Drs. Baldwin and Hochstein would disagree; they always did. The hell with Drs. Baldwin and Hochstein, I thought. I was sick of probing into my subconscious searching for motives. This decision *felt* right. It was only for a few days. She had not asked how long I could stay; I had not volunteered the information. If things got sticky, I would make my excuses and leave.

When I reached the Grande Albergo I double-parked in front of the door and went in. No one was at the desk. From the dining room came the clatter of utensils and the murmur of voices. It was still early, and Italians take long lunch hours, lingering over wine and coffee after polishing off their pasta. I was about to reach for my room key when Angelo came darting out of the dining room. He wore his waiter's white apron over his concierge suit, and he was carrying a Tower-of-Pisa stack of cups. Seeing me, he came to a dead halt and stared as if he had never seen me before.

I said, "I'm checking out. There's no hurry—I can see you're busy. I'm going to go up and pack. When you get a minute, could you make up my bill, please?"

"Ah." Angelo pondered. Then he put the cups down and went behind the desk. Handing me my key, he said, "Your friend has come."

"My . . . Oh. No, I'm afraid not."

"You were not here last night," said Angelo. It was a simple statement of fact; the assumption was implicit, but not judgmental. Angelo made no judgments.

"I was at the villa," I explained. "The Villa Morandini—remember? I'll be staying there for a few days."

"Ah." Angelo thought this over. Then he said, "My brother is a policeman."

"That's nice," I said, wondering what on earth he was getting at.

47

"It was from him I found where the Villa Morandini is. He knows all, my brother. If your friend does not come, you would like my brother."

"I'm sure I would. But I don't think—"

"He is taller than I," said Angelo. "Taller than you. Very tall." He measured his brother's height with an outstretched hand. If the measurements were accurate, his brother could have played basketball with any team in the States.

"I'm sure he is very tall and very handsome," I said. "And I'm very grateful to him for his help. I'll let you know, Angelo."

"Ah," said Angelo. Seemingly at random he plucked a sheet of paper from a drawer, scribbled on it, and thrust it at me. "*Il conto, signorina.*"

We had a little discussion over the total. It seemed that the rates quoted on the card hanging on my closet door did not include astronomical local taxes, and a few other mysterious but (Angelo assured me) legal charges. I paid the bill and waved away the change. "Thanks for your help, Angelo. Is it all right if I leave my car here for a few hours?"

Angelo assured me I could leave the car anywhere I liked—in the street, in the lobby. "But do not put your suitcase in the car, signorina; leave it in the room, and I will bring it down and keep it at the desk. There are many thieves—many thieves. . . ." And, shaking his head sadly, he picked up the cups and rushed away.

It didn't take me long to pack. Angelo was nowhere in sight when I came down, so I hung my key back on its hook and went out into the street.

I had not intended to do any sightseeing, but in Florence you can't go far without seeing sights, whether you want to or not. I was ambling along, not thinking of anything in particular, when I turned a corner and suddenly found myself in front of the Duomo, with the great dome lifting over it as lightly as a hot-air balloon. I had dreamed of coming to Florence with Bart one day; I had pored over guidebooks and art books, so I knew what the monuments looked like. What they looked like, not what they really were. The reality was overwhelming.

Later, I came by accident on the church of Orsanmichele, with its enshrined, life-sized saints, and there was Saint George, his arm resting lightly on his shield, his head lifted, looking for the dragon. I had fallen in love with Saint George during an art history class. I felt like a groupie gaping at her favorite rock star. Even the bird droppings that whitened George's shoulders and handsome head did not mar his dignity.

Along the way I passed a bookshop. Among the books in the boxes in front of the store were a few in English, and I decided I had better get something to read. Long evenings with the contessa might seem very long indeed. Even if the villa had television, I wouldn't be able to understand the language, and although there was probably a library—what great house is complete without a library?—it wouldn't have much in the way of light English fiction.

I rummaged among the books, which had been tumbled haphazardly into the containers—secondhand paperbacks, dog-eared and in some cases missing their covers. It was a funny assortment; the flotsam and jetsam of the business, books nobody had wanted—a few mysteries, a few science-fiction novels, quite a number of romances, poetry, belles lettres. Among the latter was a copy of *The Innocents Abroad*. My father was a great fan of Mark Twain; he had tried to get me to read *The Innocents*, saying it was one of the funniest books ever written. Naturally I had refused to read it. Now I picked it up with the feeling that it was a link, however remote, with home. I selected half a dozen others, more or less at random.

Eventually I found my way into the Piazza della Signoria. It was full of tourists and pigeons and fountains and statues.

49

The copy of Michelangelo's *David* was completely ringed in by tourists, some looking, some conscientiously reading their guidebooks. There were souvenir stalls all around, even under the beautiful medieval arcades. Oddly enough, the garish banners and cheap copies of *David* (made in Taiwan) didn't seem out of place. There had always been crowds in the Piazza della Signoria, and small tradesmen selling their wares. Yesterday cooking pots and utensils; today, plastic Davids made in Taiwan.

When I sat down at a table at one of the outdoor cafés, I had collected several parcels, a small guide to Florence, and a handful of postcards. I wrote cards to several of my co-workers: "Having a wonderful time, aren't you jealous?"

The family cards came next. My favorite (and so far, only) niece couldn't read yet, but she might enjoy eating the card. I sent one to her and another to her parents, Jim and his cute wife; and another to Mike, living in bachelor indigence in Boston. I addressed the last to Mr. and Mrs. Timothy Malone. Then I sat staring at the blank half of the card, my pen poised.

They hadn't wanted me to come. Pa had yelled and pounded on the table, as was his habit. The gist of his argument was, bury the past, forget it and go on. Ma hadn't said much. It had offended her thrifty soul to see me blow the entire insurance settlement on a trip abroad. It was all Bart had left—the insurance on his car.

Pa never liked Bart. He was too suave, too well dressed, and far, far too handsome. He smiled too much, particularly when Pa asked questions that weren't meant to be funny, such as, "What do you do for a living?" Bart's answer—"As little as possible, Mr. Malone"—didn't go over too well. When I explained that Bart was trying to succeed in one of the most heartbreakingly competitive of all trades, and that establishing oneself as an actor took hard work, talent, *and* luck, my skeptical father just rolled his eyes and sniffed.

I thought I understood his skepticism and his hostility. It

isn't easy for a father to give his only daughter, the baby of the family, to another man. And when the man is a stranger, and said baby daughter shows up married, without so much as a preliminary letter of announcement... I didn't blame my father for resenting that, but Bart had wanted it that way. I would have agreed if he had suggested we get married in diving suits, with Jacques Cousteau as best man.

I took a firmer grip on my pen and wrote, "It's beautiful here. Everything is fine and I'm having a wonderful time. Love..."

It was a cop-out. But what else could I say? I hadn't told the family I hoped to visit Bart's grandmother, as I then believed her to be. They knew he had been born in Italy and they assumed I was on a sentimental journey. That was all they knew. They didn't know Bart's "grandmother" was a countess. That would have finished it for my father. He was a violent egalitarian, and when he started ranting about decadent aristocrats he sounded like the French Revolution. To explain the situation I now found myself in, or even part of it, would have taken more space than half a postcard. And it was not the sort of story I wanted the postman to read. Jack Wilson always read postcards, especially cards from exotic foreign lands. Then he went and told everybody on his route.

Since my father had demanded I give him an address, I wrote down the Grande Albergo San Marco e Stella di Firenze. That took up the rest of the empty space on the card. I was sure Angelo would hold mail for me if I asked him to.

Yet I felt as if I had stopped in the middle of some task I ought to finish. I didn't push the little button that retracted the point of my ballpoint pen. Instead I took the notebook in which I keep addresses and memoranda and tore a couple of pages out of the back. I wrote for five minutes. Then I put the pages in my purse, paid for my espresso, and went on my way.

The sun lay warm and golden on the rooftops. The shops were reopening after the afternoon break. I had not meant to go shopping, but when I found myself in front of a window piled with gloves of all colors and materials, a bizarre impulse came over me, and I went in. According to the guidebook, gloves were one of the things one bought in Florence. I bought two pairs, one brown, one soft cream. I knew I'd probably never wear the cream-colored gloves. Once I got home I would wonder what the devil had prompted me to spend such an outlandish sum on them. But I knew they were a symbol; if the contessa got on my nerves, I would wear my gloves to luncheon next time.

Then the bug bit me and I wanted to buy everything I saw. Mosaic jewelry, straw bags, little wooden boxes, copies of statues and pieces of statues—David's head, David's hands—and other parts of David, meticulously reproduced. I was tempted to get one for Mike.

The only thing I did buy, besides the gloves, was an electronic football game, the kind that can be played by one or more people. It was beautifully crafted, and it cost the earth. I reminded myself that I was saving the cost of food and lodging—and then I remembered my hostess. I ought to get something for her. But what? The gloves I had bought, though more expensive than anything of the sort I had ever owned, weren't of the quality she was accustomed to wear. The truth was, I could not afford to buy her anything of the quality to which she was accustomed. The family fortunes may have declined, but she wore silk nighties trimmed with Valenciennes lace. Even the cigarettes she smoked had monograms and gold tips.

I wandered the streets trying to get an idea, but nothing seemed right for her. The flower market was intoxicating— big fluffy bunches of spring blossoms, pink and pale blue and dazzling yellow and purest white, smelling like heaven and looking like a sunrise. She had flowers—she probably had a greenhouse bursting with orchids. The vegetable market was even more colorful, but I could hardly carry back a bag of tomatoes or an eggplant. Jewelry, perfume, scarves, boxes, handkerchiefs... For all I knew, her handkerchiefs were hand-embroidered by particularly superior nuns at a particularly superior convent.

Finally I gave up the hunt. If a brilliant inspiration did not occur to me before I left, I would send her something quaintly plebeian from America when I got back. A copy of the Minute Man at Concord, made in Taiwan.

Angelo was behind the desk when I reached the hotel, reading what appeared to be the same page of the same magazine. His feet rested on my suitcase. I asked him about postage to the States. Not only did he know the amount, he had the stamps. After some searching in the drawers, he also produced an envelope. I put the pages I had written into the envelope and addressed it.

"Angelo, will you do me a favor? It's very important." I reinforced my request by handing over a wad of hundred-lire notes. "Ten days from now, if I don't come back and ask you for this letter, I want you to mail it. Ten days, okay? *Dieci*." I held up ten fingers.

Angelo was afflicted with the momentary paralysis that struck him whenever he was caught by surprise. "Ten," he repeated, clearing his throat.

"Ten days. You promise?"

He put his hand on his heart and swore by something— I caught the word *madre*, and found that convincing. After he had carried my suitcase to the car, he stood on the step staring after me as I drove off.

I wondered what he was thinking. Did he take me for a spy or a blackmailer, or did he just think I was a little crazy, like all foreigners? *I* thought I was a little crazy. But accidents do happen, even to the young and healthy; no one knew that better than I. If something did happen—it wouldn't happen, but if it did—I did not want to vanish into infinity in the hills of Italy without telling them why I was there. Writing the letter was a catharsis in itself. I made a full confession, as Sister Ursula would have said—or, as my brother Mike would have put it, I spilled my guts out. I told them everything—things they had suspected but had never known, things they had not even suspected. Confession is good for the soul.

And then I gave the letter to Angelo. I knew if I took it with me, I'd get cold feet and tear it up.

Confession was not the only reason for the letter. The other reason was really crazy. Among the books I had bought was a little masterpiece called *Bride of the Madman*. The cover showed a girl running pell-mell down the side of a mountain. She was wearing a long white dress that in real life would have tripped her up before she had gone ten feet; and on the top of the mountain was an Italian villa, surrounded by cypresses. The artist could have used a picture of the Villa Morandini as a model.

I said, sneering, "Move over, Jane Eyre," and, with a defiant twist of the wheel, squeezed into the traffic approaching the bridge.

iv

THE SETTING sun was at my back when I started up the road that led to the villa. I knew the way now, and it was the first time I had driven the road when I was relaxed, so I could appreciate how lovely it was—and how isolated. The lower slopes of the hills framing the Val d'Arno were thickly inhabited—old villas and modern suburbs, small farmhouses and vacation homes, surrounded by gardens and the beautiful, symmetrical cypresses. The small side road might have been in another country. The branches of the trees on either side almost met overhead; sunlight filtering through the new leaves cast flickering gold-green shadows across the car. If there was another house along the road it was invisible—not even a smoking chimney.

The gates were closed. As I glided to a stop, Alberto trotted out of the lodge, tossing his cigarette aside, and opened the gates. He took his time about it, but when I drove through he touched his cap in a sketchy caricature of the salute that he gave his mistress. I put my nose in the air and ignored him. Perhaps he had not known who I was the first time I encountered him, but that didn't excuse his behavior. And I couldn't forget the way he treated the dog.

The front door opened as I approached. This time it was Emilia who did the honors, with even less enthusiasm than her husband. They made a fine pair, perfectly suited to one another. No wonder Alberto beat the dog. He wouldn't get far bullying Emilia; she was short, but as muscular as a man.

I asked her where I should put the car and she gave me the same look of contemptuous surprise with which the contessa had favored me when I admitted I had not thought of ringing for a servant. It was a look with which I was to become quite familiar. "Alberto will put away the car, signora."

I let her carry my suitcase upstairs, and gave her the car keys.

Now that the room was officially my room, my mother's prohibition no longer applied, so I investigated the drawers and the wardrobe. The doors of the wardrobe stuck when I pulled at them, but there weren't any bodies inside—not even a gown spotted with bloodstains, or a lock of woman's hair. The drawers of the dressing table were lined, rather prosaically, with sheets of *La Nazione*, the local newspaper. What, I thought—no scented, satin fabric? I put my three sets of underwear and my extra nightgown away, and hung my clothes in the wardrobe. They looked lonely, like orphan children in a cold world.

I was amused to learn that the doors of the bookcase had

been unlocked; but a survey of the books made me glad I had thought to bring my own reading materials. They were all in Italian, and the most recent had a date of 1933. The added amenities also included a vase of narcissi and hyacinths on the dressing table, and a carafe of water.

Cocktails at seven, she had said. I hoped it was not as formal as it sounded; I hadn't brought the right clothes for a cocktail party. I changed into a cotton blouse and denim skirt and then, having an hour to kill, picked up *Bride of the Madman*. By the time the hour was up I wished the madman would go ahead and strangle the girl and get it over with. She deserved strangling. I tossed the book aside, gave my makeup a final check, and started downstairs.

The contessa was decked out in a long silk gown of a rare and wonderful shade that matched her hair—a blend of soft copper and shimmering silver. After the first critical look she politely ignored my cotton and denim, and when I stumbled, addressing her, she told me to call her Francesca. We dined formally that evening, in a room that made my mammoth bedroom look like a closet. The candles on the table formed an island of light amid a black sea of shadows. On the far-off ceiling was a painting—blue skies, clouds, hovering figures—gods, saints, cherubs, I couldn't tell at that distance. The table could have seated forty people. We huddled at one end, with Emilia serving course after interminable course. The food was superb and so was the wine. "Our label," said Francesca, when I commented.

I had not expected Pete to join us for cocktails, but when we entered the dining salon, in a solemn parade of two, I saw there were only two places set. Of course I had to ask. I got the look again. "Children in America dine with adults, I am told. I fear I am old-fashioned in that respect."

I wondered where Pete ate his dinner. In the kitchen with the cook? Alone in his room? I remembered family dinners when we were kids, still living at home—the boys arguing about fine points of hockey or football, and, as they got older, about politics; Pa yelling out his opinions, my mother correcting our table manners and trying to introduce nice, safe topics of conversation that wouldn't end in a fight. . . . A shiver ran through me. Francesca noticed it, and asked if I would like Emilia to fetch a wrap. I said, no, I was fine, and added, "Perhaps I could go up later and say good night to him. Or read, or play a game."

"Not tonight," said Francesca. "He has been sent early to bed. He did not finish his lessons."

We retired to her sitting room for coffee. Francesca took a piece of embroidery from a brocade bag and inquired whether I had had a pleasant afternoon.

I didn't mention the game I had bought for Pete because I was self-conscious about having nothing for her. I burbled on about the wonders of Florence and she listened with a faint, appreciative smile, as if I were praising one of her possessions. Before long I ran down, and there was a brief silence.

"I'm afraid evenings here are rather quiet," she said. "If you have handwork you would like to do . . . ?"

I had been admiring the flash of her needle as she flicked it deftly in and out of fabric as sheer as a cloud. When she made the suggestion I laughed out loud. My current project was a sweater for Mike. I had already ripped it out three times. She looked at me inquiringly, and I explained, "I'm all thumbs when it comes to handwork. It's very popular back home and all my friends do something—needlepoint or knitting or counted thread. I've tried them all, but I can't seem to get the hang of it."

"But surely you were convent-taught?"

Convent-taught? Our Lady of Sorrows? The sisters counted the year well spent if they got through with nobody pregnant or arrested for drug abuse. I thought of Sister Ursula banging on the desk with her pointer, and tried to picture her sitting in the middle of a circle of demure little maidens, their heads bent over an altar cloth. Imagination reeled.

"Not exactly," I said. "It wasn't like that."

"You ought to learn embroidery. It is a useful skill."

"I admire it; I just can't do it." I tried to see what she was working on. Daisies? White petals on white muslin, with twining stems and tendrils. . . .

"It is never too late to learn." She put her work down and reached into her bag. "Let me show you."

She threaded the needle with bright-red floss; the delicacy of white on white was obviously beyond me—and demonstrated the stitch. I was even clumsier than usual. I had finally identified what she was making. It was a long embroidered dress, like a christening gown, for a small baby.

v

THANK GOD for Mark Twain. The sight of that tiny white garment punctured my self-esteem and made me feel like a low, crawling worm. After I had excused myself and fled to my room I reached for a book—any book—anything to take my mind off my wickedness.

I couldn't have done better than *The Innocents Abroad.* The buoyant irreverence of Sam Clemens pretending to be unimpressed by the wonders of the Old World was just what I needed. "And now that my temper is up, I may as well go on and abuse everybody I can think of," he wrote, after blasting the Church for building great cathedrals while the poor starved in the streets. "They have a grand mausoleum in Florence, which they built to bury our Lord and Saviour and the Medici family. It sounds blasphemous, but it is true. . . ."

I read on, chuckling to myself, until I got sleepy, and when I finally turned out the light I wasn't feeling quite so wormy. Francesca's tiny garments weren't pathetic, they were only an example of aristocratic snobbishness. She would embroider white gowns for a Morandini baby, but she wouldn't spend five minutes sewing for a child dying of cold and neglect.

I dreamed that night—the same dream that had tormented me for months. The setting and the details might differ, but the theme never changed. I was looking for Bart. They told me he was dead, but I knew it wasn't true. He was alive, but I could not find him. He was a prisoner, held by faceless uniformed guards; he was in a hospital suffering from amnesia; he was in flight, menaced by fantastic dangers—a volcano about to erupt, a tidal wave, a hired killer. I pursued shadows down the dark streets of dreaming, shadows that sometimes paused long enough to give me a glimpse of shining gray eyes, or let me hear an echo of mocking laughter. I never found him. I never touched him. And I always woke drenched with perspiration, as if I really had been running all the long night.

The dream that night was one of the worst. This time I saw him and heard him—the familiar laughter and the shape of his body, tall and slim-hipped, with an eel-like agility. He was so close I could have reached out and touched him when my feet went out from under me and I fell, not to earth, but down, down, through thick fog into infinite depths, lit far below by a ruddy glow of fire.

I woke with the sheets twisted around me like giant snakes. My face was wet with tears—not of grief, but of rage. I pounded the pillow with clenched fists. Damn him—damn Bart for leaving the way he had; damn God for punishing me this way; damn Sister Ursula for making me believe in the fires of hell, burning, burning for the sinner.

Like Mark Twain, I went on and abused everybody I could think of, and then lay snuffling quietly to myself, the sheets thrown back and the night breeze cooling my fevered body. The breeze carried the scent of fir needles and damp earth—

and something else. I sat bolt upright, sniffing. Something acridly sweet, unpleasantly familiar.

I got got out of bed and tiptoed on bare feet to the window. The doors onto the balcony were open. The thin inner curtains swayed gently. Nothing creaked under my feet as I moved; the floors were tiled, even that of the balcony.

The moon had set. A silvery glow behind the pointed silhouettes of the cypresses marked its passing. There was no sound except the soft whisper of the boughs.

Then I saw a small point of glowing red. It moved eerily through the darkness like a satanic firefly.

Someone was on the terrace, by the fountain. I stood motionless, scarcely breathing, as I watched the tip of the cigarette brighten and fade, glide up and down and up again.

Finally the fiery circle soared like a shooting star and disappeared. The shadow enclosing the fountain reached out a long finger across the lighter surface of the starlit stone. He came out of the dark like a swimmer rising from the water—tall and slim, with eel-like swiftness. He glided across the pale grass and was gone.

Chapter Three

"HE'S HERE. I saw him last night, from my window. I heard him laughing."

Through the remainder of that endless night I had told myself that I must state my case as coolly and dispassionately as a judge summing up. I had forced myself to wait until morning before confronting her. I had planned what I intended to say, word for word. But in spite of my resolutions I couldn't keep my voice under control, and I knew the strain of the sleepless hours was visible on my face.

For a moment her face mirrored the shock that had traced disfiguring marks on my own. She burst out, "But that is..." and then checked herself. "You dreamed," she said. "You are not yourself. Your condition..."

I felt the dangerous, deadly laughter bubbling up my throat

and into my mouth. I pressed my lips together and managed to hold it in. My condition? Fresh out of Dr. Baldwin's crazy house, had she but known. I had no intention of mentioning that episode. It would only confirm her picture of the bereaved, neurotic young widow.

I said steadily, "I was not asleep. I was not dreaming. I woke in the night; I went to the window. There was a man by the fountain. He walked across the terrace and...."

Disappeared? Vanished? Neither was a particularly good word, under the circumstances.

Her face cleared miraculously. "You saw a man—but of course you did! My poor child. You must have seen Professor Brown."

"Professor...?" The images created by words are pervasive. I had had professors of all ages and sizes and shapes, yet the suggestion was that of an old man, stooped and white-haired. Nothing like the person I had seen.

"I should have told you about him." She was smiling, speaking quickly, vivaciously. "He is restoring some of the objects in the family collections for me. I gave him permission to walk in the garden at night."

We were at breakfast, in her sitting room. She went on talking about Professor Brown. Occasionally a phrase penetrated the daze of hope and fear, belief and doubt, that filled my mind. "...most persistent in his requests...the family collections...duty to art and science...I forget he is here, I see so little of him." Then her smile faded and she actually touched me—a butterfly brush of manicured fingertips across the back of my hand. She said softly, "I should have warned you. I should have remembered. After my husband passed away I saw him often, on the street, in the shops. A chance resemblance, magnified by emotional confusion which is quite normal, quite understandable."

It was an extraordinary speech for her, warm, compassionate. What she had said was true. Other people had told me of having the same experience. Quite normal...I wanted to believe it. I wanted so badly to believe it that I dismissed the echo of laughter I had heard in the empty wing. I had heard his laughter a hundred times since that day, awake and dreaming.

"You will want to meet the professor," Francesca said. "Then your last doubt will be dispelled."

"Really, that isn't necessary. I'm sure you're right."

"No, you must meet him. He is an entertaining eccentric; he may amuse you. He spends most of his time in the storerooms. I don't go there. It is very dusty. But you are dressed suitably."

There was a little sting in the words and in the cool glance with which she studied my shirt and jeans. The outfit was shriekingly out of place in the eighteenth-century elegance of her sitting room, but I couldn't wear my brown suit all the time.

We had finished breakfast. She tinkled the little bell, and when Emilia came in she said, "Take Signora Morandini to see *il professore.*"

The title jarred me. Signora Morandini...That was the name on my marriage license. But she had said it was not Bart's name. What was it? What was *my* name? I wasn't going to become morbid and introspective about my lack of identity. I had a name, a good name, and when I got home I would take steps to make it my legal name.

I followed Emilia up two flights of stairs to what would have been the attic in an American house. It was the floor above the one on which the bedrooms were located, and it was much more than an attic; it was a weird warren of oddly shaped rooms, with stairs intruding for no apparent reason, with zigzag corridors and strange little doorways. Some of the rooms were large and spacious, others were narrow cubicles furnished with scraps of cheap furniture—servants' quarters, I assumed. Some were storerooms or lumber rooms packed with the most astonishing variety of odds and ends. If they were part of the "family collections," Francesca had chosen an inappropriately pretentious term for junk.

Emilia was short of breath when we reached the top of the final stairs, a narrow uncarpeted flight that ended in a closed door. She opened it and stood back. "*Il professore*," she said.

Piles of clutter stretched out as far as the eye could see. Mountains and hills of boxes and chests and barrels and old furniture formed a landscape as rugged as the terrain outside. The only light came from small windows blurry with dust, and from the door behind me. As I stepped cautiously forward, the door closed, and I found myself in deep gloom, with shadowy objects looming on all sides.

There was no doubt about it; Emilia didn't like me. Her gesture had the subtle malice with which people show hostility when they dare not express it openly. A claustrophobic would have collapsed at finding himself shut in that crowded space. I wasn't exactly happy about it myself. I even tried the door to make sure it wasn't locked.

Presumably *il professore* was in there somewhere. I was afraid to move or call out, for fear of bringing some teetering object down on my head. Damn the woman, she hadn't even offered me a flashlight.

Gradually my eyes grew accustomed to the dimness and I saw a faint glow of light ahead. I started picking a path between the piles of junk. It became a challenge to find a way through, and I thought what a super place this would be for hide and seek, if you were willing to take your chances on being mashed by falling furniture. Only the young and agile could get through; Emilia's stocky frame would never have made it through some of the narrow spaces.

As I drew closer to the light I heard sounds, little chuckles and smothered words. *Il professore* was talking to himself. No wonder Francesca never came here—clutter and dirt and dust and an eccentric professor mumbling to himself—or to the rats? Mice, certainly; there are always mice in old houses. I'm not afraid of mice. I was actually beginning to enjoy myself.

Finally I reached a barricade that seemed impassable—a huge armoire or wardrobe, whose roughly finished back left splinters in my fingers as I explored its surface. The mumbling was louder now, and I deduced that the speaker must be on the other side of the armoire. All at once his voice rose. "'My scrofulous French novel on gray paper with blunt type!... Twenty-nine distinct damnations....'"

There was a gap between the wardrobe and a pile of crates. I tried to squirm through and stuck halfway, hopelessly wedged in at the hips. At least I could see what was beyond.

The mumbles and chuckles had confirmed my picture of a weird little old scholar, and the final outburst—obviously a quotation—nailed it down. The figure I saw was crouched and huddled, and there were streaks of gray in its thick dark hair. He was squatting on the floor, his back to me, his shoulders bowed as he leaned forward, examining some object hidden from me by his body. I wondered how I could possibly have mistaken this middle-aged mumbler for my husband. I decided I had better give him some warning of my presence. My movements had not been noiseless, but obviously he hadn't heard them. I cleared my throat. "Hello," I said loudly.

The crouched figure exploded like a coiled spring. He moved with an admirable economy of motion, displacing nothing except himself and a cloud of dust. That was the gray in his hair—dust. The little old professor vanished, never to return. He was built like Bart—an inch or two shorter, but just as lean and almost as broad-shouldered. There the resemblance ended. His face was as comically homely as that of a gnome—snub nose, wide mouth, rounded cheeks. His jaws were dark with stubble and his ears stuck out. He wore faded jeans and a T-shirt with a design, badly worn, across the chest. He also wore horn-rimmed glasses. The abruptness of his movement sent them skidding down his nose; he caught them at the last second, pushed them into place, and squinted wildly at me through the smeared surfaces.

"I'm sorry I startled you," I said, squirming in a vain effort to free myself. "I'm Kathleen Malone...." And there I stuck, verbally as well as physically. What was my name?

The professor raised his hand in a dramatic gesture. "Of course. Kathleen Malone. Why not? There's everything else in this place; why not a lost Irish colleen? Did you take a wrong turning outside of Dublin, my darling, my serpenting beauty?"

"What?"

"Browning. I'm extremely fond of Browning. And you do look rather serpentine, wriggling through that hole. Here." He shifted a box, took my hand, and yanked me into the open. An ominous ripping sound accompanied the movement.

"Damn it," I said, clapping a hand to the seat of my jeans.

"Sorry. Did I do that?" He didn't look sorry. He was grinning. Even in repose his mouth was not small; when he smiled it stretched like a rubber band, far beyond its original limits. If the length of a smile is an accurate measure of joie de vivre, he had to be the happiest man I had ever met.

"I was snagged on something, as I would have mentioned if you had given me a chance. Do you always act so precipitately?"

"No, no. If I acted precipitately here, I'd be buried under bales and boxes, and I would become a permanent part of the Morandini collections. I doubt that anyone would ever bother to look for me. Here, have a seat."

He swiped ineffectively at a wooden box. I sat down and looked around.

He had cleared a space about ten feet square. At one end was a partition wall, with a door. On one side was a long table covered with papers and office equipment, including a file box of dark metal. The light came from a battery-operated electric lamp.

"I must apologize for disturbing you, Professor," I began.

He interrupted with a hoarse chuckle. It had sounded faintly sinister before; coming from that wide-lipped mouth, it could not be anything but funny. "I'm no professor, love. Just a humble graduate student trying to scrape up material for a dissertation. I thought a title would impress the countess, but I couldn't be lying to you, now could I? How did I miss you? Or did I stumble unawares on Aladdin's lamp and summon up a genie?"

I realized he must take me for a servant. I couldn't blame him, but here, at least, I had to be honest. I was operating under enough false assumptions with too many people as it was. I said, "I'm related to the countess, by marriage. My husband was her nephew."

His smile faded. "Was?"

"He was killed in a car crash a few months ago."

"Killed in . . . But you. . . ." The words burst out like popcorn popping. He clapped his hand over his mouth and stared at me. Then he said, "I'm sorry. Really. Sometimes my mouth gets disconnected from my brain."

I didn't mind. The awkward bluntness of his distress was far more to my taste than polished phrases of formal sympathy. Francesca's dignified acceptance of Bart's death was admirable, no doubt, but it had left me feeling flat and uncomforted. "Cool" is not a quality the Malones appreciate.

"It's all right," I said. "I'd have come up and introduced myself before this if I had known you were here. I think I— I saw you last night, in the garden. The one with the little fountain."

"I'm allowed to walk in the gardens when the gentry are safely in bed. I hope I didn't disturb you."

"No. You didn't. Anyway, I'm not one of the gentry."

"That makes two of us." He held out his hand, blissfully

oblivious of the fact that it was as black as a coal miner's.

"My name is David."

"Kathy." We shook hands. "What on earth are you doing up here?"

"It's a long, boring story, which I will tell you in complete detail," said David, sitting down on the floor.

"Please do."

"I'm here under false pretenses, actually. What I'm really looking for are nineteenth-century diaries and papers relating to English and American visitors to Italy."

"It sounds very pompous."

"Does it? Good. Doctoral dissertations are supposed to have pompous titles. They are also supposed to incorporate new research, insights, and interpretations. Now I ask you: How the hell is anybody going to find a new topic in the field of nineteenth-century English literature? I mean, my God, they've even done solemn studies on the relative numbers of vowels and consonants in the works of Jane Austen! If an unpublished scrap turns up, every scholar in the field pounces on it like a dog on a bone and tears it to shreds. So I got this bright idea. I decided.... Are you sure you want to hear this?"

"I haven't anything better to do."

"If you think that unenthusiastic response is going to keep me from lecturing, you don't know academics. I decided I'd find my own unpublished scraps. As you probably know—and if you don't, I'm going to tell you—Italy became a mecca for English and American writers in the nineteenth century. If you had any pretension to culture, you made the Grand Tour. Henry James, Fenimore Cooper, Hawthorne, the Brownings—"

Not knowing how long the catalog would continue if I did not interrupt, I said intelligently, "I get it. You're doing your dissertation on Browning."

"Don't taunt me, madam." His wide mouth drooped in

exaggerated woe. "Oh, sure, I dream of turning up a batch of letters, or a diary describing a visit to Robert and Elizabeth—they lived in the Casa Guidi, in Florence, for almost fifteen years—but Browning has been dissected too many times. The one I'm looking for is Margaret Fuller."

"Who?"

"You've never heard of Margaret Fuller? Good God, the deficiencies of our educational system! She was one of the first female foreign correspondents, and a brilliant scholar at a time when women were not supposed to flaunt their intellectual capacities. Horace Greeley hired her to write for the New York *Tribune*. She was in Italy when the war for Italian independence broke out; she had fallen in love with an Italian nobleman, the Marquis Ossoli, and had a child by him. How's that for being liberated? Unlike most of his peers, the *marchese* was a supporter of the freedom movement, and so was Margaret. During the siege of Rome he fought on the walls while she ran one of the hospitals and sent back dispatches to Greeley—at ten bucks a shot. He had raised her wages from eight dollars to ten when she threatened to quit. She was also, I hardly need to say, a fighter for women's rights. But maybe that wouldn't interest you."

"What makes you suppose that?" I demanded indignantly.

He looked sheepish. "Ignorant male chauvinism, I guess. We unconsciously assume that a young, beautiful woman—"

"Enjoys being viewed as a charming nitwit? Wake up, buster. Besides, I'm not beautiful."

He adjusted his glasses and stared at me. "No, you aren't. Your lower lip is too full and your nose is too long and your chin sticks out—"

"Only when I'm mad."

David grinned. "Scratch the chin. I don't know why you give the impression of being beautiful. It's an interesting problem. Maybe it's your coloring. Fair hair and brown eyes—

and such a nice shade of brown, like a fox's coat. 'Her locks were yellow as gold: Her skin was white as. . . .' Oops."

"White as what?"

"Wrong poem," said David, somewhat flustered. "You are a bit pale, though. Have you been sick?"

"Let's get back to Margaret Fuller."

"Oh, sure. Right. Good idea. Uh. . . ."

"I'd like to know more about her," I said, relenting.

"I'll send you a copy of my book."

"At the rate you're going, I'll probably be too old and senile to read it. It will take you ten years to sort through all this. Have you any reason to suppose you'll find material about Margaret here, or are you just amusing yourself?"

"It's not a reason so much as a far-out hunch. Like Margaret's lover, the Count Morandini of that day was a follower of Mazzini and Garibaldi. After the fall of Rome, Margaret and Ossoli came to Florence and were finally married in a little village church, somewhere in Tuscany. It's probable that Morandini knew them, since they moved in the same social and political circles; possible that he mentioned them in his letters or journals. Nobody knows where and when the wedding took place. Imagine the sensation if I could find a written report! I mean, Morandini could have been their best man, or one of the witnesses."

"It looks to me like the proverbial needle in the haystack. You'll have to investigate every box and crate in the villa."

"Right." The prospect did not appear to daunt David. He beamed radiantly.

"Maybe you ought to give up literature and go in for garbage collecting," I suggested.

"It pays better than scholarship," was the bland reply. "Remember the Dickens novel in which the dustman becomes a millionaire?"

"I never read it."

"I can see your education has been sadly neglected. Not

to recognize Browning—that's a disgrace." He went on with mounting enthusiasm, "There are tons of junk in this place! It has all the charm of digging for buried treasure without the physical discomforts. You never know what you'll turn up. I found an Aztec mask in a palazzo near Rome last fall— one of the *marchese*'s ancestors had traveled in Mexico and brought back souvenirs. I've only been here a couple of weeks, and already I've found a crate of odds and ends one of the Morandinis collected in Egypt in the 1880's. Most of them are forgeries, but there are a few genuine pieces. I wouldn't be surprised to run across a mummy tucked away in a corner."

The delight in his voice made me laugh. "You'll never write that dissertation. You're having too much fun."

"I'll get tired of junk one day," David said placidly. "But in the meantime, can you imagine a better way to spend your time?"

"Frankly, yes."

"It's a cheap way of getting a European vacation. Free room and sometimes board as well. I'm on good terms with Rosa. I wander into the kitchen twice a day looking pale and wan and she stuffs me with pasta."

"But how do you con people into admitting you to their attics? You can obviously talk the leg off a donkey, but I can't see Francesca giving a damn about Margaret Fuller. Especially Margaret Fuller."

"Oh, that. Well, to be honest with you..." David took off his glasses and looked grave. "I got carried away talking to you. It must be your kind, innocent face. You won't split on me, will you?"

"That depends on what deep dark secret you're hiding."

"You already know my deep dark secret. The contessa doesn't. She thinks I'm searching for marketable treasures, like the Aztec mask. Or better—a forgotten Bellini, or an overlooked Botticelli or a Cellini saltcellar that some ignorant

71

former count replaced with a pressed-glass bowl made in Manchester. As you may have observed from the neglected state of the house and grounds and the paucity of staff, the lady's cash flow is none too good. The same thing is true of many of the old families, except the smart ones who have turned to manufacturing cars or clothes. They've already hocked the paintings and the antique furniture and the sculpture. Until I pointed it out, they didn't realize there might be unconsidered gems in the attic. The guy whose ancestor brought back the Aztec mask is a friend of the contessa. An American museum has offered a sum for the mask that dazzles his simple aristocratic soul. Your lady friend thinks I may find something like that here."

"Will you?"

"It's damned unlikely. But one never knows." His eyes rested gloatingly on the heaped-up boxes.

I stood up. "I can see you're dying to get back to work. I won't keep you any longer."

"Not that way." He put out a casual hand to detain me as I turned toward the narrow opening through which I had come. "I don't know how you ever made it through all that stuff. I'll show you my door."

"I don't want to take you from your labor of love."

"It's time for my morning break anyway." He untangled his long legs and got to his feet. "A quick run around the garden, followed by a call on the cook. Come on."

The way out was certainly less complicated than the route I had followed coming in. Uncarpeted stairs and straight passages led down four flights. The last stairs ended in a brick-floored corridor whose walls were of peeling stucco. "Kitchen is that way," David said, lifting a thumb toward the right. "Pantries and storerooms on the other side. All unoccupied now. And this . . ." He opened a door. "This is my exercise yard."

It was a small courtyard, high-walled and rank with weeds.

A path had been beaten through the weeds around the walls, presumably by David's feet. A few tangled roses struggled out of the brush to cling to the broken bricks and a half-rotted wooden bench stood against one wall. That was the extent of the amenities.

"'Run' would be more like it," I said. "You mean this is the only part of the grounds you're allowed to use during the daytime?"

"Now, now, don't let your democratic indignation get the better of you. I'm here on sufferance, and I take what I can get. It isn't so bad; my room is over the garage, which is through that gate. I can go and come as I please. Anyhow, I'm not anxious to socialize with the gentry or the staff—especially Alberto." His dust-streaked face was grim. I wondered what the chauffeur had done to inspire his silent condemnation, but David did not elaborate.

"That other gate opens into the kitchen garden," he went on. "You can get into the house that way, or go around to the front door."

"Thanks. And thanks for the lecture."

"Any time." His wide smile illumined his face. "If you get bored, come up and help me rummage."

"I might at that. If you get tired of running around this—this outdoor cage—come and play football with me and Pete."

"Pete?"

"I should say Pietro; the contessa doesn't care for American nicknames. Actually he's the Count Morandini, but it sounds silly to call a ten-year-old boy by his title."

"You mean there's a kid living here? A ten-year-old?"

"Haven't you seen him?"

David shook his head.

I LEFT David doggedly jogging around the path. Four circuits made up half a mile; he'd paced it off with a pedometer.

Seeing him in daylight, I realized how distant was the resemblance I had fancied. He didn't look anything like Bart. They were about the same height and build; that had been enough to deceive me. Even when dusted, David's brown hair was several shades lighter than Bart's; he moved without Bart's smooth actor's grace. Running, he looked like a loose-jointed, long-limbed marionette, a *Petrouchka* puppet with a cheerful clown's face. He should have had freckles. Maybe there were freckles, under the dust. Even if it had been clean, his was not the kind of face women looked at, the bolder staring openly, the well-bred sneaking little sidelong glances. Women did that to Bart. I remembered the smug satisfaction with which I had clung to his arm, watching other women yearn for what was mine.

I made my way to the walled garden where I had found Pete playing. It was quiet and deserted. There was no sign that a child had ever been there—no forgotten balls or toys lying in the long grass, no swing or trapeze hanging from the limb of a tree.

David's blank surprise at the mention of a child had left me with a queer feeling. He kept to his own part of the house and grounds, of course. He was in the attic most of the day. Still, it bothered me to think that the boy was so invisible. Maybe he was away at school. Maybe he had been home for vacation the day I saw him, or he attended a boarding school during the week and was only at the villa on weekends.

I decided I might as well do a little exploring. As Francesca had indicated, I was dressed for it, and I couldn't get any dirtier after my visit to the attic. Besides, I wanted to find out where the garage was located so I could get my car without having to apply to Alberto. I must remember to retrieve my keys, too.

I went back to David's exercise yard. He had finished his jogging and gone, presumably to beg a snack from Rosa. Through the gate he had pointed out I saw a stone-paved yard with the old stables on the far side. They were part of the house itself, the lower level of a wing that extended away from the central block. The former coachhouse had been turned into a garage. Beyond it, rows of empty stalls stretched forlornly to the far end of the wing.

I didn't go through the gate. The Mercedes was out in the yard, and Alberto was polishing it. Sunlight reflected dazzlingly from the gleaming chrome of the grille. Too bad he wasn't as conscientious about the dog.

I wondered where the animal was kept. It must be nearby, in the work area. I decided it might be a good idea to find out so I wouldn't inadvertently wander into its run. The formal introduction hadn't convinced me of its good intentions.

The obvious course would have been to ask Alberto. Instead I backed quietly away from the gate and began looking on my own. It didn't take me long. I smelled the place before I saw it—not far from the stableyard and, in my opinion, too close to the route Pete followed to reach his bleak playground. The dog's pen was worse than bleak, it was a disgrace. There was a kennel of sorts, tin-roofed and obviously not leak-proof. Though the walls of the pen were ten feet high, the dog was chained. A narrow stretch of beaten earth, liberally sprinkled with piles of dung, marked the limits of its restless pacing. It wasn't pacing now; it lay stretched out, head on paws, next to a cheap plastic bowl containing a scant half-inch of scummy water.

He looked so bored and pathetic I almost did something really stupid. When I touched the gate he started up. The wind must have been blowing the wrong way, for he had not caught my scent. Did he jump with joy at the sight of me, the only person in his life who defended him and spoke gently to him? He jumped, all right—straight at me, jaws gaping. The chain brought him up with a jerk. He strained at it, snarling.

"You have a rotten memory," I said. "Calm down. You're not supposed to eat me; I'm one of the gentry, remember?"

I talked to him awhile, till he stopped snarling and sat down, staring at me like someone trying to remember a face. As I walked away I was so angry I was shaking. It was only sensible to keep the dog chained; he could probably jump the gate with no trouble. But the chain was far too short and Alberto didn't even bother keeping the pen clean. I wondered how often the dog was fed. From the way he had drooled at me, I deduced it wasn't often enough.

I returned to the kitchen garden and went through another gate. I had never seen a place so walled off into little compartments. Once the gardens must have been gorgeous. Even now, after years of neglect, there were signs of the features that had given each enclosure its special character—beds of roses, straggling and unpruned, in one; bulbs forcing brave emerald spears through the weeds in another; a crumbling fountain set in a mosaic-lined grotto in another. The bits of glittering mica and colored stone had been laid in concrete, but the roots of climbing vines had inserted steely fingers, and piles of fallen color littered the fountain's floor. One garden had been walled with marble and adorned with a tiny circular columned temple that must have served as a gazebo. Two of the columns had fallen; I realized that they had been built that way, one of the artificial ruins popular with nineteenth-century landscape artists. And everywhere the untended grass and the weeds were growing, to smother flowers and crack stone.

A final gate of intricate but rusted wrought iron admitted

me to the front grounds. They had been splendid in their heyday; the fountain spouting crystal streams from all the Tritons' horns, the lawn like emerald velvet, the flower beds patches of bright color. A stooped figure bent over one of the beds. It must be the man Francesca had mentioned—Alberto's assistant. I assumed he was weeding, though he didn't appear to be working very hard. I hesitated, wondering whether to approach him. There wasn't much I could say except "*Buon giorno*," nor much I could do except smile. He might not care for my condescending attentions. As I watched he got painfully to his feet, and I realized, with a shock of pity, that the poor creature was physically handicapped. Limping, one shoulder higher than the other, he set off across the lawn away from me.

It was later than I had realized. A glance at my watch confirmed the time suggested by the height of the sun. I would have to shower and change. And, I promised myself, I would ask Francesca where she was hiding her grandson. She could exile the child from her presence if she chose, but there was no reason why I had to treat him like a leper.

However, when I came down to lunch, suitably attired in blouse and skirt, Francesca wasn't there. Emilia poured the ritual glass of wine for me; when I indicated to her that I would wait for my hostess she produced a note from her pocket. The delicate handwriting informed me that I would be lunching alone. Francesca had an appointment she could not cancel. "I meant to tell you this morning at breakfast," she wrote. "I hope you will excuse my rudeness."

I could hardly blame her for forgetting, after the exhibition I had put on.

I waited until Emilia had poured my coffee before I asked about Pete. I called him Pietro, of course.

She repeated the key word. "School?"

"*La scuola.* Is *il conte* at the *scuola* today?"

She shook her head.

"Why not?" She looked blankly at me. I tried again. "Where is he?"

Her shoulders lifted in a shrug. I suspected she would not have committed that vulgarity in Francesca's presence, but vulgarity doesn't bother me; what bothered me was the utter indifference the gesture implied. "You don't know where he is?" I asked.

Another shrug. "In his room?"

I tossed my napkin onto the table with a gesture worthy of a contessa. "Where is his room?"

You'd have thought I had asked the way to the lion house. She didn't try to prevent me or talk me out of it, she simply could not comprehend why I would voluntarily look for the boy.

We started up the stairs. I decided I might as well take advantage of the opportunity to find out the answers to some of the things I was curious about, so I peppered her with questions. Yes, she said, the contessa's room was also on the second floor, at the far end of the same corridor on which my room was located, and near the door into the west wing, which was now unoccupied. Emilia's fractured English became surprisingly fluent at this point, and she went on to explain that the west wing was in a ruinous condition—unsafe, insanitary, and generally undesirable.

It was from this wing I had seen her come with her covered tray. I was tempted to ask if that was where they keep crazy old Uncle Giovanni, but I decided Emilia's English wasn't good enough for jokes. It was not a very funny joke anyway.

My room wasn't the state bedchamber after all. The suite of the reigning count and his consort occupied the entire second-floor front of the villa.

But the present count was elsewhere. I had taken it for granted that the child's room would be on the same floor as the other bedchambers; however, after I had stopped in my room to pick up the game I'd bought for him, Emilia led me up again. So Pete was in the attic, with the servants and the other junk. I was familiar with the old-fashioned custom of keeping the young as far from the adults as possible, but in this case it struck me as profoundly mistaken, not to say dangerous. That was when it dawned on me that Francesca had not mentioned a governess or nurserymaid. Who looked after him, then, especially at night?

When we reached the head of the stairs Emilia turned in the opposite direction from the one we had taken to reach the storeroom where David was working. Pete's room was on a corridor paralleling the front of the house. It was not far from the stairs, but it was a long way from Francesca's room, which was at the far end of another corridor on the floor below. She wouldn't be able to hear him if he became ill during the night—and that was probably just the way she wanted it.

I asked Emilia where she slept. She gestured—near Francesca's room. "And the *tuttofare*?" I persisted. This time her pointing finger indicated a door not far from the boy's. She added, with a twisted smile, "When she is there. She sleeps away, very often."

I didn't ask any more questions. When I raised my hand to knock on Pete's door, Emilia reached for the key. I had noticed it, but had not thought anything about it. The proper place for a key is in a keyhole. She said, "You wish to go in?"

Not trusting myself to speak, I nodded. Emilia turned the key. "When you come out, you..." She gestured, twisting her fingers. Lock him in again when you come out.

I stared at her. She shrugged, smiling insolently. "*Bene, signora*. As you desire."

I waited till she was out of sight. I thought I had heard

sounds of movement inside—soft, scuttling, surreptitious movements, like rats in the wall. Then I knocked and called out. "It's me, Pete. Kathy. Can I come in?"

After a moment his voice said, "Please."

The room had been furnished as a nursery, thirty years ago. It may have been pleasant then; there were shelves filled with toys and books, a fireplace with a fender and screen, a rocking horse, a little brass bed. There was nothing wrong with it now, except for its shabbiness and the fact that there was not one object in it that could have amused a ten-year-old boy. The window was barred.

Pete was in bed, a book open on his lap. He sat quite still, his eyes wide and watchful, his lips tight, until I closed the door.

"They didn't tell me you were sick," I said. "I'd have come to see you before if I had known."

"You are alone, signora?"

"Yes." I pulled up a chair and sat down. "How do you feel?"

"Well. I am well. I am not sick."

"I was afraid you had caught something from me. I guess it wasn't catching, though."

The funniest expression spread over his face—sly, almost prurient. It was a horrid look, even worse than the shuttered wariness it had replaced.

I had not missed the significance of the way he had addressed me. He had called me "signorina" before. Someone must have told him part of the story and hinted at the rest. I said impulsively, "You know I was married to your . . . he'd be your cousin, wouldn't he?"

"Yes, signora."

"I'm not pregnant, though."

The sly little leer vanished in a flood of surprise. He knew the word; after all, he had spent some time in an American school, and there aren't many words those kids haven't heard.

80

I went on casually, "You know, when a woman is going to have a baby, sometimes she gets sick at her stomach. I was sick yesterday. It was just one of those bugs people get when they travel. But I'm afraid someone may have jumped to the wrong conclusion."

I don't think he understood the last word, but the idea got through. His brow furrowed. "You are not—you do not..."

"Not pregnant, no. Did someone tell you I was?"

He was still flushed, but his expression was one of normal childish curiosity. He dropped the book and hugged his knees. "I heard them talk—Emilia and Rosa. When Emilia saw I was listening she said I was bad. It was not a thing for children...."

"Never mind, I can imagine what she said. She was wrong on all counts." I smiled at him. "In a way I'm sorry I'm not pregnant. I'd like to have a child."

"You like children?"

"Yes, of course. That's what I do for a living—teach children."

"Like me?"

"A little bit older than you. Junior high school. My students are between twelve and fifteen."

"What do you teach?"

"History."

His face fell. "Not football."

"You know I'm not very good at football, Pete. Oh, that reminds me. I brought you something."

He pounced on the game like a starving man on a bowl of soup. "I had it—like this—before. But it was not so—so—"

"Complicated?"

He tasted the word experimentally. "Complicated ...Yes. Not so complicated. It was broken. Let us play this now."

It didn't take him long to get the hang of it. I had already accepted the humiliating fact that most of my students could beat the pants off me at any electronic game. He skinned me four games out of six, and he would have gone on playing all day if I hadn't begged off.

"Let's play something else. Darn it, I'd like to win for a change."

"There is nothing else."

"No games—Parcheesi, checkers?"

"Only baby games." He swept the room with a scornful wave of his hand.

"What do you do all day?" I tried to keep my voice neutral. I don't think I succeeded.

"I have a radio. Sometimes I listen to the music. And I am always to study."

He indicated the book he had (not) been reading. It was a thick volume on Italian history, written for adults. There were a few black-and-white photographs.

I couldn't continue the inquisition. I had completely lost my sense of perspective, and that was bad. I had only heard one side of the case. It was hard to imagine there could be another valid point of view, but I had learned through painful experience that one could easily go astray in one's judgments, especially where a child was concerned.

His face changed pitifully when I rose to go, but he didn't ask me to stay. "Maybe you can get up tomorrow," I said. "We might have a game of real football."

"I can get up now. I am not sick."

I felt his forehead. "You haven't got a fever."

He pressed his face against my palm for a moment, then moved away. "I am not sick. They say I have to rest, but I don't. Only...only sometimes...I have bad dreams."

He must have seen from my expression how that hit me. Not only my own nightmares, but the memory of a voice, smooth and trained: "I could be bounded in a nutshell, And count myself a king of ultimate space, Were it not that I have

82

bad dreams...." Bart had always wanted to play Hamlet. What actor doesn't? And what a gorgeous Prince of Denmark he'd have made in the classic black velvet doublet and tights, with his shock of dark hair and his silver eyes, his high cheekbones and flexible hands.

A small voice stammered, "I said something bad."

"No. No, you didn't." I reached out for him and pulled him close. I needed the warmth, the closeness, as much as he did. "I have bad dreams too, Pete. I know how terrible they can be. But someday they'll go away. When you lose someone you...you love, at first all you can feel is anger. But it will pass. The hate and the hurt and the bad dreams, all of it."

As I stumbled through that little speech I knew that Doc Baldwin would have howled with horror at my uneducated attempt at therapy. How dare I meddle with something as deep-rooted and deadly as this child's sense of loss? Was I naive enough to suppose that my ignorant efforts could help?

Yes, I was. And I think they did help. He wasn't ready to let go and cry, but he held me tightly for a few seconds. Then he remembered his age and his dignity and pulled away. "It was bad for you, signora? I am sorry."

"Not as bad as it was for you." I brushed the tumbled hair from his forehead. "I think you are a very brave person."

That opened the floodgates. He started to talk, in a queer mixture of English and Italian. I got a picture of a way of life totally alien to me—a life-style I thought of as "jetset" or "beautiful people," for his parents seemed to have traveled constantly, to all the fashionable places. Either there was more money in the family than I supposed, or Mama and Papa had known how to make the most of their income, for Pete made casual mention of maids and tutors and teachers and other luxuries. He had not been left to the care of servants, though. His father had taught him to swim and ski. His mother had taken him to playgrounds and carnivals and zoos. She loved carousels. "Always she rode a white horse. When I was little she took me on the white horse with her. When I was big, I rode another horse, or a lion, or an elephant."

And he had had a dog. Bruno. His eyes filled when he spoke the name, as they had not for his parents. Seeing his distress I braced myself for the worst; but Bruno had not met a sticky end, he had been left behind when Pete came to Italy.

"Maybe you can have another dog," I said, knowing how I would have reacted to that idea if I had been in his shoes.

"I don't want a dog except Bruno. And besides, *she* would not let me have an animal. Not even a bird."

I knew who *she* was.

When the spate of reminiscences finally ran down he looked limp and exhausted. I knew how he felt; I had been in that state a few times myself. But he didn't look ill. Too thin and too pale, but that was grieving and lack of exercise—mental and physical. Again I prepared to take my leave.

"Tomorrow we'll have that game," I said. "I'll ask your grandmother tonight."

"O-kay," he said, brightening.

I went to the door. "Pete," I said.

"Yes, Signora Kathy?"

"I'm not going to lock the door. Will you stay in your room?"

He thought about it. "If I do not, they will be angry at you?"

I laughed. "Probably."

"Then I will stay. On the word of a Morandini, I swear!" He sat upright, his eyes flashing.

He looked like Bart. Horribly, dreadfully like him. I forced a smile. "See you tomorrow, Pete. Sleep well—and no bad dreams, right?"

"Right! And you, signora."

I went to my room. After ten minutes or so I stopped pacing and sat down and gave myself the lecture Pa would have given me. "Damnation if you're not at it again, rushing in to rescue people who may not need rescuing and may not want to be rescued. You remind me of the Boy Scout dragging the little old lady across the street, and her hitting him with her umbrella because she doesn't want to cross the damn street! Will you never learn to find out the facts before you act?"

I didn't think I would ever learn. Pa never had. But Dr. Baldwin and all the other specialists with whom I had worked, at school, would have said the same. Butt out. You may do more harm than good. Stop jumping to conclusions, creating imaginary dramas out of nothing.

The boy had not been physically abused. I had seen that a few times, and the signs are unmistakable. Anyway, I couldn't imagine Francesca being guilty of that kind of brutality. Her sins would be those of omission and coldness. I tried to see it from her point of view. She too had known grief. She had lost an only son. And into her quiet, ordered life had been thrust a child who was resentful and angry, confused and disturbed. Perhaps she had tried to reach out to him and had been rebuffed. It's hard to accept that treatment even when you understand the reason for it. Her methods of dealing with the boy were hopelessly wrong-headed, but they were probably well intentioned.

I put on my brown suit when I dressed for dinner. At least it was dignified, and I knew the importance of personal appearance when you are planning to start a fight. I meant to get some plain answers to some plain questions. I would try to keep an open mind, but . . .

She foiled me again. When I sailed into the ivory-and-gold sitting room, there were guests.

They were a middle-aged couple, Dr. and Mrs. Condotti. He looked like a baby pig, all pink and plump. Wisps of graying hair were brushed carefully across his high forehead. His wife was as thin as he was chubby, with a head of shimmering blond hair that looked like a carved wig.

I had learned that Italians were apt to toss titles like "doctor" and "professor" around rather casually. Dr. Condotti might not have been a medical man. But I thought he was. His wife's not-so-subtle glances at my stomach were those of middle-aged female curiosity. The doctor's look had a decidedly professional gleam.

They were a very dull pair. Only Francesca's smooth hostess manners kept conversation from limping through a long formal meal. Mercifully the Condottis left early. As soon as the door closed behind them, Francesca leaned back in her chair with a sigh. A less inhibited woman would have kicked off her shoes, run her hands through her hair, and let out a loud "Whew!"

"I hope you weren't too bored," she said. "The Condottis speak English well, that is why I invited them. They are not intellectuals, however."

"Not at all," I said vaguely.

"I must also apologize for leaving you alone all day. Perhaps tomorrow I can show you something of the countryside."

That gave me my opening. "I promised Pete—Pietro—I would spend part of the day with him."

She knew I had visited him. There was no surprise in her look, only a level curiosity. "You did not lock his door."

"No."

"More coffee?" Her hands were steady as she lifted the heavy silver pot. The fact that she had not called Emilia to perform this task told me she had recognized an unpalatable fact—she was going to have to talk to me.

"No, thank you." I had thought I was mad enough to speak plainly, but her superb self-possession weakened my resolve.

I said hesitantly, "I suppose you think it's none of my business, but—"

"You teach, I believe."

I had not told her that. I said, "You had me investigated."

"Of course. You would have done the same in my position. When I received your letters I did not know Bartolommeo was married. You might have been... anything."

"Fair enough. But—"

"I learned you were precisely what you claimed to be— Bartolommeo's legal wife. Therefore you have a position here. No, I do not believe that Pietro's condition is, as you put it, 'none of your business.' I had hoped you would not be moved to interfere, but I see now that you could not act otherwise. The qualities that lead you to do so are the qualities of youth, and I respect them, though I do not admire them."

I had never been dissected with such cool accuracy, not even by Dr. Baldwin. If she had expressed contempt or anger, I could have responded. Against that dispassionate (and just) assessment I had no defense.

She went on calmly. "You think me harsh in my dealings with the boy. My methods are not yours, and I feel no obligation to defend them. Theories come and go like women's fashions; the truths you hold today will be tomorrow's outmoded theories in their turn. To lock a child in his room is not cruel or unusual punishment. But that is not why I lock his door. I do so because he must be confined for his own safety. Twice in the past weeks he has come close to killing himself. There is insanity in the Morandini line. He has the seeds of it. The child is mad."

Chapter Four

I SAID, "I don't believe it."

"What is it you don't believe? That there is such a thing as hereditary insanity, or that Pietro tried to kill himself?"

"Both. Neither."

She smiled. Her teeth looked like icicles. "You are candid, aren't you?"

"I'm sorry. You may be telling the truth as you see it, but... You're wrong, that's all."

"My husband died in a hospital in Vicenza," she said. "He was homicidal and raving mad. His uncle—his grandfather—"

The Gothic atmosphere was so thick you could have cut it with a knife. I expected Mrs. Rochester to burst through the door howling curses. "Look," I said desperately, "I don't know much about mental illness—you don't mind if I use that term, I hope, instead of 'raving mad'? I do know there is no surer way of shattering a child's mind than telling him he's doomed to madness."

"I know that too. If I had not known, the psychiatrist Pietro is seeing—"

"You're taking him to a psychiatrist?"

Her glacial calm cracked briefly. "I know I am not your idea of a doting grandmother, Kathleen, but neither am I a monster. Will you allow me to tell you what happened without interruptions or emotional outbursts?"

"You're the one who used the word 'madness,'" I said. "Talk about emotionally loaded—"

"Touché." I expected her to show resentment, but the smile she gave me was almost friendly. "I will try to avoid such terms.

"Pietro's father was my son. My only son. He was always a practical child, intelligent enough, but without a spark of imagination—quite unlike the Morandinis, though I suppose you will frown at that reference to hereditary traits. At any rate, Guido showed some talent for business—investments, that sort of thing. I have never cared for such matters. After matriculating at Bologna he wanted to go to business school. I sent him to Columbia, in the United States. It was there he met his wife. I disapproved of the marriage. I admit it because I am sure you already suspect as much. But my reasons were not what you may suppose. I did not dislike the young woman because she was an American, I disliked her because she was the worst of America—superficial, common, incapable of appreciating another way of life. She was a good wife, however. She accompanied Guido on all his business trips."

So my image of the frivolous aristocrats jetting around the world had been way off base. It ought to have been a lesson to me.

"It was on one such trip that they were killed," Francesca

went on, without the faintest trace of emotion. "You may have read about the plane crash; it was one of the worst disasters in recent history. The airliner struck a school in a small town in Switzerland. The children were practicing for the Christmas pageant."

I remembered, of course. The media had not spared their readers and viewers any of the details; there were endless photographs of the agonized parents trying to clear away pieces of twisted metal to reach the bodies of their children. Even Bart's cultivated cool had been shaken by the story. I remembered his broken exclamations of shock and dismay. . . . Had he known his cousin was on that plane?

"Pietro had been placed at school in America. Against my wishes, of course. There is no need for me to tell you of the painful weeks following his arrival here—"

"You were named guardian in your son's will?"

"There was no will. How many healthy young people can admit the possibility of dying?"

The answer came readily, with no change in the eyes fixed steadily on mine; but for the first time I sensed she was equivocating—not lying, exactly, but not telling the whole truth.

I could hardly challenge her, though. I nodded, and after a moment she went on. "I sought psychiatric treatment for him immediately. His behavior was abnormal. Violent explosions of temper, followed by days of sullen silence. For a while he showed signs, however small, of responding to treatment. Then, when he had been here a little over a month, he ran out of his room in the middle of the night. His cries woke me. He was shouting loudly and incoherently, and laughing. By the time I had roused the servants and followed, he had left the house and climbed a tree—one of the big oaks by the gatehouse. I called to him to come down. He said yes, he would come; he would fly. He waved his arms and laughed and shouted, 'I can do it. I can fly. I will show you.'"

She picked up her embroidery. I said unsteadily, "How did you get him down?"

"We didn't. Alberto climbed up after him, but when he reached out for the boy, Pietro jumped. He landed in a mass of shrubbery, with only scratches and bruises to show for his adventure."

I could think of nothing to say. Children do try to commit suicide. Sometimes they succeed. This was worse than I had imagined.

Francesca resumed calmly, "Pietro claimed to have no recollection of the incident. A few weeks ago the second attack occurred. His door was locked—I began locking him in after the first attack. The *tuttofare* was sleeping in the next room. She was awakened by his screams and came for me. He had broken a mirror. Fragments were all around, and he was beating at the empty frame when I entered. There were bloody footprints across the floor. He had raced back and forth, from door to window to mirror, and had, naturally, cut his feet. If one of the shards had severed an artery, or if he had used his hands instead of a book to break the mirror, he might have bled to death before anyone reached him.

"Now perhaps you understand why I lock the child in his room when there is no one in attendance, and why his activities are so restricted. He goes to Firenze three times a week to a psychiatrist, and he is taking medication." She paused to set a stitch, delicately and precisely, before adding, "I may as well tell you that the medication is given to him in his food, without his knowledge. He made such a fuss, it became impossible to give it to him openly. I'm sure you disapprove of my methods, Kathleen; but I hope you will do me the courtesy of not questioning my motives."

IT TOOK a large dose of Mark Twain to put me to sleep that night, and for once I was thinking of someone else's problems instead of mine. Maybe that's why I slept like a log, without dreaming. By the following morning my idiot optimism had reasserted itself. Damn it, I just could not accept Francesca's diagnosis. I didn't care if every shrink in Europe and America confirmed it. The child had not demonstrated any symptoms of mental illness before the death of his parents; I felt sure Francesca would have mentioned that, as confirmation of her theory. He was emotionally disturbed—seriously disturbed—I had to admit that much. But a hereditary taint? I felt certain Pete's doctor didn't share that medieval belief. At least I hoped he didn't.

The conversation had cleared up another point I had wondered about. Pietro was the last of the Morandinis—except for the apocryphal embryo Francesca thought I was carrying. No wonder she was so tolerant of my presence and my criticism. I wasn't just an intrusive distant relative by marriage; I, by God, was the mother of the Heir of the Morandinis—with only a "raving madman" between it and the title.

I was in the bathroom brushing my teeth when that occurred to me, and the expression on the face reflected in the mirror was so aghast I couldn't help smiling. "Cheer up, you damned fool," I told my reflection. "Of all the messes you have got into—and there have been plenty—this is high on the list."

I couldn't hang on to the smile, though; the situation was too serious. I had a nasty suspicion I knew what Francesca was working up to. Oddly enough, our last conversation had given me a grudging respect for the woman. I honesty believed she was doing her best. Her best wasn't good enough, by a long shot, but that was a weakness, not a crime. She had a number of weaknesses, not of character but of prejudice and ignorance. She was intelligent but insensitive, subtle but not complex. Once you identified the basic beliefs that governed her behavior, you could understand, and even predict, what she was going to do. I was as certain of her intentions as if she had told me point-blank.

She wanted me to stay on. She wanted the Heir of the Morandinis born in the family mansion, under her matriarchal eye. If it turned out to be a girl, or a "raving madman," it and I could go to hell, or anywhere else we wanted to go. If it was what she hoped, then she'd start the next phase of the campaign. It would be a campaign of indirection and suggestion rather than command; she knew by now that I was not easily bullied, and of course the very idea of physical coercion was absurd in this day and age. Her methods would be more subtle: Join the gentry, enjoy a life of ease, servants to wait on you, no need to work for a living. Now she had another way of pressuring me—the boy. If I stayed, I might be able to help him.

The mirrored face was decidedly glum. It had a horrible premonition of what I was planning to do.

The question was, could I get away with it? I studied myself critically. If there was such a thing as the glow of approaching motherhood, I didn't have it. My hair was a mess. When I met Bart it had been long, falling almost to my waist. He liked it that way; he'd twine it around his hands, spread it across his body. . . . The day after the accident I took a pair of scissors and whacked it off. It was growing out now, too short to be braided or coiled, too long to hold a curl. My face was fuller than it had been, thanks to Rosa—she was a first-class cook. The problem wasn't my face or hair, it was my figure. Bart had been dead for three months. I couldn't be less than three months pregnant. Within a few weeks I should be showing signs of something more substantial than extra calories and the flabbiness of a winter's forced inactivity.

I had a month—six weeks at the outside. So, said my reflection apprehensively—you are going to stay? Saint Georgia on her white mouse, riding out to conquer the dragon and rescue a troubled child? Dr. Baldwin was right; what you need is intensive psychotherapy. Or a padded cell.

If the contessa found out I was not pregnant my departure from the Villa Morandini would be precipitate and unpleasant. I had told Pete; would he tell his grandmother? I doubted that he would tell anyone. He had already been warned off the subject. If he did tell her, then the masquerade was over. I would take my lumps and crawl away. I wouldn't sink so low as to ask him to hold his tongue.

Che sera, sera. With a shrug almost as eloquent as Emilia's, I turned from the mirror.

A remark Francesca made at breakfast confirmed my evil suspicions. We kept up the usual banal chitchat while Emilia served us. Not until we were finishing our coffee did Francesca say casually, "Pietro goes to the doctor today. Would you care to accompany us?" She added, with a faint but cynical smile, "I will arrange for you to speak with him alone."

"Thank you," I said, trying to imitate the smile. "I would appreciate that."

Deeper and deeper in, I thought. Everything I do gets me more involved; everything she does pushes me farther in. I was about to leave the room when she administered another shove. "I am going up now to hear Pietro's lessons," she said. "When he is well enough, he takes physical exercise at eleven. I believe you know where?"

I went looking for David—out and around, and up the back stairs, instead of trying to retrace the route Emilia had shown me. He was hard at work. I could hear his voice,

95

raised in amiable soliloquy, before I opened the door. When he saw me he went right on quoting. It had to be a quote; normal people don't talk that way. "'Lady, that in the prime of earliest youth, Wisely hast shunned the broad way and the green. . . .' I don't know that it's so wise, though. Why aren't you gamboling on the green this fine morning?"

"I came to invite you to join me—us, rather. The football game is on. Eleven o'clock."

"Oh, yeah? You've got yourself a man. I'm looking forward to meeting *il conte*."

"He's a sweet kid. Lonely. He lost both parents recently in a plane crash."

"I know."

"Yesterday you told me you'd never heard of him."

"Good God, but you're a suspicious wench. After I talked to you, I pumped Rosa for the story."

"Oh. I'm sorry."

"You should be. Anyone with a face like yours ought to be open, candid, and idiotically trusting. What made you so. . ." He broke off, his smile fading. "I apologize. Always putting my big foot into my bigger mouth."

"It's okay. What are those nasty things?"

The table was covered with scraps of fabric, dark brown and black, ranging from fragments a few inches across to larger pieces.

"Nasty? Nasty! Those, my ignorant innocent, are examples of Coptic and early Arabic embroidery. Not worth their weight in gold, but worth a tidy sum in silver. Part of the count's Egyptian spoils. These bits and pieces weren't popular when he was on tour; he appears to have appreciated the unusual."

"They look awful."

"To me they are as lovely as the sunrise over the Duomo." He picked up one of the scraps. "The best thing about them is that the count had the good sense not to hand them over to the estate washerwoman. Wait till I get through with them."

I sat down on my old seat. "What do you do with them?"

"Wash them, of course—but not with yellow soap and a scrub brush. I'll have to go into town to pick up some chemicals and distilled water. Want to go with me?"

"What did you say?"

"Maybe you're surfeited with the sights of Florence." He didn't look at me as he spoke, but continued to admire the filthy cloth in his hand. "If you aren't—well, I'm a good guide. I know a little bit about a lot of things."

"I'd like that. But I can't go today."

"No sweat. I can wait till tomorrow."

"Fine. Are you planning to walk?"

"Good Lord, no. As an added inducement, I am offering you a ride on my BMW bike—secondhand, but superb."

I thought of the winding, bumpy road, and the carefree habits of Italian drivers. My phobia about driving was pretty well cured, but... I said firmly, "I have a rental car. I'll even let you drive."

"Okay. Whatever turns you on."

"I'll see you at eleven, then." I gave him directions to the garden and added doubtfully, "You won't get all wrapped up in your dirty collection and forget, will you?"

"Madam, you cut me to the quick. I'll be there."

In fact, he was there before me. I had gone to my room to compose a letter to my parents. On my next trip to Florence, I must retrieve the incoherent note I left with Angelo. I couldn't remember exactly what I had written, but I could remember the state of mind I'd been in when I wrote it.

The letter took longer than I anticipated. There were so many things I couldn't mention, such as my "condition," and so many others that required careful handling, such as Pete's illness. I had to make Francesca sound like a harmless, lonely old lady who had welcomed me with open arms and affectionate tears, and I had to convince the readers that I was well, happy, and in my right mind. It took three attempts to produce something that succeeded, if only partially, in these aims. I folded the delicate, gold-edged paper and put it in the delicate, gold-edged envelope with the Morandini crest. The stationery had appeared overnight in one of the drawers of the desk-secretary—another of those little amenities to which Francesca assumed I would quickly become accustomed.

When I reached the garden they were both there, sitting on the marble bench. Pete was swinging his legs and talking a blue streak. David leaned forward, arms resting on his knees, listening with intent interest, and nodding occasionally. When I opened the gate Pete jumped up. "Go out for a pass," he yelled.

I had to run forward to catch it. "Not bad," said David critically.

"She has the good hands," Pete said. "Now throw to me, signora."

"Wait a minute, we've got to go by the rules," David said. "Boys against girls?" He grinned wickedly.

"You're a crook," I said.

Pete chuckled. "A crook, a crook. He is. How can there be two against one?"

David said, perfectly deadpan, "She throws the ball, and then runs down and catches it, while we try to tackle her."

Pete broke up. He laughed so hard he had to sit down. David jabbed him in the ribs. "Don't laugh. We might have conned her into it."

After some more low-class clowning from David we decided Pete would play offense with both of us. He was the quarterback, of course. He was also a running back and all the front linesmen. Once when Pete faked and pulled in the ball to run, David tackled him with such gusto I yelped in protest, but Pete loved it. We didn't stop until we were all red-faced and winded. The score was Pete 54 (two missed extra points), opponents 14.

David stayed on the ground after the final play, flat on his back, staring up at the sky. Pete sat on his stomach. "Are you o-kay? Did I hurt you?"

"I could breathe better if you'd get off my diaphragm," David said, rolling the boy off him with a sudden heave. Pete sat cross-legged on the grass beside him. We discussed some of the finer points of the game, and David promised to give Pete some pointers on kicking. Pete nobly admitted that kicking was not one of his best skills. Finally David said, "I'd better get back to work. Thanks for the exercise, gang; that was a lot more fun than jogging."

"We will do it tomorrow?" Pete asked hopefully.

"Sure. Same time, same place."

He ambled off without a backward look. I said, "I guess I had better change for lunch. You too, sport."

"Sport. I like that." But he looked grave, and I knew he was thinking of his visit to the doctor. I had hoped he would mention it, but he didn't; so I took a deep breath and prepared to tackle something a lot heavier than my erstwhile opponent.

"I have a favor to ask, Pete."

"Of course, signora." He looked so pleased at the idea of doing something for me, I hated to tell him what it was.

"Can I go with you to Florence this afternoon?"

His face shut up like a curtained window. "Did *she* say you should come?"

"Yes. You see..." I wanted to touch him, but he was so far away from me he might as well have been on another planet. "You see, after Bart died, I was sick. I was in a hospital for several months, and I had to see a doctor—a psychiatrist—every day. I haven't been to my doctor since I left home, and I thought—if you don't mind..."

"You were sick? Like—" One finger touched his head.

He hadn't picked that up from Francesca. Probably the *tuttofare*, or Emilia, or the cook. "Right," I said. "Sick in the head. People can get sick there, just as they can get sick in their stomachs or their legs."

"But they get better," Pete said slowly. He picked up a stick and began poking holes in the dirt.

"Oh, sure they do. It takes a while; sometimes it seems as if it takes a very long time. I'm better. But I thought since you were going to see your doctor, maybe I could see him too. Just to make sure—you know—"

He nodded. I was glad he knew. I didn't know what the hell I was talking about. But I had to give him some reason for seeing the doctor alone. I didn't want him to think I was talking about him behind his back—ganging up on him with all the other adults. I knew only too well how that felt.

He went on poking holes—nice, neat holes that formed symmetrical patterns.

I said, "If you don't want me to come, I won't, Pete."

"I want you to come."

"Thank you."

He went on, as if I had not spoken. "I want you to be better."

My breath caught. It wasn't easy to speak lightly, but I tried. "We had better get moving, then. All that exercise has made me hungry. I could eat a horse."

"No, you could not! Could you?"

I held out my hand. "I'm so weak you'll have to help me up."

He did, with much grunting and puffing. It gave me an excuse to hold his hand as we walked to the gate. Francesca wasn't the only one who was pushing me farther in. Already it gave me a pang to think of saying good-bye to Pete. And how ironic that the only person in the house to whom I had told the truth (if not the whole truth) was a ten-year-old boy.

IT WAS too warm to wear my wool suit, so I put on a cotton blouse and skirt. Next to Francesca, cool and slim in pale-green linen, I looked like the *tuttofare*.

As we were finishing lunch, Emilia produced Pete, like a parcel to be taken to the post office. He didn't look like the same child who had laughed and joked and rolled on the grass. Sullen resentment coated his features like a thin, congealed mask.

We went out to the car and Alberto leaped to open the door. His manner toward me was almost as obsequious as it was to Francesca. Her style of living did have an insidious appeal. It would be easy to fall into the habit of treating people like objects, especially when they were people you didn't like. I noticed that Pete kept as far from Alberto as he could when he got into the car. It seemed more like distaste than fear, but it annoyed me, and prompted me to commit another impertinence. When we were ensconced, with Pete, stiff and silent as a doll, between me and Francesca, I said, "Does Alberto have sterling qualities I fail to observe, Francesca? I'm surprised you keep such an unattractive person on your staff."

Pete gave me a startled look. Francesca smiled, as if she enjoyed sparring with me. Fine, I thought; I'll give her plenty of opportunities.

"He does have admirable qualities you have not had occasion to observe, Kathleen. Loyalty, for one. Unquestioning obedience, for another. They are more important to me than a handsome face or fine manners. I don't dine with him, after all."

"He would die for the Morandinis?" I asked, investing the words with ironic quotation marks.

"Yes," she said flatly.

"Isn't that rather medieval?"

"Certainly. I understand he was somewhat rude to you when you first came to the gate. It won't happen again. Naturally, if you have any complaints about him you will tell me."

I wondered if there was anything Francesca didn't know about. Well, yes—there were a few things. Pete was still staring at me with shocked admiration. I winked at him.

Francesca talked to me and occasionally addressed a remark to Pete. I talked to both of them. Pete sometimes spoke to me, but never said a word to Francesca. I could only dimly imagine what those drives must be like when the two of them were alone. Pete must dread the trip as much as he dreaded the doctor.

Dr. Manetti's office was in a building that had once been a Renaissance palazzo, but the office itself was as modern as any I had seen. Like his colleagues the world over, the doctor appeared to be making a good living. The waiting room was furnished with lush plants and handsome pseudo- (or genuine; how would I know?) antiques. We were the only ones there, and when the door to the inner sanctum opened, it was the nurse, who told Pete to come in. Presumably the previous patient had been spirited out a back door. That's how Dr. Baldwin had arranged it.

Pete went with a little squaring of his shoulders that I found infinitely touching. He did not look back.

We waited for the regulation fifty minutes. Francesca looked through the magazines on the table, commenting now and then on an article or a picture. Not until the "hour" was almost up did she say, "I will meet Pietro in the outer office. I have explained to Dr. Manetti why you are here. Take all the time you like, ask whatever you wish. He has been instructed to tell you anything you want to know."

She had timed it perfectly. The last word was hardly out of her mouth when the nurse reappeared. "Signora?"

Francesca put her magazine down, smoothed her gloves, and went out.

I had assumed Dr. Manetti spoke English; there would not have been much point to my seeing him if he didn't. His greeting was not only fluent, it was flawless, with scarcely a trace of an accent. "It is a pleasure to meet you, Mrs. Morandini. May I express my condolences? I had not the pleasure of knowing your husband, but the contessa has often spoken of him."

He was much younger than I had expected, and not at all like the conventional stereotype of a psychiatrist—unless it was the television-movie stereotype. He wore slacks and a white shirt open at the neck, with an emblem on the pocket. It fit his muscular body like a second skin. His face and throat and arms were a gorgeous golden bronze and his hair was only a few shades darker. He was almost as handsome as Bart.

He held a chair for me and then, instead of retreating behind the professional barrier of his desk, sat down on the couch, his pose deliberately casual. "It's good of you to take an interest in the boy," he said. "Do I understand that you have worked with emotionally disturbed children?"

I admitted the limitations of my experience and mentioned Francesca's idée fixe about hereditary mental illness. Manetti laughed good-naturedly. "She is a remarkable woman. Very modern in many ways, and yet these old superstitions linger."

By the end of the hour we were on first-name terms. He was very easy to talk to—subtly flattering in his keen attention, quick to agree with my statements—and then, discreetly, insinuating reservations, or "redefinitions," as he called them. When I found myself moving toward the door

103

I realized I had been given a standard fifty-minute hour. No doubt Francesca would have to pay for it. I can't say that idea upset me very much.

He started to open the door, then paused and said in a sudden change from his professional smoothness, "I wonder... Would you perhaps... Would you do me the honor of dining with me one evening? I am very proud of my 'home town,' as you say in America, and I like to show it off to visitors."

I was surprised, but not at all averse to the idea. I said I'd be delighted. He said I was very kind. I said not at all, he was kind to ask me. He said he would telephone. I decided not to mention the invitation to Francesca. He probably wouldn't call anyway.

When we got down to the street the car was nowhere to be seen. Francesca looked vexed. "I told Alberto to be here at four."

"He's probably stuck in traffic," I said. "There's a café— why don't we have some ice cream? I think we deserve it, don't you, Pete—Pietro?"

Francesca's expression was that of a woman who has been offered a dish of pickled mice, and it did not change after we took our places at one end of the rickety tables under the faded awning. I must admit I was pushing her deliberately, to see how far I could go, and I must also admit she tried to be a good sport. She even ordered coffee. She didn't drink it, though.

Pete and I had the biggest sundaes on the menu. They weren't called sundaes; I forget the names. We selected them from a card, complete with color photographs displayed next to the door of the café. The flavors were a little peculiar to American taste buds—a touch of black currant, a touch of coconut, and some kind of liqueur. I couldn't finish mine, so Pete kindly offered to finish it for me. He also kindly allowed me to mop his chin with a napkin dipped in the glass of water

I had requested. A shudder rippled through Francesca's body, but she didn't say anything.

Except for an occasional wary glance at his grandmother, Pete behaved like a normal child while we ate our ice cream. As soon as the car appeared and we got in, he relapsed into silence. Alberto mumbled apologies for being late; Francesca cut him off with a brusque gesture.

I did most of the talking on the way home. Francesca replied courteously to my questions about the places we passed, but did not volunteer any information until we turned into the narrow, upward road, and I commented on the wildness of the area.

"It's part of the estate," she said. "From the turn to the top of the hill and beyond."

"All that? It must be hundreds of acres."

"We have not yet been forced to give up all that was ours. Many other families have sold the land; it is now occupied by cheap little houses and shops. That may happen here one day, but I hope I am not alive to see it."

For once there was genuine emotion in her voice. She cared more about places than about people.

iv

SEBASTIANO—DR. MANETTI—did call, the following morning, a little before nine o'clock. He apologized for calling so early. It was a nice touch of flattery, implying that he had awakened at dawn, panting with desire, and had barely managed to control himself until a decent hour. I accepted an invitation to dinner the following evening.

"I don't have any formal clothes with me," I warned him.

He laughed. "It is time you learned something about modern Italy, Kathleen. The only time I wear evening dress is when I must attend some boring professional dinner party."

I said I would look forward to it; and I meant what I said. My social life was certainly improving. Football and rag-picking with David, dinner with the shrink.

Francesca was obviously curious about the call, which had come while we were at breakfast, but she was too well-bred to ask outright. Instead she dropped a sly hint. "It would be courteous, Kathleen, if you would tell Emilia when you plan to be absent at mealtime. Ordinarily I wouldn't ask it of you, but with my small staff..."

"I understand. I'll make a point of doing so."

"Dr. Manetti tells me that you are a good influence on Pietro."

She must have telephoned him as soon as we got home. I smiled modestly; she went on, "He approves of the games, and the time you spend with the boy. He said he had cautioned you about certain matters—"

"I'll be careful, Francesca. I'm not as stupid as I look, honestly."

"I don't think you are at all stupid," she said.

After breakfast I went up to the attic to remind David we had a date to tackle each other at eleven. At least that was one of my reasons. There wasn't much else to do. My embroidery bored me, I had read most of the books I had bought, and exploring the desolate gardens had only limited appeal. So I offered my services as assistant scrounger.

He looked at me doubtfully, scratching his chin. He had shaved that morning, but he was just as dusty. "If you're going into this with some expectation of unearthing a box of rubies and diamonds, forget it. There is a method to this apparent madness, and I insist on following proper procedures."

"I will obey orders to the letter."

"Okay. That's what I'm looking for—letters. I found a box of miscellaneous papers that has to be sorted. There's all kinds of stuff here—newspaper clippings, patterns for ladies' bonnets, accounts. I want it sorted, first by category and then by date. If you're in doubt about anything, put it in the miscellaneous box."

The miscellaneous box was overflowing when I finished. I apologized for my lack of skill; David said I'd get the hang of it—which I doubted—and we went to find Pete. He was a little late that morning—a nasty session with Italian history, I gathered—but his glum expression brightened when he saw us waiting, and he put us through a stiff workout. At noon David called a halt.

"I've got to go to Florence to pick up the stuff I told you about," he explained to Pete, man to man. "See you tomorrow?"

"I cannot," Pete said with a glance at me. I gathered that his appointment had been changed, and that he was to see the doctor in the morning.

"The day after, then," David said. "That's Saturday. You don't have lessons on Saturday, do you? We'll start early and have a good long practice."

"O-kay!"

After he had gone David said, "I'm going to do you the honor of changing my clothes. Meet you in fifteen minutes."

"But I thought—"

"You forgot. Or you changed your mind?"

"Neither. I thought you had forgotten."

"I had planned to leave earlier, but we couldn't disappoint the kid. It doesn't matter; we can have lunch in Florence and do the shopping later. I know a great trattoria. Cheap."

"O-kay," I said. "I wonder where Alberto put my car. He's got the keys, too."

"The car is in the garage. I'll extract your keys from Alberto and pick you up out in front, like a proper chauffeur. Unless you don't want to be seen fraternizing with the hired help."

"Don't be silly. Make it twenty minutes."

I met Emilia in the hall and was pleased to inform her I would not be in to lunch. It really was short notice; if I had been as rude to my mother, Pa would have let me have it, but Emilia murmured a meek "thank you."

It took me a little longer than twenty minutes. David was waiting. He came to a snappy salute when I appeared, but his expression was sour. "What's the matter?" I asked.

"Nothing. I always look like this after I've chatted with Alberto."

"What did he say?"

"Never mind."

"Something about me?"

"It wasn't so much what he said, it was the way he said it."

"Oh. I trust you punched him in the nose for insulting a lady?"

"Are you kidding? I'm the original chicken. He may be twenty years older than I am, but he is also forty pounds heavier, with a reach like a gorilla's. Probably learned commando warfare under *il duce*."

"Is he that old?"

"I don't know or care how old he is. Let's not talk about him."

I had such a good time that afternoon I never thought what a good time I was having. David knew the back streets of Florence the way I knew the alleys of Wayford, Massachusetts; and if his casual greetings were any indication, he knew half the inhabitants of Florence, too. Beggars, street cleaners, waiters, guides...When I commented he explained solemnly, "I'm a charter member of the fraternity of the poor. It's an international association, confined to people who know what it's like to be hungry—really hungry, not just a little peckish. I can always count on a handout from a fellow member. Generosity is a quality restricted to the impoverished, you know. The rich scatter largesse when they need a tax deduction, and then make pious remarks about how superior they are to the lazy, shiftless recipients of their charity."

It was one of the longest speeches he had made on any subject except Margaret Fuller. I said, "I suspect you are a radical socialist."

"Absolutely."

"You'll have to meet my father."

We had lunch at his favorite trattoria, where the waiter greeted him like a long-lost buddy. We saw some of the standard tourist sights, and some that were not so standard. At the Accademia he lectured me on Florentine sculpture, and when we stood in front of the *David* he flexed his biceps and asked if I noticed the resemblance. He hadn't been boasting when he said he knew a little bit about a lot of things, and his enthusiasm was contagious. It was late in the afternoon before we finally got around to his errands. They took us to a dark little shop in a back street where, after a long discussion, David loaded several armfuls of bottles and packages into the trunk of the car.

"This is really a help," he said as we drove away. "I manage okay with the bike, but its trunk space is limited."

"Stock up on supplies any time."

"Thanks, I may do that. It's none of my business, but are you a rich heiress, despite your demure and modest appearance? I mean, if you want to turn the car in you could save yourself a few bucks, and I'd be glad to take you into town whenever you are reluctant to make use of Alberto's services."

It was a thoughtful and generous offer. There was no sense in my keeping the car; it was costing a small fortune, and I didn't really need it. I don't know why I should have felt a frisson of panic at the idea of giving up a means of escape. . . . Escape? Say rather mobility—independence.

"I'll keep the idea in mind," I said, and was obscurely relieved when he didn't press the point.

I had told him I needed to pick up something at my former hotel, so we went there after we had finished with the chemist. There was no one on duty at the desk; after I banged and yelled, a scrubwoman shuffled out of a back room and informed me that Angelo was not there. I had already deduced that. Thanks to David's superior Italian we learned that Angelo was next door, at the coffee bar, so we went in search of him.

Angelo was drinking coffee as if he were being paid to do so. He probably needed gallons of caffeine to get through his work schedule. When he saw me his face didn't exactly light up, but it became a shade less pensive.

"Ah," he said. "The friend has come."

I looked at David, who looked back at me with amused curiosity, and decided not to explain. I simply smiled noncommittally and introduced them. The title *il professore* did not impress Angelo. After all, his brother was a policeman.

I asked about my letter. Angelo pressed his hand to the pocket of his shirt. "It is here, signorina. Always, next to my heart."

"You can give it back to me, Angelo. I'm very grateful for your help."

"You want it? You don't want I should mail it?"

"No. But thank you."

Angelo's face became, if possible, even blanker. He was thinking. After a while he arrived at some conclusion—I didn't ask what it was; I didn't want to know. He nodded. "Ah. Now the friend has come...."

He handed me the letter. It was somewhat the worse for wear. Apparently he had not exaggerated when he said he always carried it next to his heart.

David suggested another cup of coffee, an offer Angelo was quick to accept. However, he rejected David's suggestion that we sit down. "There is an extra charge, professore. The coffee is the same if we stand; why pay more?"

110

The two of them entered into an animated conversation, while I shifted from one foot to the other and tried to catch a few words. I wouldn't have blamed David for being curious about the byplay with the letter, but the occasional word I did understand suggested that they were discussing something else. We parted with friendly salutes all around and Angelo's assurance that if I ever again wanted to leave a secret message with him, he would be happy to oblige.

On our way back we were fighting through the traffic at the Piazza della Indipendenza when David waved at the white-uniformed policeman perched on a perilous little platform in the center of the maelstrom of cars and motorbikes. "Was that Angelo's brother?" I asked.

"What gave you that idea?"

"I caught the word *fratello* during your conversation. Angelo is very proud of his brother."

"And rightly so. He's no mere traffic cop, but an honest-to-God plainclothes detective."

Perhaps that explained Angelo's mild obsession with secrets and mysteries. But it didn't explain David's gesture; I persisted, "Do you always wave to traffic cops?"

"I happen to know that guy," David said, grinning. "A slight contretemps concerning the right-of-way in a traffic circle. . . . But I always make friends with cops when I can; you never know when a friend in the force will come in handy."

When we arrived at the villa we found the gates had been closed. David stopped the car. "What do we do now?"

"What do you usually do?"

"Go in the back door, of course. There's a gate on the north side, big enough for the bike."

"Watch." I leaned on the horn.

At first I was afraid my gesture was going to fall flat. Then the shrubs behind the lodge shook violently, as if they had been struck by a miniature, invisible whirlwind. A grotesque figure burst out into the open. Capering and crooning in a tuneless, high-pitched monotone, he wove a fantastic pattern of stumbling steps across the gravel.

"Good God," David breathed. "Who the hell is that?"

"Alberto's assistant. Haven't you seen him before?"

"Never at close range. Do you think he's going to open the gate?"

"I think he's working up to it."

The stooped figure wore clothes that looked like Alberto's cast-offs. They flapped loosely around his body, and the cap came down to the bridge of his nose. From under the cap long, lank hair tumbled onto his neck and over his face. Without interrupting his pathetic travesty of a dance he opened one of the gates, and, after another interval of hopping and singing, dealt with the other.

David reached in his pocket; but when he pulled up a few feet and offered the crumpled bill to the temporary gatekeeper the man let out a screech of terror and fled.

"Don't chase him," I said, as David started to open the door. "You'll only frighten him more."

"I guess you're right." We drove on in silence. I assumed David's thoughts ran along the same path as mine—wondering how Alberto treated his unfortunate assistant—and suspecting the worst.

David put the car in the garage, next to the Mercedes, and handed me the keys. I handed them back. "Hadn't you better unlock the trunk first? I'll help you unload."

"That's okay, I can manage."

"Thanks for today. I had a marvelous time."

"Me, too."

He unlocked the trunk and put the keys into my hand. Our fingers touched, and for a moment we stood without moving or speaking. I hated to have the afternoon end. The Malones are great huggers and kissers; but somehow I couldn't give him the casual, friendly embrace I would normally have offered. We parted formally, thanking one another again in voices that had become strangely reserved.

I treated Francesca to another scathing critique of her servant that evening, describing the condition of the dog's pen and questioning his fitness to supervise a mentally handicapped person. She appeared faintly amused by what she would probably call my "qualities of youthful idealism."

"I assure you that the person to whom you refer is not abused by Alberto," she said. "As for the dog, discipline is necessary for a guard dog. The animal is not a pet."

"Discipline is one thing, cruelty is another. A dog doesn't have to be vicious to be a good guard dog."

She promised to speak to Alberto and then deftly turned the conversation to a subject she knew would distract me. It was so good of me to take an interest in Pietro. No doubt I had encountered other disturbed children when I was teaching. She would be happy to listen to any advice I cared to give.

There is one form of flattery to which everyone is susceptible: being asked for advice. She let me babble on, interrupting only to ask questions that proved she was listening with close attention. I was feeling pretty full of myself when I went up to bed. Smug is hardly the word. A few more weeks and I'd have everybody straightened out; then I would make a dignified exit, bowing, amid the plaudits of the crowd. The dog would lick my hand, Alberto would apologize and promise reform, Francesca would thank me for showing her the light, Pete...I would hate to leave Pete. But he would be o-kay. Thanks to me.

Even youth is no excuse for that kind of conceit.

I had finished Mark Twain. I shuffled through the rest of the books and realized I had read the lot. I should have bought more when I was in Florence. No more Gothic romances, though. The heroine of *Bride of the Madman* was a perfect fool. Sticking grimly to her job in spite of stones that rolled off

cliffs, narrowly missing her; in spite of the sinister housekeeper; in spite of the hero, scarred and brooding, who wasn't
the type I'd have cared to spend an afternoon with, much
less a lifetime. I tossed the book contemptuously aside.

I often thought back on that gesture. As I said, it's a good
thing I'm not superstitious.

v

THE MATTRESS yielded gently. Bart was sitting beside me.
The moonlight streamed in the window, showing every feature in stark detail. The flash of even white teeth as he smiled,
the little mole on the sculptured curve of his left cheekbone,
the hollow under the bone, the scattering of black hairs across
his chest.

His fingers brushed my breast and shoulder in a pattern
achingly familiar. He had such smooth hands. Not soft, like
a woman's, but smooth like warm ivory, without the tiny
calluses and roughness of normal flesh. Brushing and touching, gently at first, then firmer, with little, knowing pressures
here, there.... Moving up to my throat and cheek, into my
hair.

Sometimes I had dreamed of waking into nightmarish reality, and fought to wake again. I had followed his retreating
figure down endless shadow streets and wakened weeping
with frustration. Now I had found him; and it was worse.
My lips parted, my throat tensed to cry out. His mouth muffled the cry. For a split second I felt his lips, tasted them.
Then all sensation was blotted out.

I woke with the echo of a scream in my ears and knew it
had been my own. The room was almost dark. The moonlight
was dim, the gauzy curtains were closed. The straps of my
nightgown were pulled down, baring my body to the waist.

* * *

It took me a good five minutes to find my purse and the little bottle lying at the bottom under a jumble of other things. I swallowed one of the capsules and sat down in a chair to wait for it to work. I had turned on every light in the room, but I couldn't force myself to get back into the bed. A faint scent still seemed to linger around it—the scent of the after-shave Bart had used.

Why hadn't Dr. Baldwin warned me this might happen? Well, but he had hinted at it when he questioned me about my sexual impulses. At the time I didn't have any. Not surprising, he said soothingly. (Nothing surprises a psychiatrist.) I was a young, healthy woman. Someday...

Fine. But I had not expected that when the day came it would be Bart's ghost that aroused me.

As the drug began to take effect, relaxing muscles and dulling horror, I decided I might survive this too. Maybe it was a stage of convalescence. Maybe I had to dream about Bart making love to me before I could dream of someone else. Maybe my dead husband was a symbol of that someone else. David? Sebastiano? I wasn't conscious of wanting to go to bed with either of them, but they were both attractive men, in very different ways. A lot of people would tell me that was what I needed—a good, satisfying roll in the hay, without emotional commitments. And maybe they'd be right.

I went to the window. The moon hung tangled in the cypress tops, a lopsided ellipsoid, a silver football. I couldn't see David's window, but I pictured him scrubbing his nasty little bits of fabric, or sitting up in bed, reading—culling new scraps of wisdom from the nineteenth-century poets. Somehow it made me feel better to know he was there.

But I spent the rest of the night sitting up in the chair.

115

Chapter Five

S UNLIGHT MIGHT have improved my state of mind, but there was none the next morning. The skies were a soft pearly gray. Francesca said rain was predicted for that evening.

She seemed a little distraught—nothing definite I could point to, but not her usual self. Always the perfect hostess, she did not fail to notice my hollow eyes, though I thought I had hid the signs of sleeplessness rather well.

I admitted I had not slept well. I hadn't meant to tell her the reason, but her look of concern seemed genuine, and I desperately needed to tell someone—not the whole truth, but part of it. I said, "I had a bad dream. A nightmare, actually. About Bart."

The lines in her forehead deepened. "To dream of someone you love—is that a nightmare?"

"It can be."

"Will it help you to talk about it? I have not asked about him, or about the accident..."

"It doesn't really help. I've already..." I pushed my chair back and went to the window. "I guess you're entitled to know, though. You were fond of him."

"Yes."

I didn't turn. "When we were married Bart moved in with me." He had moved in before, actually, but why mention that? "I had a little house—it was the guest house of an estate. Only two rooms and kitchen and bath, but I was delighted to have found it—in the country, yet close enough to make commuting feasible. There was even a bus line at the bottom of the hill. Sometimes I took the bus when the weather was bad. The road to my house was a private road, narrow and steep. After a heavy snow it could be dangerous. Bart... Bart enjoyed driving it. It was a challenge to him, especially when it was slippery with ice."

"He was an excellent driver," said the calm voice behind me.

"I know. He told me he had driven racing cars. The first time he took me up that road, in a heavy snowstorm, I was scared to death. He was laughing."

"It was on such a snowy day that the accident occurred?"

"We had six inches of snow the day before. It was wet snow, packed down; cold temperatures during the night froze it solid. He—he'd been away. He came back that morning, not to stay, just to pick up some things. I was outside shoveling the walk. When he drove away I stood watching...."

I saw it now, vivid as reality. The sun, blindingly bright on the snowy slopes, the dark band of trees at the foot of the hill. The car, a splash of brilliant crimson in the stark black-and-white landscape, appearing and disappearing around the curves, growing smaller with each appearance. The road shimmering with colorless brilliance, empty of traffic. The final appearance of the tiny, toy vehicle as it swung—too fast, out of control—into the main road far below.

I turned. "We quarreled. I was angry because he hadn't come home the night before. He said he'd tried to call, that the lines were down because of the storm. But I was angry anyway. I said things.... And he wasn't the man to take criticism meekly. The last thing I said to him was—was something hateful. He always drove too fast when he was furious. He was driving too fast that day. I had seen him cope with conditions as bad, or worse. If he hadn't been angry—if we hadn't argued..."

I did not expect absolution from her. There was neither sympathy nor condemnation in her voice when she replied. "I thought as much. I won't insult you by pointing out that your feelings of guilt are both normal and unnecessary. Your doctors must have said the same."

"You know about that, too."

"Of course. Are you ashamed of it?" She gestured. "Sit down and finish your coffee."

I needed the caffeine; I was still groggy from taking the Valium so late at night.

Instead of asking more questions she began to talk about Bart. She didn't take out pictures of babies on bearskin rugs or coo about how cute he had been; but the relationship I had pictured became clearer as she went on. Bart had been several years younger than his cousin Guido, but always in their encounters he came out best. His sayings were wittier, his laughter more engaging; he ran faster, hit a tennis ball more accurately, swam more strongly. Guido sounded like a singularly dull lad. When I asked, Francesca showed me a photograph of him, taking it from a drawer. The only photo on display was the one of Bart.

The cousins stood side by side, not touching. Bart must

have been about twelve then; he was already almost as tall as his cousin. The contrast between the two was painful. Guido had none of the family good looks. His long, mournful face resembled that of an amiable horse. He stood stiff and unsmiling, arms at his sides. Bart's head was thrown back, laughing.

My preconceptions about Guido couldn't have been more inaccurate. He was probably as dull as he looked—steady, dependable, reliable—all the boring virtues. Pete didn't resemble him at all. Nor, except for those startling silver eyes, did Pete look like the Morandinis. Maybe that accounted for Francesca's indifference to him.

Francesca did not invite me to go with them to the doctor that day. However, she did mention the matter of transportation. Alberto was available to take me to Florence whenever I wished; did I want to return my rental car, or have him do it for me?

I finessed the question, but it bothered me. This was the second time in twenty-four hours someone had worried about that car. It was uncharacteristic of Francesca to do so; why should she care what it was costing me?

After she had gone I jogged around the drive a while, getting some much-needed exercise. The air had the breathless hush that often heralds a storm, but I knew the clouds weren't heavy enough for that; the breathless, restless feeling was not in the air, it was inside me. I wanted to do something, but I couldn't think of anything I really wanted to do. The options were limited: sort junk with David, jog up and down the drive, explore the grounds. Finally I went to my room to review my wardrobe. I didn't want to do that either, but I had to find something to wear to dinner. My clothes were whisked away, laundered and returned, almost as soon as I took them off; even so, I had very little to choose from. I had not been concerned about clothes when I packed, and I certainly had not given much thought to the season. I might have known it would be cold in Florence in April, part of the time at least. Everything I had was too big or too lightweight or too shabby. I should have gone to Florence with Francesca to buy a decent dress. I should go now. I didn't feel like doing that either.

Thoroughly disgusted with myself, I slammed the wardrobe door. I knew what was wrong with me. My treacherous body still tingled with the memory of my dream.

A cold shower is the conventional remedy for what ailed me. I wasn't that Spartan, so I decided to try cold air. It was getting on toward the time when David took his morning break. If he was jogging around his exercise yard, I would jog with him.

I went out the front door and around the house. David wasn't outside. Feeling like a child who has no one to play with, I wandered toward Pete's so-called play yard. A sudden sharp yelp from the dog made me jump, it sounded so close. I heard Alberto's voice and the dog's response—a burst of excited barking. I had never heard it bark before, and curiosity drew me toward the sound. When the dog stopped to draw breath Alberto laughed—either that or he was scraping a rusty metal bar across a stone. They seemed to be having a jolly time, but there was a quality in the dog's barking that made me uneasy—a frenzied note of excitement. If Alberto was teasing him, I'd have a word or two to say....

Then I heard something that made me break into a headlong run—the high, piercing screams of an animal in pain or desperate terror.

The gate wasn't locked. I burst through it like a cannonball and skidded to a stop. The dog was loose. Its chain lay coiled on the ground beside it. It was facing away from me, crouched, its haunches quivering with eagerness, but restrained by the stick Alberto held. He stood a few feet beyond the dog, the stick in one hand. From the other, raised high above his head, dangled a small ball of bedraggled fur. The ball of fur was screaming. The dog must have already got to it; blood dripped from its side.

The next few seconds were a blur. When I got my wits back, I was standing next to Alberto with the kitten clutched to my chest. All ten of its claws stuck into me, tiny needlepoints pricking. Alberto hadn't moved. The stick still hovered, the other arm was still raised. I used to play basketball with Mike and Jim, but I never made a jump like that one.

How long the tableau would have held I do not know. Alberto was paralyzed by surprise; the dog didn't know what the hell he was supposed to do, if anything; I was so furious I couldn't catch my breath, so furious a red haze clouded my vision. The spell was broken by a bellow of alarm and a flying body. An outthrust arm sent me staggering back. The dog began to bark, the kitten screamed and dug its claws in deeper; David knocked the stick out of Alberto's hand, and Alberto pulled back his fist and hit David in the face. David tumbled over backward. The dog leaped for his throat.

I was afraid to let go of the kitten, or carry it close to the dog. I kicked Alberto in the leg. "Get him off," I yelled. "*Avanti, pronto*—move it, you—you—"

I couldn't think of any name bad enough to call him. He gave me a startled look and then reached for the dog's collar, lifting it as easily as he had lifted the kitten.

David lay on his back, knees drawn up, arms crossed over his face and throat. He said, "Is it off me?"

"Yes, it's off you. Are you all right?"

David scrambled to his feet. He examined his shirt sleeve and said indignantly, "My shirt's torn."

"Small loss," I said, eyeing the faded garment. Out of the corner of my eye I saw Alberto quietly backing away, dragging the dog with him. Suddenly the full enormity of what had happened swept over me like a huge wave, and I had trouble controlling my voice. "Are you really okay?" I squeaked. "I can't believe—"

"The dog knew me," David said. "I suspect it wouldn't have been long before auld acquaintance was forgot, but he was confused enough to hold back for a few seconds. What a damned fool thing to do!"

"It certainly was. Alberto wasn't threatening me."

David sputtered. "I wasn't referring to myself, I was referring to you. I heard what was going on and was rushing to the rescue. The damned gate stuck, and I was trying to open it when you came barreling in. My God, Kathy, you sailed past that dog's jaws with an inch to spare. You ought to know better than to startle a neurotic animal like that. Not to mention Alberto. He might have—"

"Well, he didn't."

"Don't you ever stop and think before you jump?"

"Not often enough."

His face softened. "Oh, what the hell. Let's see what you've got there."

He held out his hands. I said, "It's stuck to me like a burr. Oh, David, I'm afraid—"

"It couldn't hold on that tight if it were badly hurt," David said reassuringly. "Come on up to my room. I've got some first-aid stuff, and some milk left over from breakfast."

David's voice and touch finally persuaded the little creature to let go. The milk helped too; it practically fell into the saucer, it was so hungry.

The only cute thing about it was its size. Otherwise it was a mess, skinny and dirty, its coat dull and matted and full of burrs. It was so young it didn't know how to drink properly. It kept sneezing and putting its front paws into the milk. David filled the saucer a second time when it had been licked clean. Neither of us spoke. Finally the frantic lapping slowed. The kitten lifted a milky muzzle, and after a moment we heard a faint, uncertain purr. I burst into tears.

A short time later David said, "'The book of female logic is blotted all over with tears.'"

I mumbled into his shoulder, "I didn't know Browning was such a male chauvinist."

"Thackeray, not Browning. Nor Brown, for that matter. I merely meant to point out that there's nothing to cry about now."

I moved away from him. "Sorry," I said snuffily. "It was just..."

"I know." One arm still rested on my shoulders. He gave me a quick, brotherly squeeze, and then took his arm away. "Let's see about some first aid, shall we?"

The kitten was howling again by the time he finished, but its shrieks sounded more indignant than pained. The cut on its side wasn't as bad as I had feared. David smeared on antiseptic lotion from his kit and, despite the kitten's furious struggles, dunked it up to its nose in a basin of warm water. When he took it out, the water was black with dead fleas.

"How did you learn to do that?" I asked, as he set about drying and grooming his victim.

"Oh, we always had animals around. My sisters and I dragged home all the neighborhood strays."

"Sounds like my family. Is that your comb?"

"It's the only one I've got," David said cheerfully. "Too bad I don't own a hair drier. I've never gone in for that sort of elegant grooming. But it's a warm day; he won't catch cold. He looks better, doesn't he?"

He had rolled the kitten in a towel; all I could see was a pointed face and two big ears. The eyes had a distinctly resentful expression. The face was prettily marked, however. The dark M of the tabby markings stood out against a silvery gray background, and the pink nose and spiky whiskers were set in a symmetrical frame of white. The eyes blinked and started to close.

"He's pooped," David said. "I guess I'll take him to the vet now, while he's too limp to resist."

"You're nuttier than I am. What are you going to do with it—him?"

"Keep him, I guess. What else is there to do?"

"Bring him to me when you get back from the vet."

"But you can't—"

"I'm going to give him to Pete."

By the time I had fetched the car keys for David and changed my clothes, I was late for lunch. I didn't care. I felt marvelous. There is nothing like a storm of rage to clear away the clouds of depression.

I told Francesca what had happened, without mincing any words. "I don't think it's the first time. I've heard about people who train fighting dogs that way, by letting them kill smaller animals."

Her face wore an expression of fastidious disgust. "Naturally I would never have permitted such a thing had I been aware of it."

I believed her. But she wouldn't have been aware, or made any effort to find out. I said, "Do you mind if I am present when you speak to Alberto about it?"

"You think I will not be forceful enough?"

"I just want to watch him squirm," I said.

She smiled faintly. "I will tell Emilia to bring him here after we have finished."

It was a delightful interview. I enjoyed every minute of it. I couldn't understand what Francesca said, but her voice crackled with anger, and by the time she finished with him Alberto was practically groveling. He had not once looked in my direction.

"Are you satisfied?" Francesca asked.

"One more thing," I said. "Tell him I'm holding him responsible for the cat. If anything happens to it—anything—I will assume he's to blame."

She raised her eyebrows, but did as I asked. Alberto looked at me then, a quick, lowering glance from under his heavy brows. I expected him to show resentment; I was the one who had got him in trouble, and it really wasn't fair to hold him accountable for the animal. It might run away or be injured by some wild creature. But I saw no resentment on his face, only the same fawning humility he gave Francesca.

She dismissed him with a curt command and then looked at me. "You are keeping the animal?"

"I'm sorry. I forgot my manners. I tend to do that when I'm angry. I'd like to give him to Pete, if you have no objection."

"So long as he keeps it out of my way. I do not care for cats. But are you sure it is wise?"

"What do you mean?"

"You seem to be fond of animals. Do you think this one will be safe with Pietro?"

"I know it isn't realistic to expect a child that age to take proper care of a pet; but I'll explain it to him, and the cook—she seems like a kindly person—maybe she could help out—"

"That is not what I meant. I'm sure you believe that my fears about Pietro's mental health are unfounded, and that he needs only a few simpleminded panaceas, such as a pet and a pat on the head, to be fully recovered. But what if you are wrong? Twice he has tried to injure himself. When the next attack comes—and it surely will—he may injure something else."

NATURALLY—NATURALLY!—I paid no attention to this depressing suggestion. I was waiting on the terrace when David drove up. He leaned across and opened the car door, and I climbed in next to the sleeping cat.

"Here's the loot," he said, indicating a canvas carryall. "Cat food, medicine, the lot. Are you going to take him to Pete now?"

"Why not?"

"Can I come?"

"Why not," I said, laughing.

The kitten woke when I picked it up. It wasn't a beauty, but it looked a hundred percent better. We went into the house through the kitchen and stopped long enough to introduce the new resident to Rosa. She reacted as I had hoped, tickling it under the chin and giving us a saucer and a glass of milk to take up with us. David translated her comment. "It is a good house that has a cat. Better than mousetraps."

"Mice," I said.

"The place is riddled with them. Are you afraid of mice?"

"No. But I don't like to find dead ones in front of my door."

"Better brace yourself. It's a demonstration of affection, I'm told, and this guy sure owes you."

I can't describe Pete's face when he saw the kitten and realized it was for him. I still get choked up thinking about it. I managed to keep my emotions under control, however.

The kitten was not averse to more milk, so Pete fed it, and David explained the proper use of the things he had bought. "Don't try to put the medicine in its ears by yourself, Pete. It's a two-man job. Cats hate the stuff."

"O-kay." Pete stroked the cat's back. It tried to purr and drink at the same time, sneezed, spat, and rubbed its nose irritably. Pete laughed. "Is it a boy or a girl? How old is it? What is its name?"

"Boy," David replied. "About six weeks old. You're the owner; what do you want to name him?"

Pete hesitated. Then he said, "Joe. His name is Joe."

"Namath?" I guessed. "If you're going to name him after a quarterback, there are other—"

"Not a quarterback. Joe is what his friends call my father. His name is not Joe, you understand, but that is what they call him in America."

"That's a very good name," I said, clearing my throat.

"It is not bad, to name an animal for your father?"

"I think it's a great compliment," David said seriously. "I have a pig named after me. He's a very handsome pig."

"I will call him Joe David," Pete said. "I have two names, so he can have two names. I cannot call him Kathy. He is not a girl. But when I get a girl cat or a girl dog..."

"That's a promise," I said. "Don't forget."

"I picked up a few toys too," said David, clearing *his* throat. "Ball, catnip mouse. Here's some string; what you do is, you tie something on the end and—"

"I know." Pete seized the string eagerly. "I know how to do it. My aunt Vera had two cats. I played with them. Like this."

He dangled the string. When we left he was laughing and watching the kitten pounce fiercely on the end of the string. It was the first time I hadn't felt wretched about leaving him alone.

Aunt Vera. His mother's sister? It had not occurred to me that he might have living relatives on that side of his family. The seed of an idea put up a tiny green tendril in my all-too-fertile mind.

"Hey," David said. "We forgot something."

"What?"

"Litter box."

"Oh, lord, you're right. Not that I care if the cat poops on the floor. Emilia will have to clean it up."

"I'll dig up something," David said. "Literally."

We parted with mutual expressions of esteem and a promise to meet next morning for football.

David headed down the back stairs and I went the other way, to the front stairs and my room. When I turned onto the landing I saw Emilia ahead of me, about to start down. Where the devil had the woman come from? She certainly hadn't been with Pete, and there was no other reason for her to be on the top floor.

I called to her to wait. I felt fairly certain she had been spying on me, or on the child. Some people are natural sneaks, and Emilia probably justified her prying and spying on the grounds that her mistress ought to know what was going on in her own house. It would have been pointless to accuse her, though. Instead I told her I was going out for dinner and asked what time she locked up.

"You will be late, signora?" she asked.

"I don't know when I'll be back. That's why I'm asking."

"*Naturalmente*, I will not lock the house until the signora has returned."

I thanked her and went on down the stairs. Alberto must have told her about being raked over the coals. He might not resent my interference, but she did; the sullen hostility in her eyes was now open instead of half-concealed.

I wondered if she would put snakes in my bed or forget to clean my room. Probably not; as long as I was on good terms with Francesca I was safe—hated but sacrosanct. All the same, I thought, I'll look under the covers before I get in bed.

SEBASTIANO WAS picking me up at seven. I decided to wait for him downstairs. The idea of being summoned by Emilia and perhaps being invited to join Francesca for a drink before we left didn't appeal to me.

I was trying to decide between a bare-shouldered sundress, in which I would freeze, and the inevitable brown suit, which made me look ten years older, when there was a knock on the door. "Who is it?" I called.

"Francesca."

"Oh. Come in, please."

I pulled the dress over my head as I spoke. The vexing question of what to wear was settled, anyhow. The zipper stuck as it always does when you're in a hurry, and when Francesca came in I was squirming around, both hands behind my back, like Laocoön fighting off unseen snakes.

"May I?" she asked.

"Oh; thank you. I'm afraid it's stuck."

It took her about two seconds to free the catch. I thanked her again, and tied the belt. She said nothing more, just stood watching me. I knew what she wanted, but—naive me—I put it down to curiosity, and her habit of authority.

"I hope I gave Emilia enough notice—about not being here tonight," I said after the silence had become embarrassing.

"Yes."

She waited. It was against her principles to ask outright, but this time I was not going to make it easy for her.

"It may be raining before you return," she said finally. "Do you wish Alberto to drive you, instead of driving yourself?"

"No, thanks." There was no sense in stalling; he'd be at the front door in less than half an hour. "Dr. Manetti is picking me up."

"Manetti!"

I decided to go on the attack. "Is there something I don't know about him? Vicious habits, drunk driving, dead wives in the closet, like Bluebeard?"

She was not amused. She began, "Bart is—"

"Bart is dead," I said harshly. "Three months dead. I'm sorry if your notions of propriety are offended, Francesca, but at home we don't go in for formal periods of mourning and I find such observances hypocritical. You needn't worry, I'm not going to...do anything you'd disapprove of. I only met the man two days ago. We'll probably spend the evening talking about Pete—Pietro, I mean."

"That is your only interest in Dr. Manetti?"

"I'd be a liar if I said yes, and you'd be very naive to believe me. He's an attractive, interesting man. But I'm not in the habit of jumping into bed with someone the first time I go out with him—or even the second time."

"I see." Lines of worry scarred her forehead. She said, as if to herself, "There is no hope of dissuading you. I can give no reason..."

"I'm afraid you can't dissuade me, no. I could meet him on the sly, but I've no intention of behaving like that."

"I see," she repeated. "Well, then...Perhaps it will be acceptable...."

And with that peculiar remark she walked out, closing the door softly behind her.

I thought of another old adage: Just because you're paranoid it doesn't mean somebody isn't following you. What a strange interview that had been. It hadn't occurred to me that Francesca might disapprove of a woman so recently widowed dating a man.... Well, to be honest, it had occurred to me. I had thought she might not like the idea, but I had not realized it would matter so much. Yet she had seemed more worried than angry. Perhaps Manetti did have a bad reputation. The Florence Strangler? The Marquis de Sade of Tuscany? I felt sure she'd have told me anything to his discredit.

I picked up my purse and my shabby old raincoat, which was all I had, and hurried down the stairs. I caught a glimpse of a black skirt whisking out of sight as I crossed the stairs. Emilia again. Damn the woman, I thought. How does she find time to get her work done? Or is spying on me her chief job?

It felt good to get out of the house, even though the shadows were closing in and the air was heavy with pent moisture. I had intended to walk to the gate, but after seeing how dark it was I decided not to. I was wearing rather high heels and the gravel was not the best of surfaces for walking.

He was early. I saw the headlights of his car appear and blossom into brilliance. They caught me full-on, and I put up a hand to shield my eyes. He was out of the car before I got over being dazzled.

"What are you doing out here?" he asked, handing me in. "It is dreary, chilly—"

"The atmosphere inside was chillier." I settled back into soft, gray velvet comfort.

"Oh? But I should have known. Was Francesca angry?"

"Not so much angry as upset. It doesn't matter."

"She is difficult to understand," Sebastiano admitted. "So sophisticated, so modern, and yet there are these pockets of traditional belief. I hope you weren't disturbed by her attitude."

"Is that a professional question, Doctor?"

He laughed ruefully. "It is a hard profession, mine. When I ask a simple question, the question of a friend, I am accused of probing. When I don't ask, I am thought cold and unsympathetic."

"You have a point," I admitted.

The big car—it was a Cadillac, brand-spanking-shiny new—went so lightly down the steep road that I hardly felt the bumps. A glare of headlights burst out at us, and Sebastiano pulled sharply to the right to let the oncoming car pass. He swore in Italian, and then said, "I hope you didn't understand what I said. He was coming too fast for such a narrow road. But you need not worry, I am a careful driver."

"I have a mild phobia about fast driving," I said.

"I do not ask why."

"Good for you."

He laughed; then I could laugh too. I was much more relaxed with him than I had expected to be. After a moment he said, "If you don't want to talk, that is fine. If you want to, then talk as you would to any friend. And I won't send you a bill."

It began to rain as we passed through the village, a soft drizzle that barely moistened the windshield. He handled the big car expertly. I don't remember what we talked about, but I remember that we laughed a lot. But it was not until we reached the restaurant, and we had checked our coats, that I really began to appreciate him. I had felt self-conscious about my off-the-rack cotton dress. Sebastiano was wearing an equally unimpressive suit, and his shirt was open at the neck. The other diners were more formally dressed; I had to believe that Sebastiano had deliberately dressed down to my level so as not to embarrass me.

The headwaiter greeted Sebastiano with the enthusiasm reserved for old and valued customers and we were shown to a table in a shadowy corner. I asked him to order for me. It was all superb—the wine, the food, the deft, unobtrusive service, the beautifully appointed table. I couldn't help thinking of the meal I had had with David. Plastic tablecloths instead of snowy linen, coarse white plates instead of fine china, a harsh, biting Chianti instead of—whatever this superb vintage might be. But the two men had one thing in common—the ability to make me feel relaxed and at ease, the ability to make me laugh. And if Sebastiano's charm was practiced and professional, I couldn't have cared less.

I refused dessert, though he urged me to have something. "You are too thin," he said, his fingers tracing a line along the inside of my arm. "I speak medically, you understand. Doesn't Francesca feed you?"

"Too well. Rosa is a good cook." But there was a reason why I had enjoyed this meal more than usual. Every bite I took in that house stuck in my throat. I had not thought about it until that moment, but it was true. Breaking bread with another person has time-honored emotional connotations. Offering food is a gesture of friendship; accepting it is a sign of trust.

"You are thinking thoughts that are not pleasant," Sebastiano said softly. "I don't ask what they are. What shall we do to take your mind off them? Would you like to go dancing?"

"I'd rather not, if you don't mind."

"I don't mind at all. Although I am a good dancer. But not so good as your husband, perhaps."

I looked up from my plate. He clapped his hand to his mouth in mock consternation and then said, "I can't help it. Forgive me."

"You're forgiven," I said, laughing. "Bart did love to dance, and he was marvelous. He was an actor, you know; every movement he made was trained, graceful."

"I didn't know. Francesca has spoken of him, but only of his childhood and adolescence. I am something of a movie buff; I'm surprised I have not recognized the Morandini name or features."

"He had had a few small parts in television shows, but most of his work was on the stage."

"Ah. New York?"

"Well . . . It was mostly summer stock, dinner theaters, that sort of thing. Luckily he had a private income or he'd have starved. It takes not only talent, but contacts and luck, to break into the theatrical profession."

134

"True." He waited a moment and then said tentatively, "If I were to suggest a film, it would not..."

"No, that would be fine. But my Italian is practically non-existent."

"There is a cinema that shows old British and American films. I don't know what is playing, but we could go there and see."

The movie was an old Marx Brothers film—*A Night at the Opera*. Sebastiano had not martyred himself on my account; he laughed so hard I thought he'd choke. When we came out of the theater it was raining heavily. He suggested a drink, or coffee. "I guess I'd better not," I said reluctantly. "Emilia will be waiting up for me. I can't stand the woman, but it isn't fair to keep her up half the night."

The streets were slippery. He had taken my arm; now he gave it a squeeze. "You are a very kind person, Kathy."

My laugh had more than a touch of wryness.

The gates were closed, but before Sebastiano could sound the horn Alberto came out from the lodge and opened them. The rain had slackened, but he got pretty wet. Sebastiano said, "Is your tender heart concerned for Alberto too?"

"I just wish the rain were boiling oil," I said.

"*Dio mio*, how vicious you are! What has he done to deserve that?"

"Lots of things. I don't understand why Francesca employs a man like that."

"His personal habits would not concern her so long as he performed his duties faithfully. I believe he and his wife have been with her for years. It is hard to keep servants, especially when one doesn't pay high wages." He brought the car to a stop in front of the stairs.

"Don't come in," I said quickly. "I'm sorry, Sebastiano—that sounded awfully rude; I didn't mean it that way—"

"It did not sound rude and I know why you said it. But I must see you to the door."

"It's stopped raining. I'd rather you didn't. Really."

"That bad, eh?" He sat back, his hands resting on the wheel. "Do you mind if I smoke? Will you join me?"

"And you a doctor," I said. "It's very bad for you."

"It is a bad habit. I try to cut down—it is my first of the evening, if you notice."

I accepted a cigarette. I didn't want it, but it seemed boorish just to say thank you and leave after such a nice evening.

"I haven't smoked since I got here," I said proudly. "I don't want to start again; I was smoking too much for a while."

"How long has it been?"

"Since I quit? Only a few days, actually."

"You know what I mean. And you know I am not asking as a doctor."

"Sebastiano—"

"Six months? A year?"

"Three months." I choked on the smoke like a teenager with her first cigarette.

"I didn't know."

"Francesca didn't tell you?"

"No. And that is not strange, for we do not talk of family matters very often. When she called to ask if I would see you she said only that you were her nephew's widow. I was taken aback when I saw how young you were. I knew you could not have been married long, but I had no idea...."

"You wouldn't have asked me to dinner if you had known?"

"Oh yes, I would." The answer was prompt and heartfelt. I laughed a little. Then I said, "Perhaps after all you share Francesca's idea about the propriety of someone so recently widowed going out."

"I don't make rules. All cases are different. In your case, it shows a healthy attitude. One cannot mourn forever."

"How true." I put out my cigarette. "I'd better go in."

"Yes, the poor servants whom you hate so much will be kept waiting," he said mockingly.

136

"Thank you for a wonderful evening. I really enjoyed it, Sebastiano."

"Then we will do it again. Tomorrow?" Before I could reply, he clicked his tongue and said irritably, "I forgot. I am going away for the weekend. Monday, Tuesday...Tuesday for dinner?"

"I'd love to."

"Good. I will telephone." He went on with scarcely a pause, "If I try to kiss you, will you consider it an affront to your hostess?"

I was laughing when he took me in his arms, and the kiss was more intense and prolonged than I had planned. It wasn't at all like Bart's kisses.... The fact that I could think of that, in the middle of a thoroughly satisfactory and enjoyable embrace, was not a good sign, but I didn't let it keep me from responding. Not until Sebastiano's hands moved under my loosely belted coat did I pull away.

"Right move, wrong place," I said a little breathlessly. "Emilia is probably looking through the keyhole and Alberto is ticking off the minutes until you drive out."

"Since we will be blamed anyway, why not enjoy it?"

The first fine careless rapture was gone, though. I had a prickly feeling at the back of my neck, as if we were under hidden, intense surveillance. Which was ridiculous. The lantern lights flanking the door of the villa were some distance away, and the interior of the car was dark. When I drew away the second time, Sebastiano didn't insist. I refused another cigarette. He lit his; the flame trembled perceptibly. "Get out, then," he said lightly. "You won't let me come to the door, you won't...Next time it will not be so easy for you to run away."

Despite the light tone and the smile that accompanied the words, I knew he was annoyed—at me, at Francesca, or at both of us. I didn't blame him. He waited until he saw the door open, and then pulled away with a roar of the exhaust.

Emilia had indeed been waiting for me. She had the door open before I reached the top of the stairs. I felt like an adolescent who has violated a curfew, and I found myself self-consciously straightening my coat and tightening my belt as I crossed the terrace. The rain had stopped, but the wet stones were slippery.

Emilia stood back with exaggerated deference, holding the door. I had barely entered the house when I heard it—a scream of tortured metal that seemed to go on forever, and a dull, crunching crash.

For a few seconds I was frozen, flung back into a memory of past horror. But when I turned there was no flame, no column of smoke. I started to run. Emilia followed. I heard a voice call out: "What is it? What has happened?" The voice was Francesca's. She had waited up for me too. I didn't pause to reply.

The Cadillac was halfway between the house and the gates, where the drive curved. The hood was jammed against a tree trunk. The headlights still shone; one went off at a drunken angle, shedding a weird theatrical light up into the leaves.

I saw a man leaning against the driver's side of the car looking in the window and thought it was Alberto, until the gatekeeper came running up, calling out. Sebastiano straightened. He spoke to Alberto, and then started violently as I caught his arm. I stammered out a series of questions, the conventional inquiries, to which he replied that he was unhurt.

Francesca was the last to arrive on the scene. She had delayed to put on a coat and—with her usual good sense—to find a flashlight. She turned it on Sebastiano. He was pale and his hair was disheveled, but his face, at least, was unmarked.

He insisted on inspecting the damage to the car before he did anything else. It might have been worse. One of the headlights was out of line and the hood was crinkled, but there did not appear to be anything wrong with the engine. It would cost a pretty penny to repair the body, though.

We went back to the villa, leaving Alberto trying to straighten the headlight. When Francesca got a good look at Sebastiano she announced flatly, "You have cracked a rib. You had better stay here tonight. I will call a doctor."

"I am a doctor," Sebastiano said, with a forced smile. "It is not broken, only bruised. I was thrown against the steering wheel."

He refused her invitation to stay, or to let Alberto drive him back to Florence. Somewhat to my surprise she didn't insist.

"But you shouldn't drive," I protested. "Even if you are physically able, there may be damage to the brakes or the steering or—"

He cut me short with uncharacteristic abruptness. "I will drive carefully. There is little traffic at this hour. Good night, Kathy—Francesca. I regret having inconvenienced you."

"It is I who should apologize," she said expressionlessly. "The drive must be in poor condition. I will have Alberto look at it."

I don't know how she managed in such innocuous words to convey the impression that the accident was his fault— that he must be drunk, or drowsy, or distracted. I knew he was none of the above, but I couldn't understand how it had happened. The drive was not in first-class condition. There were slippery spots where the gravel had been worn away, but only excessive speed would cause a car to skid out of control.

Sebastiano kissed Francesca's hand, wincing as he bent from the waist, and shook mine with ostentatious formality. His eyes avoided me. He telephoned an hour later, as Francesca had asked him, to let us know he had arrived home safely. Emilia delivered the message. He didn't ask to speak to me.

Chapter Six

WOKE up sneezing. I had not caught cold; there was a cat
sitting on my face. Somebody giggled, and a voice said,
"You have a mustache. A black-and-white-striped mustache."

I removed the cat's tail from under my nose and sat up.
The kitten slid down my front, rolled over, and attacked my
knees. I made a grab for it. Pete got to it first and hugged it
protectively to his chest.

"Joe did not mean to hurt."

"I was thinking about the sheets." Ruefully I examined the
perforated silk. "Your grandmother isn't going to like this.
I'm afraid Joe will have to have his claws clipped."

"Clipped?" The silver-gray eyes widened in horror.

"It won't hurt him. A scratching post might not be such a

141

bad idea either." I sank back onto the pillows, yawning. "You little demon, don't you know that people who wake up their friends by putting cats on their faces are not popular?"

"But you sleep too late. Today we have the football, and also washing of David's things. He said we could help. What do you call them—the things from the storeroom?"

"Darned if I know." It had been late before I got to sleep, following the accident and its aftermath, but the beaming face that peered at me from over the cat totally disarmed me. He was reacting to a Saturday off like any child freed from the appalling boredom of studies.

"You have a mustache now," I said. "Okay, buster, scram out of here and let me get dressed. I'll be with you soonest. Am I allowed to eat breakfast first?"

A knock sounded at the door, and the boy's face altered so unpleasantly I reached out a hand to him. Emilia came in before I could reply. "You are ready for breakfast?" she asked. "I have—" Then she saw Pete, who had retired behind the bed curtains, and burst into a tirade in Italian.

"I asked him to wake me," I said sharply. "That will be all, Emilia. I'll be down in fifteen minutes."

"The contessa has eaten an hour ago. I will bring a tray to you."

Pete didn't come out from his shelter until she had closed the door. "You don't have to go," I told him. "Wait for me if you like."

"No, I will put Joe in my room. Then I will go to David. He is in his room, at the garage. You will come?"

"As soon as I can."

He scuttled out, clutching Joe. He didn't want to encounter Emilia again, even with me there to defend him.

When I came out of the bathroom my breakfast tray was on the desk. For all her bulk Emilia could move quietly when she chose. I wasn't sure I liked that idea.

The scientists were hard at work when I arrived. David had put his rags to soak. A row of trays filled with muddy liquid lay on the table. Pete was peering onto one of them with an expectant air that was, in my opinion, hardly justified. All I could see was dirty water.

"Just in time," said David. "The great unveiling is about to take place. Nothing up my sleeve, lady and gent..."

He flexed his hand, reached into one of the trays, and came up with a fragment about a foot square. He dunked it in a tray of clear water to rinse it. "Voilà."

The colors seemed to leap up off the surface of the water—bright crimson, clear green and buff against a background of rich dark blue. Careful stitching outlined a woman's face and shoulders. Her features had the big-eyed stiffness of a Byzantine painting, and her hair, of soft auburn, was surmounted by a fillet of twisted gold threads. A border of flowers and leaves framed the portrait. At least David claimed it was a portrait.

"Fifth century if it's a day," he murmured rapturously. "And in perfect condition."

"What do you mean, perfect? The stitching's come undone here—"

He stepped back with a look of horror as I put out my hand. "Don't touch it!"

"I was just pointing. Goodness, what an old granny you are."

"I've been called worse." David deposited his treasure tenderly on a piece of blotting paper and went on to the next. The fabrics—some woven, some embroidered—had a certain charm, especially the squares and roundels with running animals—cats, hares, greyhounds—which, according to David, had been stitched to clothing. I found them mildly interesting, but only mildly, and Pete soon got bored.

"Let us play football," he said.

143

"Don't tell me you aren't having fun," David said with a grin.

"I like that—" His finger indicated the embroidered cat. "But to wash clothes, it is a woman's work."

"Male chauvinist," I said.

"What is that?"

"Well...It's like saying girls can't play football because they're girls."

"But they cannot. Except you," Pete added.

"You'd better quit now while you're ahead," David advised him. "I'll be through in a minute, Pete. Can't stop in the middle of a job, you know. How about getting rid of the used solution for me? No, not out the window, you lazy cuss— in the sink."

He indicated the door behind him.

"You've got plumbing?" I said, as Pete lifted the tray, spilling only a quart or so.

"All the comforts of home. This used to be the chauffeur's quarters. Alberto being a happily married man, and Emilia being vital to the contessa's comfort, they live in the villa."

I helped Pete empty the trays and rinse them. David refilled them with distilled water and mixed some assorted chemicals. "That's the lot," he announced, dunking the next batch of scraps. "Now we can get on to the important business of the day."

Pete had the football with him, of course. He clattered down the stairs ahead of us. "Who called you worse things?" I asked.

"Huh?"

"When I said you were an old granny I was being chauvinist. I apologize. You said—"

"Oh, yeah. Think nothing of it, dearie. My old man had more pejorative comments to make when I took up my profession. He went so far as to impugn my masculinity, if you can believe it."

"What did he want you to do?"

"Follow in the paternal footsteps. He manufactures bolts—those fifty-cent bolts the Pentagon buys for nine hundred bucks."

"Oh." Another stereotype gone west. The starving academic was, or could have been, one of the idle rich. "A matter of principle?" I inquired.

"I don't like bolts," David said.

Pete decided he wanted to practice kicking that morning. I let David talk me into holding, though I ought to have known better. Pete kicked my hand as often as he did the ball, so after a while I persuaded him it wasn't fair for me to have the honor of being the holder all the time, and David and I changed places.

The sun was high in the sky before Pete could be persuaded to stop. I reminded him that Joe would be waiting, and he gave in with reasonably good grace. "To take a nap is not so bad with Joe," he admitted. "Joe must sleep lots, he is young."

After he had gone I dropped onto the bench. David sat beside me. "Nap?" he said. "He's too old for an afternoon nap, isn't he?"

"I would say so. But his grandmother has some idea he's delicate."

"Delicate, my foot." We had ended the session with some passing and tackling. David had been tackled. "Is that why he isn't in school?"

"I guess so." I felt sure David's question wasn't prompted by idle curiosity or love of gossip. But it was not my place to tell him about Pete's emotional problems.

"This is a lousy setup for a kid," David muttered. "He'd be better off in school. Hasn't he got anyone to play with? Not even a pet, until you came up with the kitten."

"I'm working on it," I said briefly.

David's wide, *Petrouchka* smile split his jaws. "I'll bet you are. Little Miss Fix-It."

145

"I've been called worse than that."

"By your old man?"

"Especially by him. You'd like him," I added after a moment.

"Maybe I'll look him up when I get back."

"When will that be?"

"June, July—whenever the money runs out."

"Oh."

"Any chance that you'll be there?"

"At home with the folks? That depends on the job situation. If I can teach summer school I will; I need the money. If not, I suppose I'll scrounge off my mother and father, and sling hash at the local diner."

"Then you won't be here?"

"Not on your life. I—" His eyes shifted, but not quickly enough. I glowered at him. "Who have you been talking to? Rosa?"

"I was not prying into your personal affairs, if that's what you're thinking. Rosa volunteered the information. She's all excited about it."

"Damn," I said.

David went on, "She keeps talking about what joy it will bring to the house when the baby is born, and all like that. I got the impression you were going to stay until . . . that you were going to stay."

"No."

"I didn't mean to—"

"I don't want to talk about it."

"Okay." He stood up. "See you."

After he had marched off, visibly offended, I regretted having been so brusque. Apparently my interesting and fictitious condition was now public knowledge, and it wasn't his fault if Rosa liked to gossip. I could not imagine Francesca chatting with the cook; presumably Rosa had heard the news from Emilia. I should have known it would happen. It didn't alter the situation, but somehow the fact that David was now one of the deluded majority brought the whole dubious business into sharper, uglier perspective.

I had been kidding myself when I thought I could prolong the lie for another month. Every day brought the possibility of a painful confrontation that much closer. If Francesca asked me flat out I would have to tell her the truth. When the situation first arose she had been a stranger to me, a stranger I didn't much like. Now she was a person I knew, with feelings that could be hurt. I might not sympathize with those feelings; I couldn't even say truthfully that I was fond of her. But when I thought of seeing her face change, her eyes harden with contempt—no, I couldn't contemplate that. I had to leave, soon. I had done all I could for Pete; Lord knows it wasn't much, but there wasn't much I could do except talk. And I had done plenty of that.

As I showered and changed I rehearsed the speech I meant to make to Francesca: graceful thanks for her hospitality, apologies for remaining longer than I had intended. Then she would say something like "Not at all, it was a pleasure." And I'd say, "It's been great getting to know you, but..." But I have to get back to my job? But my mother broke her leg and she needs me to take care of her? But I feel another nervous breakdown coming on?

No. That was my guilty conscience thinking I needed an excuse to leave. What I needed was an excuse for barging in and staying so long. A polite hostess doesn't ask a guest when she is planning to go. Maybe my cynical and melodramatic theories about the matriarch and the Heir of the Morandinis were all wrong. Maybe she would be glad to see the last of me.

I revised the dialogue.

"Thank you so much for your hospitality, Francesca."

"Not at all. I've enjoyed having you here."

"I've enjoyed it too. But I've trespassed long enough."

"I'm sorry you must go. When are you leaving?"

"The end of next week."

The end of next week. Set yourself a deadline and stick to it. Don't let an unhappy child or a handsome doctor stop you.

The only trouble with pre-planned conversations is that the other guy never says what he's supposed to say.

I went downstairs early, wanting to get it over and done with. Francesca was not in her sitting room. I paced the floor nervously, picking things up and putting them down. Bart's photograph followed me with smiling eyes. I tried not to look at it.

I heard the telephone ring. The instrument was on a table in the hall; I suppose Francesca didn't want such an intrusive, modern vulgarity in her lovely room, where she might have to answer it herself instead of letting Emilia screen the callers.

The door opened. "It is a telephone for you, signora," said Emilia.

It had to be Sebastiano. Who else would be calling? I picked up the telephone and said brightly, "How's the rib today?"

There was a moment of silence. Then a voice said, "Which one? I've got eleven or twelve of the cursed things. They seem to be all there, but I've better things to do than ask them how they are feeling."

"Pa!"

"So you know me, do you? But you weren't expecting the old man, oh no. Whose ribs was it you were inquiring about so sweetly, may I ask?"

"Oh, Pa, it's so good to hear your voice! How did you find me?"

"With great difficulty. And it's costing me a pretty penny even on a Saturday, so don't be wasting my time in idle chatter."

"Who's wasting whose time? How are you? Is everyone all right? What's wrong?"

"Nothing is wrong *here*," said my father with heavy significance. "It's yourself that must be wrong, I'm thinking, to foist yourself on a poor woman who never saw hide nor hair of you till you turned up on her doorstep. What the devil are you up to? Never mind; don't tell me, I don't dare think about it. When are you coming home?"

"Soon, Pa. Did you get my letter?"

"What letter? I got a postcard with a dozen words on the back, and thank you for the effort. When I telephoned your hotel I had a very strange conversation with a young man who seemed to know more about your affairs than your own father. When is soon?"

"I don't know exactly."

"Aha. You're flat broke, is it, without the means to buy a ticket."

"For God's sake, Pa, I'm not eighteen years old. I have my return ticket—"

"Then use it. When?"

"The end of next week."

"You mean it?"

"Yes. Friday or Saturday—maybe Sunday. I'll call as soon as I get a reservation. Honest."

"Humph," said my father.

"Let me talk to Ma for a minute."

"She's not here."

"I'll bet she doesn't know you called. I'll bet she said, 'Leave the girl alone and don't be treating her as if she was a baby.'"

"Humph."

"I adore you, Pa. I'll call you in a few days."

"You damn well better," said my father.

I heard the click as he replaced the telephone, more than

149

five thousand miles away. I was so homesick I felt dizzy. Friday. I'd try to get on a plane Friday.

Then I looked up and there was Francesca on the stairs, staring down at me.

I said stupidly, "That was my father."

"So I gathered." She came down the stairs. "I apologize. I could not help overhearing."

She walked right past me toward the door of her room. Emilia materialized in time to open the door. I followed, though my first cowardly impulse had been to flee.

We took our seats. Emilia poured wine. I said with forced brightness, "He's mad because I've been gone longer than I planned. As you may have heard, he wants me to come home."

"Friday or Saturday, you said."

"If I can get a reservation. I've trespassed on your hospitality long enough."

I was back on track. Unfortunately she failed to pick up her cue.

"I had assumed you would stay on."

"Oh, my goodness, I don't know what gave you that impression. I haven't any—"

"You are Bartolommeo's wife. This is his home. It is yours, for as long as you like." A faint frown wrinkled the serenity of her brow. "Perhaps I should have made that plain from the beginning. I assumed you would understand."

Worse and worse. She was talking to me the way she would to a simpleminded child. And the kindness, the open-hearted generosity...Don't be a boob, I told myself. It isn't generosity. It's the old European assumption that a woman is her husband's property, to be moved from place to place at his convenience. That his child belongs to his family, not his wife's.

"You are very kind," I stammered. "But I must go home. My—my mother..."

I verily believe I would have dragged out that stupid lie if she had not interrupted me. "Ah yes. You want to be with your mother. I can hardly hope to take her place at such a time. It would be different, of course, if Bartolommeo were here."

"Oh yes, of course." By that time I didn't know what I was saying. I snatched at the excuse she had offered. "That would be different. But as it is—"

"Friday?"

"If I can get a reservation. Do you mind if I call this afternoon?"

"Emilia will place the call for you," she said abstractedly. "The telephone system is difficult."

My appetite wasn't very good. Francesca did not raise the subject again, but I expected her to at any moment, and my stomach was a mass of fluttering butterflies. It did not improve matters when Emilia came in with a long white florist's box, and Francesca held out her hands, and Emilia said dourly, "For the signora."

I had to open it then and there. The flowers were freesias, a rainbow glory of peach and pale blue, pink and yellow, smelling of springtime. The card said only, "Until Tuesday."

Francesca murmured, "How charming. Give them to Emilia; she will take them to your room and put them in water."

Emilia took the flowers with a curl of the lip that indicated what she thought of the gift, the giver, and the recipient. No doubt the conventional red roses would have impressed her more; but these soft, fragrant blossoms were more to my taste. That Sebastiano knew they would be—that he wasn't annoyed with me—improved my mood considerably.

I told Francesca I would let her know about the reservation. She only nodded, without speaking. I was on my way out of the room when I thought of something. "Francesca?"

"Yes?"

"I'd appreciate it if you wouldn't tell Pietro I'm leaving. I suppose it's vain of me to think he will care—"

"He will care."

"But he must know I can't... Anyway, I'd rather tell him myself, if that's all right with you."

"Certainly." She smiled. "I have not given up hope of persuading you to change your mind."

ii

WELCOME BACK, Jane Eyre, I thought. But that was just my neurotic conscience reacting to what had only been a courteous conventionality. Coming from a sinister housekeeper, or a villain twirling his mustache—or the scarred, brooding hero of *Bride of the Madman*—it might have sounded like a threat.

I decided to go to Florence. It was a beautiful day, a good day for shopping and sightseeing, and a very good day for avoiding the members of the household. There wasn't a single person I could face. I had even been rude to David.

The flowers were in my room, filling the air with their sweetness. I grabbed my purse and coat and went out. Emilia was in the hall when I got downstairs. The damned woman was everywhere. On a sudden impulse I told her I would not be in to dinner. I couldn't endure another meal like the last.

There was no one in the stableyard, no sign of life at David's window. No doubt he was in his beloved dusty attic. It felt good to be behind the wheel of a car again. If no other positive feature had resulted from this visit, that phobia at least seemed to be cured. The car represented freedom, independence, mobility, escape.... From my own folly, what else?

When I reached the gates, they were closed. Alberto was

nowhere in sight. No reason why he should be on duty; he had not been told I was going out. I got out of the car.

There was a bar on the inside, but after I had hoisted it out of its supports the gates still wouldn't open. I pushed and tugged without result, and then looked more closely. There was a lock. There was a keyhole. There was no key.

Surely Alberto wouldn't carry the key on his person. If he did, I'd have to go back to the garage and look for him, and I was averse to that idea for more reasons than one. I heard something moving in the shrubs behind the lodge. I called, "Alberto?" and went around the shrubs to have a look.

The man behind the bushes wasn't Alberto. He was on his hands and knees, crouched like a beast of prey. Locks of greasy flaxen hair fell over his face; and as I stood watching he began crooning to himself.

I took a grip on my nerves. The poor man couldn't help it if he looked like a creature out of a horror film. I didn't know his name. I said slowly, *"Pardone, signore. La porta è chiusa. Io desidererei..."* I couldn't think of the word for key.

He didn't look up. He started crawling back and forth, snuffling like a dog on a scent. It was really a ghastly performance, and my voice was a trifle unsteady when I began again, *"Scusi—"* That was as far as I got. The man sprang to his feet, arms flailing wildly, and ran straight at me. I caught a flashing glimpse of a face twisted by some strong emotion— fear, perhaps. His eyes were shut, his mouth was an open, gaping hole in his face. He passed within a foot of me and rushed on, limping dreadfully, but moving at surprising speed. A harsh cackle of manic laughter drifted back to me.

I finally found the key hanging on a nail inside the lodge door. It was eight inches long, and I had to use both hands to turn it. Then I had to return the key to its place, drive out the gates, get out of the car, close the gates. I couldn't lock them. I decided that was just too damned bad. Why all the fuss about security, anyway? Barred gates, a vicious killer dog, a surly brute of a human guarding a run-down mansion whose portable treasures had long since gone to the pawnshop....

The green shadows of the tunnel-like road reminded me that I might be unfair to Francesca. The house was certainly isolated. For all I knew, the quiet countryside might be a hotbed of vice and crime. Perhaps she needed the dog and the gates.

As soon as I came out of the trees my spirits improved. Under the spring sun I saw the lovely smiling landscape I knew from photographs and paintings. The hills were flushed with the pale green of new growth; the dark gray-green shapes of the cypresses looked like an ornamental frieze, too symmetrical to be natural. The small piazza in the village was crowded—women shopping, or pushing baby carriages, men filling the tables at the outdoor café. I drove at a crawl, responding to the friendly nods and smiles and the curious stares of passersby.

What a pity my visit had been spoiled by personal difficulties—most of them, I had to admit, brought on by myself. Someday perhaps I could return. I'd like to see Pete again. But Francesca would probably never forgive me when she learned the truth.

I forced Francesca from my mind. This was my afternoon off. I was going to play tourist, shop for souvenirs, see the sights. I had not much time left. Five days, or six.

I had forgotten one little detail until the clerk at American Express reminded me of it. Yes, I could get on a flight from Rome on Friday, if I was willing to pay an extra hundred-plus dollars. My ticket was an excursion-type, with a minimum number of days. If I wanted the lower rate, I would have to wait until Monday.

Luxurious living hadn't blunted my thriftiness. What was a couple of extra days, after all? I made a reservation on a train to Rome Sunday afternoon, and another on the Rome-to-New York flight Monday. There were lots of flights from New York to Boston; I wouldn't need a reservation for that leg of the trip. That job done, I turned to the important business of the day. I had no intention of spending the glorious sunlight hours in the Uffizi or the Pitti Palace. I wanted to go shopping.

Many of the shops were closed; they would reopen later in the afternoon. But the open-air stalls in the Piazza San Lorenzo were doing a thriving business, and I bought presents for everybody—a real leather purse for Ma, a silk shirt for my father (he wouldn't wear it, but he would brag about owning one), toys for the baby, souvenirs for brothers and sister-in-law—and a dress for me. I intended to dazzle Sebastiano on our next—our last—date. The dress was peach-colored silk with a jacket trimmed with braid of the same fabric. My souvenir of Florence.

Later in the afternoon I found myself in my old neighborhood and decided to stop for a cappuccino at the coffee bar near the hotel. I hadn't been there long when Angelo came in. I invited him to join me. He glanced doubtfully at the table and the chair and I said expansively, "I'm buying, Angelo. Today is the first day of the rest of my life."

"Signorina?"

"Just a figure of speech, Angelo."

"Ah," said Angelo. He looked to my right, to my left, and then, for reasons known only to himself, over my head. "The friend is not with you."

"No."

"The friend is gone? My brother—"

"I'm sure your brother is very nice," I said. "But I won't get a chance to meet him this trip. I'm going home soon."

"He is handsomer than your friend," said Angelo. "Your friend is nice fellow, but not handsome. You are going home?"

"I have to work for a living too, Angelo."

"Ah yes. You have more secret letters for me, signorina?"

I thought of telling Angelo I was not a secret agent or an undercover cop, and decided there was no need to disillusion him. Let him enjoy his fantasy.

"Not at the moment, Angelo. But I appreciate the offer."

"*Prego, signorina*. I am always ready. I am always at your service. A secret message, a room, if you wish to be private, no one knowing where you are..."

"I may take you up on that," I said.

He swallowed two cups of espresso in quick succession and then announced he had to get back to work. "Any time, signorina. Remember. You take advantage of me."

It was nice to have a friend, even if he liked me for the wrong reasons—as did most of the people I had met recently. Angelo thought I was a spy, Francesca thought I was pregnant, David and Sebastiano...I had not been completely candid with them either. They might not like me as well if they found out what I was hiding. Thank heaven for Pete. Pete liked me.

That thought didn't cheer me up one bit.

I took my parcels back to the car, which I had left in a public parking lot. I couldn't return to the villa yet. I had told Emilia I would not be in to dinner. It was too early to eat, but the shops had reopened. I still needed a gift for my hostess, and I wanted something to read. Perhaps I could find a book for Pete too.

Secondhand paperbacks weren't difficult to locate, but I had to go to an expensive foreign-language bookstore to find children's books in English. I had no idea at what level Pete was reading, so I avoided the heavier classics and settled for the Hardy Boys, a book about cats with lots of color photographs, and one real prize—a book called *Famous Quarterbacks of the NFL*. I felt sure he'd struggle through that text, even if it was too advanced for him.

Sometime later I was unconcernedly lost in a maze of narrow streets behind the Duomo. The narrowest were no wider than sidewalks, and here, for the first time, I began to get the feel of the medieval city. The houses were flush with the pavement; occasionally I could see flowers and fountains through open archways. There were a few jarringly modern touches; through the open windows came, not the gentle tinkling of a lute, but blaring rock 'n' roll, from radios whose volume switches had been turned up as far as they would go.

I wandered along, pressing against the wall when a motorbike roared past. Then I saw something in a shop window, illumined by a ray of sunlight that had squeezed through a gap between the high buildings opposite. It was a scrap of embroidery that looked as if it had been cut from a larger piece. A spray of silvery-green leaves and pale-pink flowers curved across a background of ivory silk. The flowers were shaded with such skill that the individual stitches blended, like a painting. On a sudden impulse I opened the door of the shop and went in.

I had tried my hand at the bargaining I knew was customary in the smaller shops, without much success; but I did not have to counterfeit the consternation that seized me when the genteel lady clerk told me the price of the scrap. "It is Lyon silk embroidery, signorina, over two hundred years old. Very rare."

"It's just a scrap," I protested. "Not even big enough for an evening bag, or—"

She looked shocked. "One does not *use* such rare pieces, signorina. One exhibits them. It is a manufacturer's sample, not a scrap!"

I got it for a little more than half the price she had originally quoted, only because I didn't really want it and she knew I didn't really want it. I was almost out the door when she made her final offer. As I filled in traveler's checks I was already regretting my purchase. I must have embroidery on the brain; without David's lectures and Francesca's attempts to instruct me, I'd never have noticed the wickedly expensive trifle. And Francesca would probably consider it a tacky, inappropriate gift.

iii

IT WAS dark when I got back to the villa, and as I drove into the garage I saw that David's window was alight. That surprised me; I had expected he'd be out on the town on Saturday night. I was unloading my purchases when I heard his door open and the clatter of feet down the stairs.

"Hi," he said tentatively.

"Hello."

"Are you still mad at me?"

"No. I was rude, David. Sorry."

"That's okay. Hey, you really went on a shopping binge, didn't you? Let me take some of those things."

"I should have bought a shopping bag. They don't give—" The paperbacks I was trying to balance slipped and fell. David bent to collect them. I had left my headlights on; he examined the books as he gathered them up. One cover was particularly lurid; I seem to remember it featured a decapitated head with tongue protruding and eyeballs rolled up till only the whites showed.

"Tsk, tsk," David said. "Your taste in literature is deplorable."

"Who asked you?"

As we walked toward the back door David said, "Pete was looking for you."

"I didn't tell him I would see him this afternoon."

"Why so defensive? I know you didn't. He's lonesome, that's all. He seemed upset."

"Thanks so much for telling me."

158

David opened the last gate and we went into the kitchen garden. "There's a carnival in Fiesole tomorrow. We could take the kid."

"What an irresistible invitation."

"Are you sure you aren't still mad at me?" David asked mildly.

"Damn it—" He cringed in mock terror as I turned on him, and I had to laugh. "Sorry again. I'm not in a very good mood, I guess. I'd love to go to a carnival, and I know Pete would get a kick out of it. I'll check with Francesca to make sure it's all right." After a moment I added, "Thanks."

"*Prego, signora.*" He opened the kitchen door.

The room was dark except for a flickering bluish-white light that came from a small television set on one end of the long kitchen table. Beside it sat Rosa, a bottle and glasses in front of her. She called out a greeting in Italian, then saw me and lumbered to her feet. David flicked on a light switch.

"So this is how you spend your evenings, carousing with Rosa," I said. "Tell her to sit down, for goodness' sake. And give me those books; Francesca would have a fit if you took them upstairs."

He handed them to me. "Don't worry, I know my place. Sure you won't join us for a nice lowbrow evening? You haven't lived till you've seen 'Dallas' in Italian."

"Each to his own lowbrow tastes, thank you. I prefer to wallow in crime and in chocolates. Have one?" He shook his head. I offered the bag to Rosa, who had returned to her seat and was watching me somewhat warily. She accepted a piece of candy and crunched it between her teeth with such relish that I put a handful of it into a dish. "I can see you're a fellow chocolate fiend, Rosa."

David translated, and Rosa's face broadened into a grin. She nodded vigorously. "*Grazie, signora—molto grazie.*"

I patted her on the shoulder. "Enjoy yourselves. *Buona notte*, Rosa. Good night, David."

Before I so much as closed the door they were deeply involved in the drama. The screen blurred and flickered, but it didn't seem to bother them; Rosa shook with laughter at some quip of J. R.'s and nudged David. I was tempted to stay. They looked so comfortable—so happily lowbrow, like me.

The house was quiet and deserted. I barely saw Emilia's apron fluttering around a corner.

I had to shift my parcels to turn the doorknob. The books slipped again and I made a rush for the bed, reaching it just in time to spill books and parcels onto its surface. Then I jumped back with a gasp. My fingers had touched something wet and slimy.

There was a lamp on the bedside table, but I wanted to get as far from the foul thing as I could. And I had thought I was being morbid when I speculated about snakes in my bed! I found the light switch by the door, and pressed it.

It wasn't a snake. It was the mutilated remains of my pretty flowers, crushed and torn, oozing sap like blood from their broken stems.

Chapter Seven

MY ANGER wasn't of the speechless variety this time; I swore at some length, using several expressions of which my father would not have approved. ("Big as you are, don't think you can use swear words in my presence, young lady—and it's no lady you are to say such things.")

Francesca had disapproved of my going out with Sebastiano, but I didn't suspect her of committing this vulgarity. It was worse than vulgar, it was obscene. The flowers had been so fragile and pretty. They had been not only crushed, but wrenched and ripped by hard, spiteful hands. I was sure the hands had been Emilia's; but was it Francesca who had prompted the destruction? Like Henry the Second and Thomas à Becket—"who will free me from this turbulent priest?"

I couldn't leave the mess, it was smack in the middle of

the velvet spread. I cleared it away, but it left a disfiguring stain, like the stain of memory in my mind that could never be forgotten.

The fit of rage on top of an active day and little sleep the night before left me exhausted. I got undressed and climbed into bed with my pile of books and my chocolates and my carafe of water on the table beside me. Eating chocolates always makes me thirsty, and I intended to eat every last one of them. The water had looked stale, beaded with tiny drops and hazy with sediment, so I rinsed it out and refilled it.

The nice proper English detective story or the decapitated head? I sorted through the pile, trying to decide, and realized I had acquired an extra book. As soon as I saw the title I knew how it had got there. *Collected Poems of Robert Browning*. David must have brought it down with him intending to give it to me, and sneaked it into the pile. What a nut he was.

I tossed it aside and opted for the detective story. Decapitated heads were too suggestive of my murdered flowers. But the detective story was dull, and by the time I had eaten my chocolates (filled with peculiar combinations of liquor, nougat, and marzipan) I decided I didn't care who had murdered Lord Billingsgate.

The only Browning I could remember reading was *My Last Duchess*. It had been a requirement one year in high school. I had hated it. At the time I didn't understand why I hated it; it takes a certain experience to comprehend fully the chilling, subtle evil of the Duke. As I leafed through the book I found other familiar lines that I hadn't known were Browning's. "God's in his heaven, All's right with the world." Says who, Robert Browning? With a little snort of laughter I recognized the line I had overheard the first day I met David. "My scrofulous French novel, On gray paper with blunt type...." Poor Brother Lawrence, in his Spanish cloister!

I remembered David saying that the Brownings had lived in Florence. I must ask him to show me the house, if it was still standing. Although I had never had much use for Robert, I had adored Elizabeth, especially the sloppier, super-romantic sonnets. "How do I love thee? Let me count the ways." Robert must have had some good qualities to inspire those words.

Actually, he wasn't such a bad poet himself, I decided after a while. I read "Andrea del Sarto" and "Fra Lippo Lippi" because I recognized the names—they were Florentine paint-ers—skipping a lot, because the poems were awfully long-winded. There were some good lines, though. The ending of "Fra Lippo Lippi" rather caught my fancy; the old rascal is on his way back to the monastery after an unclerical night on the town when he is stopped by the watch. "No lights, no lights," he begs. "The street's hushed and I know my own way back. Don't fear me! There's the grey beginning...."

I wished I could be sure I knew my own way back. I had taken the first stumbling steps, but the end of the road was lost in darkness, without any sign of the gray light of dawn.

When the sounds woke me it was the dead, silent center of the night. The moon had set; faint starlight delineated the window. The sounds were coming from inside my room. The hair on the back of my neck lifted as I listened.

I sat up in bed and turned on the lamp. He was huddled on the floor just inside the door. Both hands clutched the leg of the chair in a grip that whitened his knuckles. His pajamas stuck to every fragile bone; they were soaking wet, as if he had stood under a shower. The sudden burst of light dilated his pupils to black, hiding the silver-gray. He forced one word out of his distorted mouth. "Help..."

I ran to him and scooped him up bodily. His bones felt like the hollow bones of a bird, and waves of shivering ran through him.

"Pete! For God's sake, honey, what is it? What happened?"

"Don't let them..." His teeth were chattering so violently

163

he couldn't get the rest of the word out. His crooked fingers dug into me like the kitten's claws.

"Don't be afraid. I won't let anybody do anything. It's all right...." I went on crooning meaningless words of reassurance as I carried him to the bed, meaning to wrap him in the blanket. Luckily I was still holding him when it happened. Every muscle in his body went into a spasm, hardening like wood. The hands that had clung now struck out at me. His flattened palm cut a stinging slash across my cheek. At first I thought he was having an epileptic seizure. Then I saw his face, and reeled, almost losing my hold, as his fist smacked into the side of my head.

We fell onto the mattress, with me on top. My body pinned his arms to the bed, but he continued to struggle, writhing and kicking with an unnatural strength. I must have outweighed him by fifty pounds, but I could barely hold him down. That was all I could think to do, and all I could manage—hold him, keep him from hurting me or himself, until the attack passed. But every now and then I could have sworn that something flickered behind the eyes that were narrowed with rage—something frightened and bewildered, begging for the help he could not request in words.

The fit passed as suddenly as it had erupted. His eyes closed. I thought he had lost consciousness, and was about to shift my weight when his dark lashes fluttered. He whispered, "Are they gone? Are they gone?"

"There's nobody here but me," I said, fighting to keep my voice calm.

"Signora?"

"Yes. It's all right, honey."

His lashes stuck together in wet points. I rolled over and took him in my arms. "It's all right. Everything is all right now."

It wasn't all right, though. He couldn't look at me. He risked one quick glance, and then scuttled on hands and knees to the farthest corner of the bed, where he huddled against the headboard with his hands pressed to his eyes. When I tried to touch him he let out a thin mewing scream, like a rabbit cornered by hounds.

Sometimes, during that long night, I looked at the clock. The hands didn't seem to move. It was still dark outside when at last he ventured to open his eyes. I was sitting as close as I dared, ready to grab him if he went into another convulsion. But it was over—whatever it was. His chest rose in a sharp sigh. "Signora."

"It's me."

His arm lifted, with painful slowness. I took his hand, but that wasn't what he wanted. His fingers squirmed free and reached for my face. They traced every feature, as a blind person might. He could see, though. His eyes were focused and aware.

"It is you," he said. "I am very sleepy, signora."

"Me too. Get under the covers. You can stay here the rest of the night."

He rubbed his eyes fretfully. "No. I must be there, in my bed. I must see where Joe is."

My heart gave a painful lurch. If Francesca had been right— if he had struck at the kitten as he struck at me... "Okay," I said. "I'll carry you."

I couldn't manage it. He was too heavy and the stairs were too steep. We staggered up them together, leaning on one another. His door was closed but not locked. The kitten was nowhere in sight.

Pete went straight to the wardrobe and opened its door, to be greeted by a reproachful yowl. Like a true philosopher Joe had whiled away the hours of his imprisonment by sleeping. He rose in one of those fabulous stretches only felines can achieve, back arched, tail stiff. Pete dropped to the floor. "He is safe," he murmured. "Joe is o-kay. They didn't..."

He fell asleep sitting there. I caught him as he swayed and

lifted him onto his bed. With a businesslike air, Joe headed for the litter box. I found clean clothes in a drawer and changed Pete's pajamas. His muscles were relaxed like those of any sleeping child. His lashes lay soft on his cheeks. I had to lift him to get his arms into the pajama top. His eyes opened a slit. A smile curved his lips. "I came to you," he murmured. "I did it. To you."

I spent what was left of the night lying on the rug by his bed. Joe kept me on the qui vive, walking up and down my body and nibbling my hair. Not until the room grew light did I get stiffly to my feet. The child was deeply, peacefully asleep, the cat curled up against his back. Through the barred window I could see the cypresses taking shape against the gray dawn. "There's the grey beginning. . . ." But not here. Not in this room.

ii

I DIDN'T expect to sleep, but I did, instantly, like someone who has been hit over the head. From the angle of the sunlight streaming in when I woke I knew it must be late. Memory returned, total and horrifying. I got out of bed so fast my head swam, and I had to sit down for a minute.

Finally I opened my door and looked out. The house was as silent as a tomb, but Emilia must have been waiting for me to show signs of life, for she appeared instantly. "You are awake, signora. You wish breakfast?"

"Please. Where—where is everybody?"

"*Alla chiesa, signora.*"

Her expression and her tone implied that I should have been at the *chiesa* too. I couldn't have cared less what she thought of my devotional failures. I said, "And Pete—*il conte*—is he at church too?"

"*Sì, signora. Naturalmente.*"

I closed the door, practically in Emilia's face, and collapsed into the chair. Naturally *il conte* was at church. Naturally.

Then he was all right. He was functioning normally. No one had noticed anything wrong.

I sat staring at my bare feet until Emilia came back with my tray. The coffee restored a few of my wits. Could I have dreamed the whole ghastly episode? My aching muscles denied that comforting solution. There were bruises on my shins, where he had kicked me, and a tenderness behind my ear. It had not been a dream. But how could a child go through an attack like that and be fully recovered in the morning? If Francesca was to be believed, there had only been two comparable episodes, weeks apart. Had there been others she didn't know about? Other times when he fought it alone, locked in his room, or sought help and comfort from...

From whom? "I came to you," he had said. He had known it was coming. He had shut the cat in the wardrobe, so it wouldn't be hurt, and struggled down the stairs to my room.

I hardly need say that by that point in my meditations the tears were streaming down my cheeks and dripping into my coffee cup. I wiped my face, wincing as my fingers touched another sore spot where his open hand had hit me.

I knew I must tell Francesca. I knew it, and I had no intention of doing it. I should be ashamed to admit that, even in the light of what happened later. It was nothing less than criminal negligence. But I could not bring myself to betray the boy. That was the word that stuck in my mind—betrayal. He had come to me, with God only knew what effort and courage. What would Francesca do if she knew what had happened? Lock him in his room, increase the dosage of the drug he was taking—the same old remedies, only more of them. I couldn't see that her methods were proving particularly effective.

It was a strange coincidence that his door had not been locked last night. But coincidences happen. Someone had forgotten, that was all. Thank God, thank God, he had thought of me. Thank God he had come to me instead of...

I was leaving in five days.

By the time I got myself under control my coffee was too salty to drink. I reminded myself that the situation had not changed. He was no worse than he had been before I arrived on the scene. He might even be better. Relapses were only to be expected. It was consummate egotism on my part to think that my half-baked therapy would restore him to perfect health overnight. Things like that happened in movies, not in real life. I would talk to Sebastiano—really talk to him, not exchange compliments. That was all I could do, except make the next few days as happy as possible for Pete.

And then walk away clean, jeered my conscience.

What the hell can I do? demanded my common sense. I'd take him home with me in a second if I could. I can't. I have no right.

My conscience had no answer to that one, but it wasn't satisfied. I could feel it rumbling unhappily, like an empty stomach. An empty conscience is much more uncomfortable.

I was getting dressed when the churchgoers returned. Their arrival was heralded by an altercation in the hall—Pete's shrill voice, and Emilia's growl.

I rushed to the door. She had him by the arm, although he wasn't doing anything except arguing. He looked like a child model for an expensive catalog—shirt and tie, polished shoes, three-piece white linen suit.

"What's going on?" I asked.

"I wanted to see if you were awake," Pete said.

"I told him he must not disturb you, signora."

"You knew I was awake. Let go of him."

"*Sì, signora*. As you desire."

The look she gave me didn't match her submissive reply. She walked away.

He looked tired. There were dark stains like bruises under

his eyes. He looked at me shyly from under his fantastic lashes. "I dreamed of you last night, signora."

"Did you? What did you dream?"

It was hard to speak casually, but I must have succeeded; he gave me another long, measuring look and then shrugged. "It was a funny dream. I don't remember. Will we do something today?"

I threw caution and common sense to the winds. "How would you like to go to a carnival?"

iii

FRANCESCA AGREED to my request that I be allowed to take Pete to the carnival, but expressed some concern that the crowds might be too much for me. She had heard there was a great deal of pushing and shoving at such affairs, coarse language, rude overtures to young women. . . .

I could almost hear Jim and Michael howling with laughter. After Celtics and Red Sox games, with beer bottles, fists and epithets filling the air, I felt sure I could cope with a carnival crowd. I explained that David was going with us.

Francesca nodded approvingly. "Yes, he will do very well. I will see that he is suitably rewarded."

As I withdrew from the presence I told myself I must repeat that condescending comment to David. He would be highly amused.

Not to my surprise I found David hanging around the kitchen. Rosa was baking—some variety of crisp little brown cakes that smelled divine—and he was eating them almost as fast as they came out of the oven.

"You sure took your sweet time," he said when I walked in. "Is Pete—" He broke off, staring.

"That bad?" I said.

"You look like the morning after the night before."

169

"Your gallantry is remarkable. I didn't sleep well."

"Hm."

"We're all set." I handed him the car keys. "I'll collect Pete and meet you out in front."

Excitement had made Pete so hyper he didn't notice how tired he was. We ate the most awful, indigestible combination of food—"American hot dogs," which didn't taste like hot dogs, but some variety of sausage—slabs of pizza, lemonade, soft drinks, taffy sticks twisted into red-and-white columns. Most of the stalls and rides were typically tawdry affairs, but the carousel was wonderful—real old wooden horses, the kind they put in museums in the States, lovingly repainted and gilded. I had forgotten there would probably be a carousel. By yelling and sliding around on my horse and generally making a spectacle of myself, I managed to keep from waxing sentimental; and if Pete was reminded of his mother he kept his feelings under better control than I did. There weren't any giraffes or elephants or lions, just horses. Some white.

I went bravely on a couple of the rides, the kinds with little cars that bump into each other or swoop sickeningly around a central pole, and then I copped out. David gave me a meaningful look when I said wanly that I would prefer to sit down for a while, but he didn't say anything.

Pete did not want to leave, of course. He whined and complained like any rotten, normal youngster until David said equably, "Cut that out or I'll slug you."

Pete grinned. "Would you?"

"Sure," David said.

"O-kay," Pete said.

He was sound asleep before we had gone a mile, curled up beside me with his head on my lap.

"Now you can tell everybody back home you saw the sights of Fiesole," David said. "It's a popular tourist spot."

"What else is there besides a carnival?"

"Nothing much. A famous cathedral, with frescoes by Rosselli, tomb sculptures by Mino da Fiesole—boring stuff like that."

"Oh well. Any woman of sense would prefer roller coasters and diseased hot dogs."

"We could go back this evening. Have a quiet dinner someplace, stroll in the piazza under the light of the moon."

"David, I can't. I've been a rotten guest; tonight is my night for being polite to my hostess."

"Some other time, then."

Within another mile I was asleep too.

iv

I WOKE when the car stopped. The first thing my sleepy eyes saw was Alberto opening the gates. It was not the most auspicious welcome.

I had been able to conquer my forebodings during the horseplay and activity of the afternoon. Now they came back in full measure, and I had to keep telling myself I was being overly protective. There was no reason to suppose that another attack would follow so close on the last, or even that they inevitably occurred at night.

When David stopped to let us out, the front door opened. Emilia was there; and she wasn't the only one. David muttered, "Oh, oh, here it comes," as Francesca's slim, erect figure crossed the terrace and descended the stairs.

But she was smiling. "Did you enjoy yourself?" she asked.

Pete nodded. He never spoke to her if he could help it. He was certainly no advertisement for the quality of my childcare: crumpled, sleepy and sullen, spotted with various foodstuffs. Francesca studied him. "I see you did," she said dryly. "Thank *il professore* and the signora and go with Emilia. You will sleep well tonight."

171

"I don't know whether he'll eat his supper, though," I said, watching the small, stiff figure ascend the stairs.

"I suppose an occasional orgy of self-indulgence is good for all of us," Francesca said. "I came to thank you personally, Professor, for your kindness. Please join us for cocktails this evening."

I gathered she considered that the suitable reward she had mentioned. It sounded more like an order than an invitation. David said meekly, "Yes, ma'am. Thank you."

"Seven o'clock." She dismissed him with a gesture only slightly less brusque than she used for Emilia and Alberto, and turned away. David winked at me and rolled his eyes in pretended awe.

Francesca waited for me at the door to make sure I didn't linger to chat with the help. I told her I had my reservation, and would be leaving Sunday. "I'll turn my car in at the station," I explained. "So Alberto won't have to drive me."

"Whatever you like."

Her remark about persuading me to stay on had been only a meaningless courtesy after all, and my apprehension had been groundless. "You see?" whispered the shadow of Sister Ursula. "Honesty is the best policy. Now if you will tell her about the other..."

Shut up, Sister Ursula.

When I went to my room I found a surprise waiting for me. The vase had been placed near the window and the setting sun struck full upon the flowers, making them shine like carved garnets. Not rubies; the roses were deep, deep red. There was no card.

If they were an apology, they weren't good enough. If they were a reminder, they were a piece of damned impertinence. I moved them to a dark corner and collapsed on the bed for a nap.

Prompt upon the hour of seven I descended the stairs,

172

washed, brushed, and properly clothed. I hoped David would be the same, and I also hoped he would be able to restrain his irreverent sense of humor.

He was on time, at least. Francesca and I had exchanged only a few words when he appeared, escorted by Emilia. It would have been hard to say which of them looked grimmer. I studied him in exasperation. He was clean—but neat? That depends on how you define the word. From the remains of the once-gaudy scene plastered across the front of his T-shirt I deduced it was a souvenir from one of our national parks. Much of the color had washed out, but I could see the shape of a mountain.

Francesca wasted no time. "How is your work progressing, Professor?"

"Oh, fine. Great. I'm finding all sorts of things."

"What sorts of things?" There was a slight edge to her voice. David looked terrified. He had selected a chair that was too small for him, and he perched uneasily on its edge, knees together, holding his glass of wine as if he were clutching a beer can. The pose and the expression were so exaggeratedly awkward—the country bumpkin in the china shop—that I suspected he was putting on an act.

"Uh," he said. "Well, er . . . I've been working on the Egyptian collection. So far there's nothing particularly interesting except the Coptic embroideries."

"Embroideries?" A spark of interest warmed her face.

David expanded. "The Copts were Christian Egyptians. They used embroidery on robes and clothing for the most part, sometimes for cushions and wall hangings. The surviving pieces date mainly from the third to seventh centuries, though some are as old as the first century A.D. The dry climate explains why so much survived. . . ."

He rambled on, sounding as stiff and dry as a textbook, until Francesca cut him short. "I would like to see them."

173

"Oh? Oh, sure. I'm cleaning them now. Kathy can tell you. It's a slow process, you have to use special chemicals and distilled water and let them dry—"

"How long will it take?"

I didn't blame her for interrupting, since he appeared prepared to continue talking till someone stopped him; but I was a little surprised at her peremptory tone. David blinked. "A few more days. There's another crate I haven't opened, and it might have—"

"I'm afraid that whatever you are working on will have to be finished by the end of the week," Francesca said. "More wine, Professor?"

"Uh—thanks."

"I am going away for a while," Francesca explained. "The house will be closed."

My astonishment was scarcely less than David's. She had not mentioned her plans to me. A wild and horrid suspicion flashed into my mind. Surely she wouldn't pursue me and the apocryphal embryo into the wilds of western Massachusetts.

Francesca went on, "When you came we left the duration of your stay indefinite. I had no plans at that time, but now the situation has changed. I hope it does not inconvenience you, Professor."

"Yes, yes—I mean, no. I mean—whatever you say, of course. The end of the week?"

"That will give you time to finish whatever you have begun," she said complacently. "And you will let me know when the embroideries are ready for display?"

"Oh, sure," David said bleakly.

She let him finish his wine, and then eased him firmly out the door.

I knew that if I didn't find out what she was planning I wouldn't get a wink of sleep that night. My uneasy conscience might even drive me into premature flight. Sneaking down the stairs at midnight, shoes in hand; hitching a ride to Florence; appealing to Angelo for a room, secret, no one knowing I was there....

With Machiavellian subtlety I said, "Francesca, I hope I'm not interfering with your plans. If you want to get away earlier, I can easily stay at a hotel for a few days."

"That is not the case at all. The idea did not even occur to me until you told me you were planning to go home."

That wasn't reassuring. I abandoned subtlety. "Where are you going?"

She answered readily. "I haven't decided. Switzerland, perhaps. Or Austria. Paris is impossible these days."

I felt so lighthearted with insane relief that I dared make a joke. "Too many American tourists?"

"Too many tourists," she corrected, unsmiling. "I have no prejudice against Americans, Kathleen. I know several who are very pleasant."

"Some of my best friends..." I didn't speak the words aloud; her sense of humor wasn't exactly uproarious. A new worry penetrated my selfish euphoria, and I said, "What about Pete?"

"Arrangements will be made for him."

I daresay I would have put my foot in my mouth and asked what arrangements if she had given me time. She pressed the bell, saying pleasantly, "I hope you didn't overindulge in carnival food. Rosa has prepared one of my favorite dishes tonight."

At home we'd have called the dish a seafood casserole, but the seasoning and the delicate wine-flavored sauce made that term too commonplace for such a culinary masterpiece. Francesca was in an excellent mood; she even made a few dry, cynical little jokes. We were finishing dessert, another heavenly concoction consisting primarily of raspberries and

175

whipped cream, when she said, "It is good of you to take such an interest in Pietro, Kathleen. You have strong maternal instincts."

I wanted to get her off that train of thought. "He's a very nice kid," I said.

"You would like to see him again, in the future?"

"Yes, very much."

"We must see if that can't be arranged." She smiled, as if nursing a pleasant little secret.

I excused myself early, saying I was tired, and for once I was telling the truth. It had been a long day and a longer night. Instead of going to my room I went on up the stairs to the top floor. I expected Pete would be asleep by that time, but when I put my ear to the door I heard voices, so I knocked.

A voice I didn't recognize—a woman's voice—answered in Italian. I assumed she was telling me to come in, so I did.

It was the *tuttofare*. I had forgotten her name. She was sitting on the bed watching Pete toy with the contents of a tray lying across his legs. When she saw me she got quickly to her feet.

"Hello," Pete said, sounding pleased. "I was sick."

"You were...Oh. I'm not surprised. Eating all that junk food, and then the roller coaster."

"It all came out," Pete said, making a graphic gesture. "The pizza, the hot dog, the *gelato*—"

"Never mind, I get the picture. Only too clearly."

"So now they say I must eat this." He scowled at the bowl on the tray. It appeared to contain some pale substance like mush. "I do not want it."

"I don't blame you. Is it as bad as it looks?"

"Try." He offered an overflowing spoon.

"I will if you will." The *tuttofare* giggled as we finished the mush, turn and turn about. It didn't taste bad, or good. It didn't taste at all. When the bowl was half empty I said, "That ought to be enough. Is she waiting for the tray?"

176

The boy's eyelids lowered. "Always she waits."

No knives, no glasses that could be broken...I gestured at the girl. She picked up the tray, started for the door—hesitated—spoke to me.

"She asks if you stay here?" Pete translated.

"Yes. *Sì.*"

The girl started to speak, then broke off with a nervous laugh. "She wants," said Pete, "to tell you to be sure to lock the door."

It wasn't the girl's fault. She was just obeying orders. I dismissed her with a nod and a stiff smile.

Pete got out of bed and opened the door of the wardrobe. Joe emerged, tail high, whiskers indignant. "She made me put him there so he would not eat the food," Pete explained.

"Get in bed and I'll tuck you in. I'll bet you're tired."

"Yes. It was a good day."

Joe thought the tucking-in process was a game for his benefit. He pounced on my hands and rolled himself up in the blanket. His antics cheered us, but I kept thinking of that damned key, and after I had turned out all the lights except one by the bed I said, "I won't lock the door if you don't want me to."

"I want you to."

I couldn't see his face, except as a pale oval beyond the limited circle of the lamp. "Are you sure?"

"Yes. And," he said, "please take the key."

Chapter Eight

CALLED Sebastiano the following morning to thank him for his flowers—and for other reasons. The nurse informed me he would not be back until Tuesday. I thanked her and hung up without leaving my name.

Just as well, I told myself. I knew—how well I knew!—that it was difficult to talk with psychiatrists during working hours. I had a lot to talk about. I needed plenty of time and Sebastiano's undivided attention. We had a date for dinner Tuesday. It was only one more day. One more night.

Francesca was working at her desk when I joined her for breakfast. She apologized. "There is so much to do when one is preparing to leave for an extended period. One of the things I would like, Kathleen, is to show you something of the city. What do you say to a thoroughly frivolous view of Florence—shopping, hairdressers?"

I had never seen her look so young and carefree. She's probably happy at the prospect of ridding herself of the woman who came to dinner, I thought.

"I guess I need a beauty shop at that," I said, smoothing my flyaway locks. "My hair needs cutting."

"Only trimming and shaping. You mustn't cut it short; it is beautiful hair."

"I'd love to go to Florence with you," I said, tactfully avoiding the question of how to style my hair. "Let me take you to lunch."

"You are my guest. Today?"

"That would be fine."

After breakfast I left Francesca working on her lists and wandered out onto the terrace. It was a lovely morning. You could practically see the flowers jumping up out of the ground. My fingers itched for a trowel. I love gardening, though I have been accused of not being able to tell a weed from a flower, and one of the charms of my little house on the hill had been its minuscule garden. I looked at my hands. They had become white and soft over the past months. A lady's hands.

The sight of Alberto's unfortunate assistant languidly at work on the front flower beds killed any lingering ambitions at horticulture I might have had. It wasn't his fault he was a pitiable creature, but he made me nervous.

I had returned the key to the lock of Pete's door early that morning, just after daybreak. I had not been able to resist a quick look inside. He was sound asleep, curled awkwardly around the cat, who was, in the manner of cats, lying in the precise center of the bed.

I decided to go up and extract him for an extra hour of football, or washing antiques, or whatever he had in mind. He had no doctor's appointment that day, and it wouldn't hurt him to miss an hour of such schooling as Francesca provided.

His face lit up when he saw me, and I concluded I would postpone telling him I was leaving for another day. He wasn't studying; the heavy Italian history book lay significantly crumpled against the wall and he was playing with Joe, pulling a string to which a piece of paper had been tied.

"Shall we play football now?" he greeted me.

"You really ought to be studying. Oh, the heck with it. It's too nice a day to stay indoors."

"Shall we find David? It is better with three."

"He's probably in his room washing rags," I said, remembering Francesca's ultimatum. "We could stop by and see if he has time to play."

Joe would have been happy to accompany us. A wail of frustration arose when we closed the door on him. Pete said seriously, "I do not let him go out. I am afraid he will run away."

"You're a good pet owner," I said approvingly.

"David has told me. When an animal is young it does not have good sense, David says. There are many dangers here. Cars on the road, wild animals in the woods, or even..."

He didn't finish the sentence. I had not told him about Alberto and the dog, for I felt it was too grisly a tale for a child. Either David had hinted at potential danger from the animal, or Pete was perceptive enough to have figured it out for himself. He went on, "And also, David says, it could climb a tree and not know how to come down. Is that true? If a cat can climb *up* a tree, why can't it climb *down* a tree?"

I explained the physiological mechanism involved, as I understood it, and added comfortingly that most cats managed to get down sooner or later. I did not tell him about a feeble-minded feline we had once owned, who really didn't know how to climb down. We'd once left him up the big sycamore in front of the house for three days, hardening our hearts to his shrieks after all efforts to entice him down had failed. Ma insisted he'd come down when he got hungry, but even she was relieved when Michael finally shinnied up, at extreme risk to life and limb, and retrieved old Bill.

Pete and I stood in the stableyard and yelled for David. At last his head appeared at the window. "What a racket!" he said. "Why didn't you come up?"

"We thought you might be busy," I said.

"Besides, it is more fun to yell," said Pete.

"True. Aren't you guys early today?"

"It is too nice a day to stay inside," Pete informed him.

"True again. I'll be with you in ten minutes. Have to finish this lot first."

I was glad of the interlude because it gave me a chance to ask the boy some questions. I had been puzzling over that enigmatic comment of Francesca's—that she hoped I would have the opportunity to see Pete again—and a possible explanation had occurred to me.

I sat down on the bench, and Pete rambled around kicking at the ball. "You said something about your Aunt Vera," I began.

"Yes. She is the sister of my mother. You go over there and I will kick the ball to you."

"In a minute." I caught his arm and pulled him down beside me. "What's her name?"

"I told you. Aunt Vera."

"Doesn't she have another name?"

"Oh, yes. It is a funny name. It is Hassel-berg. Her husband is Uncle Ben Hassel-berg."

"Where does she live?"

"In America." Pete began to squirm. He wanted down off the bench.

"Where in America?"

I finally pinned him down. Aunt Vera and Uncle Ben lived in or near Philadelphia. "That is where I went to school," Pete said. "Phila-delphia. I had to remember the number of her house, if I was lost."

Aunt Vera sounded like a sensible woman. I wrote down the address and the name. Then I said, "You were living with Aunt Vera when you were going to school in the States? I thought it was a boarding school."

"You mean where you live in the school. I did live there. But I went to Aunt Vera on holidays and on the week endings." He was silent for a moment, remembering. His eyes were wistful, his mouth had a sad little droop to it. "I liked it with Aunt Vera and Uncle Ben. My cousins were older, but on the week endings they played with me sometimes. Evan (he pronounced it with a long *e*, Ee-van) was going to teach me basketball. In his school he was a basketball *star*. And when Uncle Don came, in the summer, he was going to teach me baseball. He was a baseball *star*, when he was in his school. And Aunt Vera let me play with the cats and the dogs, and Bruno was there, and I was going to be a cub."

I assumed they hadn't offered him a position on the Chicago team, so I suggested, "Cub Scout?"

"Yes. They wear clothes like soldiers."

"The eternal male animal," I said.

"What? Oh, there is David! David, hurry, we are ready."

He leaped up to greet his receiver and I sat pondering what he had told me.

It was only a hunch, but I thought I understood why Francesca had equivocated when I had asked her about her son's will. He may or may not have had such a document, but I seriously doubted that he had meant Francesca to be Pete's legal guardian. Guido and his wife might have put the boy in an Italian school, near his grandmother, so he'd have a relative close by in case of illness. Instead they had picked a school near his mother's family. After the death of the boy's parents, Francesca had taken Pete from the Hasselbergs. Had they agreed, or had she simply scooped him up and walked out with him? Possession is nine tenths of the law, and it would be difficult to extradite a child from a foreign country if the person in charge of him was a close relative, and a distinguished citizen of the country in question.

As yet I had no proof of this theory, but it gave me an idea with which to calm my indignant conscience. The minute I got home I would look up the Hasselbergs. If Pete had been taken from them against their wishes, and if they were willing to fight to get him back, I would help them.

It might not be necessary. Francesca's hints could be interpreted as meaning that she intended to return the child to his aunt and uncle. Perhaps she had acted on impulse, not realizing what she was letting herself in for. Finding the boy a burden and a nuisance, she might be willing to let someone else take over.

I surpassed myself at receiving that day. Even Pete was impressed. "Someday you may play quarterback," he promised. "After you have practiced some more. See, you hold the ball like this, with the laces so..."

He had the theory down pat, though his hands were too small to encompass the girth of the ball. He remembered his cousins' lectures on sports word for word, though he couldn't seem to get a grip on his history lessons. Not uncharacteristic of boys of any age or nationality; some of my worst students could reel off statistics of prehistoric games played long before they were born, including such crucial details as Bronko Nagurski's height, weight, and yearly stats.

Before we finished the game the skies had clouded over and a cool breeze was chilling my bare arms. "It's going to rain," said David, with the dour satisfaction some people display when announcing bad news.

"Darn. I guess you always expect the sun to shine when you're on vacation."

"The weather has been very unusual," said David pontifically. "Usually it rains cats and dogs all through April and May. Innocent travelers think of Italy as sunny and semitropical, but the northern parts have the same climate as—"

"It feels like home," I agreed, shivering. "Come on, Pete, we'd better get inside. You're perspiring and I don't want you to catch cold."

"If you two are bored this afternoon you can come up and help me," David offered. "I've got a lot of work to finish before I—"

I shook my head warningly. The boy scampered ahead, and I said in a low voice, "He doesn't know we're leaving. I don't want to tell him until I find out where he'll be going."

"Her ladyship hasn't deigned to inform you?"

"Not yet."

"That's strange, isn't it?"

"Not at all. The decision is hers, and she's not accustomed to discussing her plans with other people."

"Hm," said David.

I read that noncommittal sound correctly. "Look, I'll find out. If she doesn't tell me, I'll ask. She isn't used to children. She doesn't realize they have to be carefully prepared for dramatic changes in their lives. I get the impression she's planning it to be a surprise—a treat—so it must be something he'll like."

"The contessa's idea of a treat may not coincide with the kid's," David said dryly.

"I said I'd find out." I added pointedly, "Even though it really isn't any of my business."

"Or mine?"

"You're a nosy, bossy, impertinent son of a gun, aren't you? I'll talk to Francesca this afternoon. We're going shopping in... Good heavens, we're going shopping! I'd better hurry and change."

"Wear your raincoat," was David's parting shot.

It rained, heavily and persistently, all afternoon, but I didn't need my raincoat. Money and status can even protect you from the weather. Alberto drove us from place to place and parked smack in front of the door, in flagrant violation of the traffic signs—to which nobody in Florence seemed to pay much attention anyway. When we had to cross a foot of open pavement he unfurled a big black umbrella and escorted us through the danger zone. Instead of enjoying this, I wanted to grab the umbrella and close it, lift my face to the cold rain.

We lunched exquisitely and leisurely in a small restaurant that made the place Sebastiano had taken me to look like a slum. I think it was a private club; Francesca was greeted like one of the Medicis. I had no opportunity to raise the subject of Pete's future, for there were always at least two waiters hovering.

The next stop was at Francesca's hairdresser. It looked more like a medical clinic than a beauty shop. A grave middle-aged man with the manners of a diplomat inspected me; he and Francesca engaged in serious, low-voiced debate while I sat feeling like a patient who has delayed treatment too long. "If you had only come to me six weeks ago, madam, I might have been able to save your leg." I got the impression the two disagreed, though I could not follow the rapid speech. Finally the diplomat threw up his hands. Francesca smiled at me and vanished into the adjoining cubicle.

When she had gone I had the nerve to tell the diplomat I wanted my hair cut short. Apparently he didn't understand my vigorous gestures. He left it shoulder-length in back, shaking his head firmly when I pantomimed the use of the scissors. I had to give up. The result was certainly a hundred-percent improvement.

Francesca was waiting when I came out. She looked exactly the same as she had when we entered, every hair in place. I guess that was the idea. When I reached for my purse her hand closed over mine. "Please allow me to deal with this, Kathleen."

It's vulgar to argue about money in some circles—not mine—but this was not my ambience, so I gave in. But at the next stop I forgot my manners when I realized what she was up to.

The place was a dress shop. I didn't identify this function at first, for the room resembled a beautifully appointed *salone*, with not a garment in sight. After we had seated ourselves, a series of young women emerged, to posture and stroll, displaying the clothes. I like clothes. I mean, not just as methods of avoiding cold and damp and getting arrested; I like pretty clothes. I had never seen anything like this display. Even my uneducated eye observed the genius of line and tailoring in the most seemingly simple costume. The fabrics were absolutely sensuous—wools soft and light as silk, silk shimmering with imprisoned light, pure linen, even a few humble cottons—for scrubbing floors, I presumed—but they were the sleek, fine cottons I associated with names like Liberty of London.

I enjoyed the novelty of it so much that it took me a while to notice that the women were all about my age and my size, and that the garments did not resemble Francesca's tailored conservative tastes. She consulted me as the parade went on; I thought she was asking my opinion for herself. Then she said decisively, "The apricot suede suit, I think—that is a good shade for you—the blue linen, the amber silk, and the velvet coat."

"Francesca," I said.

"Fittings are so tedious, I know. But it must be done today, if the clothes are to be ready by the weekend."

"No. You... Your generosity overwhelms me, I mean it; but I can't let you—"

"I am not making you a gift, Kathleen." She paused just long enough to let a furious blush of embarrassment drench my face, before going on. "As Bartolommeo's wife you are entitled to whatever your position requires."

Such a thing had never occurred to me. Bart always had

enough money for what he wanted, but when my father, acting for me, checked out the assets he had owned at the time of the accident, they consisted solely of a few dollars in a bank account and the small insurance policy that had paid for my trip abroad. I stammered, "You mean his father—"

"I will explain it later. Please go now and try on the clothes. If there are any others that appeal to you..."

She went into the dressing room with me. So did the fitter and the owner of the establishment. I couldn't go on arguing in front of that audience.

The process dragged on interminably. I turned and pivoted and raised my arms and lowered them, and wondered what the devil I was going to do. It was out of the question for me to accept such a munificent gift; I could only dimly imagine how many million lire the collection would cost. No wonder Francesca hadn't invited any of her friends to meet me—except the doctor, for obvious reasons. Probably she was ashamed of the way I looked.

The suit needed few alterations. Francesca indicated an almost invisible pucker across the shoulders and pointed out that my waistline was half an inch higher than that of the jacket. To me it looked like a perfect fit. I had never tried on an outfit like that, much less owned one. The sight of my image in the mirror sent not one but a few dozen cracks across the surface of my resolve. Maybe there was family money owed Bart. Why shouldn't I take Francesca's word for it, especially since she was determined that I should?

I still hadn't decided what to do when we left the shop. She took my blank-faced, dazed manner for fatigue and proposed a cup of tea. "I hate fittings," she confided, girl to girl. "But it is necessary. These will do for you to go on with."

On with until when? I wondered. Till I visited my favorite couturier in Paris or New York, to pick up my summer wardrobe? At any rate, the fittings proved that Francesca had abandoned her fantasy about my being pregnant. She could count as well as I could. The clothes she had just ordered wouldn't have fit for more than a few weeks, if I had been expecting a baby. Nobody, not even a spoiled aristocrat with more wealth than her run-down living quarters had suggested, would blow a small fortune on clothes that would be outgrown in a few weeks and outdated next season.

Would she?

It didn't matter. The important thing was that she had accepted my imminent departure without argument or hard feelings. Had she something on her conscience that had prompted the expensive gift? I toyed with fantasies. Bart the heir to immense wealth which she had usurped, in her role as Pete's guardian; an aristocratic lover waiting impatiently in the wings for the trespasser to go—to be bribed, so she would not be tempted to change her mind? The first was pure fantasy, but the lover was entirely reasonable. Francesca was still relatively young and more than relatively attractive. Perhaps that was where she was going, to meet *il principe* or *monsieur le comte*, or *Graf von und zu* something, in a Swiss hideaway.

Speculations of this sort kept me preoccupied during the drive home. Francesca was silent, apparently wearied by the effort of selecting clothes, and the view was nothing to brag about in the rain and lowering fog. Mist veiled the dripping tree trunks and swirled in ghostly patterns among the brush. It was pleasant to come in from the dull twilight and the damp air to find a fire burning in my fireplace. I looked forward to a quiet evening with my books.

When I went down to dinner I took the scrap of embroidery I had bought for Francesca. I was tempted to bury it in my suitcase; it seemed so paltry an offering, especially now. "It's not the gift, it's the thought behind it," I quoted to myself— my mother, not Sister Ursula, though the latter would undoubtedly have agreed.

At any rate, Francesca appeared pleased. I expected she

would express her thanks graciously, but her reaction was a little warmer than that. She pointed out some of the technical excellences of the stitching and assured me that examples of that kind of work were increasingly rare. "I must start a collection," she said, smiling. "With this and the Coptic embroidery the professor has discovered, I have a good beginning."

She was in such a charming mood I ventured to bring up the subject I had neglected all day. "Have you decided yet what plans you will make for P-Pietro?" I got the Italian name she preferred out with only a slight stutter.

"I have thought he would be better off at school. There are places for such people."

That had an ominous sound. "Yes, but where?" I said. She frowned a little at my peremptory tone, and I added, "The reason I ask is that I know of several excellent schools in the States for children with emotional problems. It occurred to me that you might be thinking of sending him back to his aunt—"

"His aunt! How did you hear of her?"

"Pete—Pietro told me. Of course I don't know anything about his mother's sister or her family; they might not be the proper people to take charge of him, even temporarily. But if you had thought of sending him home—to the States, I mean—I could take him. That would solve one difficulty for you, wouldn't it?"

Her forehead smoothed out as I recited this speech. She listened attentively, nodding from time to time. "You would be willing to have him with you?"

"Of course. I'd love it."

"Such arrangements cannot be made quickly."

I was tempted to ask why she hadn't begun them, then. "I could stay on—as long as you like." The corners of her mouth twitched as if she were trying not to smile. I felt myself flushing. "That sounds as if I'm looking for an excuse to prolong my stay, doesn't it? Honestly, Francesca—"

The smile came into the open. Her eyes shone with amusement—more amusement than my blunder warranted, in my opinion, but if she was enjoying herself, who was I to complain? Actually, I was pleasantly dazed by her reaction to my admittedly high-handed suggestion. I wasn't accustomed to having people respond so amiably to my attempts to run their lives for them. She must be really desperate to get rid of the child.

"You need not explain," she said. "The suggestion certainly has a number of positive aspects. Suppose you let me think it over and take certain preliminary steps before we reach a decision?"

I liked the delicate touch of irony with which she invested the word "we." "Of course," I said quickly. "It's your decision. I only wanted—"

"I understand. I appreciate your concern."

She didn't refer to the subject again, but I hoped I had made an impression. Now the trick was to leave her alone and refrain from nagging. What a marvelous solution that would be—not only for me, selfish creature that I was, but for the boy. He couldn't be worse off than he was here. He'd be with a family, with people who cared about him. And I could see him sometimes.

When I went up to his room there was no sound within. The door was locked. After only a moment's hesitation I removed the key and took it with me.

ANOTHER NIGHT safely passed, I thought, as I crept back to my room in the gray dawn, after looking in on a sleeping child and restoring the key to the lock. Only a few more nights to go. If Francesca wanted me to stay on I would, but I couldn't see why it would take long to arrange for Pete's return. He must have a valid passport; it had been used within the past year. Communication with his aunt and uncle was only seconds away, thanks to the telephone. Maybe we could make it by Sunday after all. Four more days.

I refused to think about the alternative—catching my plane as I had planned, leaving him behind.

I was so excessively charming to Francesca at breakfast I'm surprised she bothered to add sugar to her coffee. I did not protest about the clothes, even when she coolly informed me that I had an appointment for a final fitting on Thursday. I did not mention my date with Sebastiano. I'd have canceled that—anything to make Francesca think better of me—except for the fact that I wanted to talk seriously to Sebastiano about Pete. I needed all the information I could get if I was to be responsible for him, even for a few days. I even—"The Good Lord curse you for a hypocrite, Kathleen Alice Malone"—I even brought my embroidery down and asked Francesca to straighten out the mess I'd made of it.

She removed the faulty stitches and showed me where I had gone wrong. "I'll never be any good," I said dismally, watching her deft fingers.

"If you don't care to do it, of course you must not. But perseverance and practice will bring skill, and I assure you it is a restful activity. Good for the nerves," she added, her head bent over her work.

The almost-colloquialism of the comment surprised me, as

did the sentiment itself. Good for whose nerves? I wondered. Hers? She didn't appear to have any.

She ordered—I suppose I should say asked—me to bring the wretched scrap with me that evening, so we could work on it together. I didn't tell her I would not be there that evening. Assuming that eventually she would inspect the product to see what I had accomplished, I put in a tedious hour pricking myself and taking out more stitches than I put in. I knew the theory, but practice wasn't having any discernible effect on my lack of skill.

When I tossed the damned thing aside I saw that it had stopped raining. The skies were still swollen with clouds ready to release their burden, and a stiff breeze was blowing; the tops of the cypresses bowed and curtsied. I got my coat and went up to extract the prisoner from his cell. It would do both of us good to get out. If I could persuade him to practice kicking instead of tackling, we wouldn't get quite so wet.

I was surprised to find Emilia with the boy, stuffing him into an assortment of outdoor garments that would have been more appropriate for a winter day in Montana. "He must have the fresh air," she informed me, as I stood staring at the motionless bundle. Between the knit cap and the scarf covering his mouth Pete's eyes blazed with rebellion.

"Oh, I agree, Emilia. A little wet never hurt anybody. You run along. I'll finish—er—dressing him."

She obeyed, shutting the door with a slam. Pete snatched off the scarf and threw it on the floor. "Eevan never wears a scarf. Even in the snow."

"You don't need it," I agreed. "Haven't you got a lighter coat?"

The coat followed the scarf onto the floor. "I will not wear a coat! It does not snow."

I found a light jacket of waterproof material in the wardrobe, and we compromised on that. The cap would have gone the way of the scarf and the coat if I had not agreed to wear its mate. It was too small for me, and I had to tie it on with a babushka. My appearance sent Pete into spasms of laughter, and he forgot to argue about the gloves and the boots.

Joe emerged from under the bed; obviously he had been avoiding Emilia, which only went to show what an intelligent animal he was. He dragged the despised scarf into a corner and began chewing it. Pete was all for that, but I explained wool was not good for cats, and took it away. "He's really getting handsome," I said, stroking the sleek fur on his neck. "A few more weeks and he'll be fat as a tub of butter."

"I comb him every day," Pete said proudly. "And catch the fleas. That is fun, to catch the fleas. They pop when you squeeze them."

We sneaked out the door while Joe was investigating a ball Pete had tossed under the bed. Pete gravely rattled the door to make sure it was latched. He was taking his responsibilities seriously. The kitten had been a godsend. I had hoped it would entertain him—I hadn't thought of the fascination of popping fleas—and increase his self-confidence and self-worth and all those other desirable attributes our school psychologist kept talking about. (I don't disagree with the theory, but sometimes I get awfully tired of professional jargon.)

The boots made a satisfying clatter on the stairs. Pete went up and down a couple of times while I contemplated a problem I had overlooked, the problem of Joe. Pete would kick up a fuss if he had to leave the cat behind, wherever he was destined to go. And he'd be right to fuss. You don't teach a child responsibility by allowing him to discard a living creature if it becomes an inconvenience. I had no idea what formalities were involved in transporting an animal across the Atlantic. There was no six months' quarantine in the States, as there was in England, but Joe would probably need shots and a certificate from a vet. The ticket was no problem. I would happily shell out for Joe's ticket.

You see, I had already assumed that Pete and I would be leaving together. Optimism is an incurable disease.

David didn't want to leave his work. "It's wet out," he protested like a little old lady.

"A little wet never hurt anybody," said Pete, who had a memory like an elephant's for convenient clichés.

"Why don't you come up here and help me?"

"I helped you before. It is boring," said Pete, dancing up and down with impatience.

When David appeared with a shabby windbreaker as his concession to the chill air, I said, "Your work isn't going well?"

"The damned scraps won't dry in this weather," David grumbled. "I promised her ladyship a show tomorrow, and I can't use artificial heat, it warps the fabric."

"Too bad," I said.

"Ha," said David.

"Come *on*," called Pete.

We concentrated on kicking and going out for passes, but we got pretty wet all the same. Once or twice a feeble ray of sunlight tried to struggle through the clouds, but it was quickly vanquished. Thanks to the boots and the jacket, Pete didn't get too soaked, but his pants were drenched, since he kept falling down in dramatic, unnecessary lunges for the ball. I called a halt earlier than I would otherwise have done and sent him in. "Ask Rosa for a cup of cocoa, or something hot," I suggested.

"She's probably baking," David added encouragingly. "She said she meant to this morning."

Pete ran off, promising to save a few cookies for us. "Come up and have a cup of coffee," David said.

He had a small electric heater. We sat in front of it and steamed gently while we drank our coffee. It was instant, and tasted awful after the espresso I had become accustomed to drinking. But it was hot.

"Any news?" he asked, after a while.

"What about?"

"Your imminent departure. Are you really leaving this weekend?"

"I think so. Sunday, possibly."

"What about Pete?"

"I'm working on it."

"Oh, you are, eh? You look awfully pleased with yourself. What have you been up to?"

"I can't tell you till I know for sure. But I am pleased. I think—I hope—something nice is going to happen."

"Nice enough to make you forget your recent bereavement?"

The abrupt brutality of the question took my breath away. He went on in the same savage voice, "You don't look like a grieving widow. What was he like, this husband of yours? Handsome, intelligent, sexy—"

"All those things." I slammed my cup down on the table and stood up. "How dare you!"

"Wait." His fingers wrapped around my arm as I spun toward the door. "I'm sorry, Kathy. Sit down."

I had very little choice in the matter. He kept hold of me after I had seated myself, but the angry contempt had left his face. "Forget I said that, will you? You must know why I said it."

"Innate boorishness, I assume. Let me go."

"Not until you've heard me out. When you showed up that first morning I couldn't believe my eyes. I was only half kidding when I said that about rubbing a magic lamp and getting a free wish. After you told me about your husband, I figured I had better take it slow. But it didn't take long for me to realize that, slow or fast, it was all the same; I was never going to get anywhere. You're still in love with him. You can't get him out of your mind. He was everything I'm not."

"Yes," I said. "You aren't...any of the things he was."

"Then you do understand why I spoke out of turn? I didn't mean it. It's only a few more days, Kathy. I'll probably never see you again. Can we go back to what we were, for those few days?"

"We can't ever go back. But I understand."

"It's okay, then?"

"Yes. I think I'd better go now."

"See you tomorrow?" His face was anxious.

"Yes. Sure."

I headed for the kitchen door, so deep in thought I hardly noticed where I was walking. I was in the kitchen garden, treading blindly on baby lettuces and sprouting carrots when the door burst open and Pete came flying out. His face was as gray as his jacket.

He flung himself at me. "Joe. Joe is gone. Did you see him?"

"Why, no. He must be in the house somewhere, Pete. I'll help you look—"

He was off, pelting down the path, water spraying up from the puddles struck by his flying feet. He was out of sight before I could collect my wits.

Then I heard him scream.

I reached the stableyard before the echoes of his cry had died. The kitten flew across the cobblestones like a ball of animated fur, hardly touching the ground. The dog was close behind, but Pete was closer, moving on an oblique line and running as I have never seen a child that age run. Without pausing he scooped up a stone. He pitched it underhand, wildly; instead of hitting the dog, it struck the ground several feet away. But the impact and the sound it made caused the animal to break stride, just long enough. Pete got through the gate into the garden and slammed it shut.

I didn't stop running, but I was still twenty feet away when the dog crouched to jump. It is difficult to run and yell at the

197

same time. I was trying to do both. Where the hell was David? Pete's first cry should have brought him down from his room.

The dog didn't make it on his first try. The second attempt succeeded. The gate was a wooden grille, I could see through it. My stiff fingers fumbled with the catch. Pete had pulled himself up into a tree. Joe was nowhere in sight. I kept wrestling with the gate, but my racing heart began to slow. They were safe. The cat must have climbed the same tree. My cries had been heard; there were voices, footsteps running.

The dog was snuffling around the trunk of the tree. He jumped again. He missed the boy's feet by a good yard, but Pete lost his head and tried to climb higher. His hands slipped on the wet bark and he fell, landing across the limb on which he had been standing, his legs dangling down.

I could see the drops dripping from the leaves, the quiver of the muscles in the dog's haunches as it crouched, the white terror on the boy's face as he struggled to draw himself up. I could even see Joe, half camouflaged by the leaves where he crouched on a branch high in the tree. All my other senses cut out. I couldn't feel my hands or my feet, I couldn't hear anything except a high, distant ringing. I couldn't hear my own voice; but I must have called to the dog, because it turned to look at me.

The gate opened and I walked into the garden, slowly, not running. The dog stared at me. It knew my voice; but mine was not the voice it had been trained to obey. The words were not the right words of command. I stooped and picked up a fallen branch. With a sudden pop my hearing came back, the way it does when you swallow hard at a high altitude. I heard myself say, "Good dog. Sit. Stay. That's a good boy.... Pete, just take it easy. You got up there once, you can do it again.... Sit, good boy. Stay."

The dog's hindquarters sank down. It was not sitting; it was getting ready to attack.

The mind works oddly at moments like that. I felt as if I

had all the time in the world to decide what to do. I doubted that I could make it to the gate. Better to stand and face what was coming. One arm over my throat, one shielding my eyes. Try to get the stick in its mouth.

The dog was in mid-leap when the shot cracked like a thunderclap. The shock was so great I staggered, feeling as if the bullet had hit me. The dog twisted and spun, and fell in a tangled heap.

I stood as if rooted to the ground, too scared even to faint. My ears rang with the echo of the shot—or had there been several shots? Pete had dropped down out of the tree and was running toward me. When his frantic arms went around me my legs gave way and I sank gently to the ground.

Chapter Nine

O UT OF the chaos, faces slowly took shape. Alberto, cradling the rifle and smirking with pride; David, staring not at me but at the twisted body of the dog; Rosa, wringing her hands and invoking a pantheon of saints; Emilia; Francesca, her ashen face contrasting bizarrely with the lacquered perfection of her hair.

Having assured himself I was unharmed, Pete stood up. "I am going to be sick," he announced.

I sat there like a broken doll, my legs doubled up under me. It was David who lifted the boy and held him close. "No, you aren't," he said. "Take deep breaths. You're okay, I'm okay, Kathy is okay. So what's to worry about?"

From the face pressed against his shirt came a muffled voice. "Joe."

"Joe?"

"Joe," I said, in a voice that didn't sound like mine, "is also o-kay. But I doubt that he'll want to come down out of that tree in the near future."

"I can't say I blame him," David muttered. "Well, Pete, Joe isn't in any danger now. Suppose I carry you up to bed and then I'll come back and—"

"No. Joe will run away."

David looked inquiringly at me. I looked dumbly back at him. My brain had gone as limp as my legs. I just wanted to sit.

Francesca touched my shoulder. "Kathleen. The dog did not..."

"Never laid a tooth on me. Thanks to Alberto," I added grudgingly. He had saved me from serious injury, if not worse, but I found it hard to acknowledge his services. Killing the dog had been the kindest thing he had done to it.

"How did the dog slip its chain?" Francesca demanded. "The whole business is unaccountable. I cannot believe—"

A babble of voices interrupted her. Alberto displayed the end of the chain, with its torn link; Emilia praised his quick thinking and superb marksmanship; Rosa raised her hands to heaven and praised the saints and the Holy Mother of God. I leaned toward her interpretation. It was nothing short of a miracle that no one had been hurt.

Francesca ended the uproar with a sharp command and gave orders all around. Rosa took Pete to her ample bosom. David shinnied up the tree and retrieved Joe, and we all went to the house for first aid and sympathy. David was the only one who needed first aid. Joe had not wanted to come down.

I went upstairs to change clothes. My teeth were chattering, not only with cold, and I accepted Francesca's offer of a warm robe, since mine was lightweight cotton. Hers was velvet. Real velvet, not polyester, in the pale ivory she favored, trimmed with what appeared to be mink.

I trailed my mink hem up the stairs and pounded on Pete's door. Rosa had put him to bed and was trying to coax him to eat. The tray held enough food for three people, every dish steaming—soup, spaghetti, milk, rolls.

"*Momentito, momentito,*" Pete said irritably. He was at work on Joe, rubbing him with a towel and trying to get the tangles out of his tail. Joe was not cooperating.

"That's good," I said. "He can finish the job himself now, Pete. I'll bet he'd like some of your milk."

"Yes, he would." Pete snapped an order at Rosa. He sounded just like his grandmother. She grinned and poured milk into a saucer. Steam rose from it. Rosa blew on the milk so vigorously the surface ruffled into white waves.

"*Eccolo,*" she said, putting the saucer on the floor. Joe sailed into it and Rosa chuckled, her fists on her broad hips.

Before I left I had the satisfaction of seeing Pete eat his lunch with a hearty appetite, having apparently suffered no ill effects from his adventure. I didn't mind leaving him with Rosa. He seemed to like her, and his autocratic attitudes only amused her. It was a pity she couldn't look after him, instead of Emilia.

I exchanged Francesca's gorgeous robe for my suit—the only warm garment I had—before I went downstairs. Francesca exclaimed in surprise when I walked in. "I was about to send Emilia to you with a tray. You ought to rest."

I had forgotten my condition. "I'm fine," I assured her.

"You appear to have taken no harm." She shook her head. "A shocking experience of that nature would have left me completely prostrate."

"I doubt it," I said, before I thought, and then added, "That was meant as a compliment, Francesca, even if it didn't sound like one."

"Thank you, Kathleen."

"I'm sorry about the dog. I hope you won't think I'm impertinent if I suggest you ought to entrust its successor to someone other than Alberto."

"You don't like Alberto. Why?"

"What's to like? He's ignorant, sadistic, crude.... I'm sorry. But the dog wouldn't have been so dangerous if he had not mishandled it. A guard dog is a potentially explosive weapon; in my opinion, animals like that shouldn't be in any house where there are children. Proper training and handling can minimize the danger, but the dog wasn't getting it from Alberto. How did it get loose?"

"Apparently there was a weak link in the chain. Seeing the cat, the animal struggled to free itself—"

"And how did the cat get out?" I had no right to quiz her, but remembering Pete's near escape I got queasy all over again. When I feel queasy I yell.

"The child forgot to close the door of his room."

"He didn't. I was with him. I watched him test the latch."

"What are you implying?"

"Someone let the cat out. Oh, it may have been an accident—the cat could have slipped through the door when the *tuttofare* went in to clean. Or someone may have let it out deliberately, hoping it would run away."

"Is it Emilia you are accusing?" she asked coolly.

"I'm not accusing anyone. The culprit won't confess now, when the consequences were so nearly disastrous. I'm only pointing out that you ought to make certain it won't happen again."

"And I might point out that giving Pietro a pet was not a good idea, since it led him into danger."

"You needn't remind me," I said wretchedly. "Don't you suppose I thought of that? But it's part of living, Francesca—at least, that's how I look at it. You take chances every time you give someone, or something, a piece of your heart. They, or Fate, may smash it. But what's the alternative? Not taking risks, not caring—not feeling?"

"I did not intend to accuse you, Kathleen. Your point of view has been argued by others more eloquent than you." She fell silent, her face remote.

I forced a laugh. "This is turning into a morbid discussion. I didn't mean it to. All's well that end's well, after all."

"Trite but true."

"I think I will rest this afternoon," I said. "It's starting to rain again; my room is so pleasant, with the fire and everything."

We were getting along swimmingly when the damned telephone rang. When I heard the far-off shrilling, I had a premonition. Sure enough, it was for me.

Sebastiano apologized for not calling earlier. "I was late getting in last night, and this morning has been busier than usual. Not a free moment! You have not forgotten our engagement this evening?"

"Of course not. Look, Sebastiano, I've been thinking; why don't I meet you? I could drive to Florence—"

"I don't often run the car into a tree, Kathy." The tinny impersonality of the connection robbed his voice of emotion; I couldn't tell whether he was joking or offended.

"I was only thinking of the time," I explained. "It's an hour up here and another hour back—"

"That is not important."

He was offended. I said quickly, "If you don't mind, then. To be honest, I hate driving in the rain on unfamiliar roads."

"Do you need spectacles that you are too vain to wear?" he asked teasingly, his good humor restored. "Never mind, vanity is a sign of mental health. I will pick you up at seven."

I thanked him and hung up. When I turned from the phone, there was Emilia at the door of the sitting room with the coffee tray. What she knew, Francesca would soon know. I decided I might as well get it over with.

"That was Sebastiano," I said, returning to my place at the table. "I'm going to have dinner with him tonight. I hope that doesn't conflict with your plans."

"You must do as you like."

"It will be the last time I see him," I explained. "I want to thank him for his kindness and say good-bye. Besides, there are a few questions I want to ask about Pietro. Supposing I should be able to take him back to the States I ought to know the best way of handling the transition."

"Yes, that is reasonable." Her stiff face relaxed.

Yet as I retreated to my room I felt like a naughty schoolgirl escaping from the principal's office. The strange thing was, I was beginning to like the woman—or rather, not dislike her as much as I had. We had nothing in common, we could never be friends. But if we had met under other circumstances, we might have felt at ease with each other. I had to admit that the present circumstances were mostly my fault.

ii

I WAITED for Sebastiano in the hall. It was raining so hard I preferred Emilia's not-so-thinly-veiled hostile glances as she passed back and forth between the kitchen and the sitting room. I wondered why she disliked me so much—or rather, why she let it show. Alberto couldn't have any better opinion of me, but he had never been less than obsequious after the first encounter, when he had not known who I was.

As soon as I saw the headlights I pulled the hood of the raincoat over my head and went out. Dusk had fallen; Sebastiano didn't see me till I opened the car door and tumbled in.

"Is this the American liberation I am always reading about?"

he demanded. "You can't allow a man to do something for you?"

"It isn't liberation, it's common sense. Why should both of us get wet?"

"I have," said Sebastiano, "an umbrella."

I remained respectfully silent, and after a moment he added, wonderingly, "Why did I say that? I sound like an English butler."

"I'll let you use the umbrella next time," I promised.

He didn't get a chance at the restaurant; the doorman had his own, a perfect monster of an umbrella, the biggest I had seen off a beach. We did not go into the city, but dined at a new restaurant on the outskirts; it had been a monastery, and the restoration was charming and whimsical. Favored patrons, of whom Sebastiano appeared to be one, had tables in miniature white-painted cells, with a discrete wooden grille on the open side.

Since I never can leave well enough alone, I proceeded to spoil the cheerful atmosphere by asking Sebastiano if his ribs had healed. After all, the last time I had seen him, he had been hobbling with one hand pressed to his side as if he expected the contents to spill out. The question brought a frown to his face, and a curt reply: He was fully recovered, thank you.

I took his annoyance for a display of wounded male ego and would have dropped the subject; but then he said, still frowning, "I suppose I must tell you. I have been debating as to whether I ought; but if you are driving yourself, especially at night... The reason I skidded is because someone ran out in front of the car."

"Good heavens! Alberto, was it?"

"Not Alberto. This was someone I had never seen before— a truly monstrous figure, like a creature from one of the old horror films. He appeared out of nowhere. I had to slam the brakes on and the car went out of control."

"I think I know who it was," I said. "Francesca has a poor mentally handicapped man working as assistant to Alberto. He has physical handicaps as well."

"Ah, I see. It occurred to me that it was a vagrant—a tramp. But in that first moment I confess I felt a touch of superstitious panic. I was reminded of the great Lon Chaney in some of his masterful performances."

"I know how you felt. I had a brief encounter with the man one day in broad daylight, and I was uneasy too. I don't suppose he realized that he was endangering himself, or you."

"I'm glad you understand. Most of the unfortunates who suffer from such handicaps are the gentlest of people. You probably frightened him more than he frightened you in the encounter you spoke of. It is a shame the public has such a distorted view of mental illness."

"Thanks in part to those horror movies you're so fond of."

"People ought to be able to distinguish between fact and fantasy." He added shrewdly, "Don't you liberated ladies have daydreams of being overpowered by a handsome pirate or highwayman? You wouldn't really want it to happen to you, though."

I didn't resent the touch of malice in his speech. He could not know why it hit so close to home.

I turned my attention to the menu. It was decorated with amusing little sketches of plump monks doing various things.... "Good heavens," I said, blinking.

Sebastiano laughed. "They are clever sketches, aren't they? I hope they don't offend you. Outsiders are sometimes puzzled by what they consider our cavalier approach to religion."

I assured him I was not offended. The approach of adolescent girls to religion is not always conventional, either. I told him about a sign one of the girls had tacked up on her locker, until one of the nuns removed it. "Holy Virgin, who conceived without sin, let me sin without conceiving."

Sebastiano chortled over that one, and we exchanged stories until we were toying with salad, which in Italy, as I had discovered, is served after the main course. I was having such a good time I almost hated to bring up the subject of Pete. I knew I was going to be scolded.

He didn't blow up when I told him about the most recent attack, but the look he gave me was not exactly admiring. "And you didn't mention it to Francesca? Kathy, I can't believe you could be so careless."

I didn't deny the charge. "I'd have called you if you had been available. Oh hell, why not admit it? I don't approve of the way Francesca is handling the child."

"I assume she is following my instructions. You are a sentimental little thing, Kathleen."

I didn't deny that accusation either, though it sparked a tiny flame of resentment. I don't like being treated like a sweet little dumb female. "Is it your idea that he live at home, without a tutor or governess or teacher? Without friends his own age? There isn't one person in that house who shows him affection, except the cook, and he hardly ever sees her."

"I suggested to Francesca that he would be better off at school. There are excellent institutions. . . ."

"Then why hasn't she done it? Why haven't you insisted?"

"Insist? With Francesca?" His laugh was tinged with bitterness. "I sometimes think a hereditary nobility is the curse of any country. They have no power; they are often stupid, uneducated; yet the aura of superiority still surrounds them."

"Francesca would be charismatic if she had been born in a gutter," I said. "I understand your dilemma; she's in charge of the boy, and you can't force her to do anything she doesn't want to do. You'll be glad to hear that she is considering a change. Within the next few days."

"What? She has said nothing to me. But," he added sourly, "she would not consider it necessary. She wouldn't notify her hairdresser or her plumber that she meant to stop his services."

"Come on now," I said. "You're a big, grown-up psychiatrist. Can't you laugh at Francesca's foibles?"

"I may be a psychiatrist, but I am also human." He shook his head. "This news disturbs me. Vanity aside, I would have expected her to consult me as to where the boy should be sent. The doctor who takes over his treatment ought to know what I have done and what results I have achieved. How soon is this change to take place?"

"Maybe I shouldn't have said anything."

"I won't mention that you told me. But I am entitled to know what you know."

He was all business, brisk and professional. I had to agree with him. So I told him what Francesca had said.

"She is closing the villa?" he exclaimed. "But then you—you too are going away."

"You must have known I would, sooner or later. This isn't my home."

"Of course. I don't know why I had the impression you were staying on indefinitely. Something Francesca said, I suppose. Then I won't see you again."

He took my hand and looked deep into my eyes. His disappointment pleased me, but it also aroused feelings I could not encourage. "Now who's being sentimental?" I said lightly. "I'll be back one day. At least I hope I will. This hasn't exactly been a pleasure trip."

We lingered late over coffee and brandy, talking—mostly about Pete, but also about the country Sebastiano loved and his regret that I had seen so little of it. "Surely I will see you another time before you go," he said.

"I had better not plan on it. My schedule is still uncertain. And Francesca doesn't like my seeing you. I won't sneak behind her back, and I don't want to make her angry."

"You are not immune to the aristocratic aura, either."

"It isn't that." I didn't want to tell him my real reasons for wanting to remain on good terms with Francesca. She hadn't actually said she was sending Pete back to the States with me; if I told Sebastiano, he might repeat my statement to Francesca, despite his promises, and she might resent my interference.

Sebastiano didn't give up easily. He continued to press his point as we drove back. "There is so much to see and do in Italy, so much to experience. It is nothing less than an insult that you are leaving so soon. You need not stay with Francesca. There are other places."

Other bedrooms, other beds. He wouldn't make the offer openly unless I responded to his hint. There was enough of the traditionalist under his modern manners to make him a little hesitant about propositioning a widow of three months—a sharer, however faintly, of that aristocratic aura he had mentioned. If it hadn't been for Pete...well, I'm not sure how I would have responded. As it was, all I could do was pretend I didn't know what he was getting at, which made me appear pretty simpleminded.

He was still at it when we stopped in front of the villa. "Don't go in just yet," he murmured. "It is still early—see, there are lights in several windows."

Making out in the front seat of a car isn't my idea of comfort. If Sebastiano had yearned to bid me a prolonged and passionate farewell, there had been a dozen places along the way where he could have pulled off the road. I knew his reason for waiting until we reached the villa, and a damned childish reason it was. He had even checked to make sure the inhabitants were awake and watching before...

One of the lighted windows was that of my room. The golden rectangle was bisected by a shadow. It was blurred by rain and distance, but I knew what it was doing. Looking down at the car.

Emilia, on her nightly errand of turning down the bed and

tidying the room? The shadowy shape looked taller and slimmer than hers.

"I've got to go in," I said.

He took my hand. "I find it harder to say good-bye than I had thought. There is a conference this fall, in New York. . . ."

I agreed to meet him in New York, to call him before I left Italy, to try to find time to see him again. I may have agreed to move in with him or help him rob a bank; I don't know what I said. I didn't linger to make sure he negotiated the drive without incident. The door was unlocked. I closed it and went straight up the stairs.

My room was empty. The fire had been built up and the bedclothes had been turned back. Across the bed . . . It looked like the sprawled body of a woman, impossibly slender, long skirts trailing, head concealed by the shadow of the curtains.

I found the switch controlling the chandelier and the room sprang into brilliant light. It wasn't a body. It was a nightgown, arranged in the faintly grotesque shape employed by chambermaids in old-fashioned, elegant hotels—waist pinched, skirts carefully spread out. Not that I had ever stayed in such places, but I had read or heard about the custom. The most interesting thing was that it was not my nightgown. It looked like one of Francesca's; silk chiffon, transparent as a drift of cloud, lace-trimmed and embroidered.

I touched the folds of the skirt. The garment looked brand-new, but the truth didn't dawn on me until I saw the other things. They lay in piles on the chair next to the bed, neatly folded, just as they had come from the shop. Bras and panties, nightgowns, slips—the finest batiste and the most delicate silk, tucked and pleated.

When I acted, it was without conscious thought. The emotion that moved me wasn't anger or resentment or pride, it was simple negation—a large, silent NO.

Carrying the nightgown, I marched down the hall to Francesca's room. She wasn't asleep. I could hear voices. The fact that I could hear them through the heavy door suggested that she was berating Emilia about something.

I knocked. Francesca answered: "Who is it?" She must have known who it was, otherwise she wouldn't have spoken English. I answered anyway.

"It's me, Kathy. I'd like to talk to you."

"Just a moment."

It was more than a moment. The seconds ticked by as I stood there. When Francesca finally opened the door I thought I understood the delay. She wouldn't allow anyone except her maid—a nonperson, by her definition—to see her au naturel. Her makeup had been so hastily applied it failed to cover the deep lines framing her mouth.

She stood back to let me enter. It was the first time I had seen her bedroom. The color scheme was her favorite ivory and off-white; it gave the room an oddly Spartan, almost monkish appearance. But the sheets on the narrow bed were silk, and the top of the dressing table was covered with cosmetics and beauty aids. The only other modern touch was a small clock radio. There was no one else in the room, so I decided I must have heard the radio. Or else Emilia had gone out through the adjoining room, presumably a bathroom, whose door stood slightly ajar.

I held out the nightgown. "I can't take this, Francesca. Or the other things. I appreciate the thought, but I can't."

Her only visible reaction was a tightening of the muscles at the corners of her mouth. Anger, I assumed. I had not been very gracious.

After a moment she said, "Don't you like the . . . things?"

"They're beautiful. But—no, they aren't what I would have selected, even if I had the money. I haven't time to hand-wash and iron lingerie."

"Money," she repeated, with a faint distaste. "As I told you, you have a legitimate claim."

Even in my present mood I was not boorish enough to say

that if there was something owed me, I'd rather have the cash. The amount that had been spent on the lacy frivolities would have paid my rent for a year.

So the discussion ended, as it had before, with my giving in—or appearing to. I couldn't afford to alienate her at this stage. I told myself I would leave the clothes in the wardrobe when I left.

As I went out I noticed that the door next to Francesca's was open. So was the door leading into the abandoned wing. Emilia could have gone that way. I had meant to ask her if she had been in my room, but the question was irrelevant now. It must have been Francesca whom I had seen looking down from the window.

A breath of cold air brushed my face from the open door. The darkness at the end of the long, empty corridor seemed to shift and curdle, like shadows trying to shape themselves into a solid form. With the cold air came sound, a breath of soft laughter, trembling on the rim of soundlessness.

When I got back to my room, breathless and shaking, I saw that the fragile silk of the gown was crushed and wrinkled where my hands had squeezed it. I threw it onto the chair and got into bed.

Then I got out of bed. Once again the hated, the too-familiar ritual—a look at a sleeping child, a turn of a key in the lock. The hallway was chilly with dampness, and some of the bulbs had burned out.

iii

I WAS beginning to count the days—and the nights. Perhaps the weather had something to do with my growing impatience to be gone. Wednesday was another gloomy, dripping day, which meant I couldn't take Pete outdoors. I should have driven to Florence and visited the museums, and the

214

other sights that draw tourists from all over the world; heaven knew when I would be able to afford to visit Europe again. Hopefully I would come back someday; but at the moment I only wanted to be somewhere else.

I decided I had a legitimate need to know how Francesca's plans were developing. I had promised my father I'd call when I got my reservation. That call had yet to be made. I faced Francesca with the question at breakfast; and, as usual, her unsmiling regard drove me into incoherent and graceless explanations that probably bored her as much as they disgusted me. "I have to let the folks know when I'm arriving. It's a long drive from Wayford to Boston, and my brothers work, and so does my father, part-time anyhow, and my mother hates to drive...."

"I understand. You have not telephoned your father?"

"Not yet. But I told him I would, and he'll be wondering."

"Would it be inconvenient for you to wait until Saturday? You see," she went on smoothly, "I am working on the arrangements we discussed earlier. I have been assured I will be notified by Friday. It may be late in the day, or evening, before I hear, but by Saturday morning you will be able to tell your parents of your plans."

She sounded even more formal and stilted than usual, and the vagueness of her reply irritated me. She must have realized this, for she added, in a more conciliatory tone, "I have every reason to suppose that you will be able to leave Florence as you planned, on Sunday, and that the other arrangement will work out as you desire."

"Oh. Oh, that's wonderful! I'm so pleased."

"You are, aren't you?" She studied me wonderingly. "I too am pleased, of course. To be quite honest, it will be a relief to have someone else take charge of the boy. I know I am not the best of guardians. I really don't care for children."

"Not even Bart?"

"He was different." She didn't say how. Perhaps she didn't

215

know herself. Parents try to love all their children equally, but often there is a quality in one child that brings out a stronger response from one parent or the other, or both.

I didn't hang around after breakfast. Francesca appeared to be preoccupied. She had asked, with only the faintest tinge of irony, if I wanted to accompany her and Pete to the doctor's that morning. It would be his last appointment, so they might be late returning; she had a number of things to discuss with Dr. Manetti. I declined, with thanks, and removed myself.

It looked like a long, boring day. The news had cheered me considerably, but had made me even more anxious to shake the dust of the Villa Morandini off my shoes. I had been mistaken when I hoped the trip would help rid me of Bart. The ghosts of the boy he had been and the man he had become haunted every corridor and moved in the shadows of the gardens. I knew that was foolish, of course. The ghosts that haunt us are in our own minds; they follow wherever we go, unbounded by time and space. But I would find it easier to exorcise that laughing shadow in some other place than this.

For want of anything better to do, I went looking for David. He wasn't in his room. The grubby scraps of Coptic embroidery covered every flat surface. He had placed lamps over some—ordinary table lamps, with ordinary bulbs. Most of the scraps still felt soggy.

The only other place he could be was the attic, so I went there, using the back stairs. As I approached I heard him muttering to himself in his favorite blend of personal commentary and poetic quotation.

I looked in. "How's it going?"

David was holding a handful of papers. He flung them into the air and said, " 'Shut, shut the door, good girl (fatigued I said), Tie up the knocker, say I'm sick, I'm dead.' "

"That isn't Browning!"

"Pope. How are you getting on with Robert?"

"Slowly." I closed the door. "I can't tie up the knocker, there isn't one, and besides, I don't know how. Are things that bad?"

"Things are worse," David said, stooping to retrieve the scattered papers. "This has really left me in a bind, dammit. I'd counted on six weeks or more."

"I'm sorry."

"Any chance that she'll change her mind?"

"I don't think so. She told me this morning that Sunday would probably be the day. I don't know when she—"

"What about the kid?"

He spoke casually, but I could see he was really concerned. "He's going with me. It's not absolutely dead certain, so don't say anything to him, but it's looking good."

"That's what you wanted?"

"Well, of course. This is a miserable life for a child. Don't you agree?"

He didn't answer, just sat there looking steadily at me, his long, thin mouth drawn down at the corners, his eyes narrowed. I prayed he wasn't going to bring up the subject we had agreed to forget. I hadn't forgotten—I never could—but his manner had been so normal since that one slip that I had been able to behave as usual.

"What's the matter?" I asked. "Is my face turning green or something?"

"Sorry. I am struggling with the impossibility of my own conclusions. Did you come to offer a helping hand?"

"I'll be glad to help if I can."

He put me to work. Real work. Whenever I stopped to exclaim over a nineteenth-century ball gown, packed in camphor, or an album of family photographs in a fat velvet cover, he yanked this treasure out of my hands and gave me another pile of papers to sort. If effort is any proof of honesty, he really was looking for manuscripts. The rest had just been fooling around. Now that Francesca had given him his marching orders, he wasn't bothering about the family "collections."

I tore myself away, without too much effort, when it was time for lunch. My promptness was wasted, however. Francesca was not there. Emilia gave me another of those exquisite notes, in which Francesca said she would also be out for dinner.

"Is Pietro with her, or did he come back?" I asked Emilia.

"He is here, signora. In his room."

"As usual," I muttered.

"Signora?"

"Nothing. That's all, Emilia. You needn't wait; I prefer to serve myself."

Still she lingered. "Is there any food for which you have a desire, signora? Any special dish?"

She might have been consulting me about the dinner menu. But she wasn't. Her eyes were fixed on my napkin-draped lap, and her smile was sly.

I told her no, and did not thank her for asking.

iv

NOW THAT the time for our departure was imminent, I found myself curious about Pete's academic capabilities. Once a teacher, always a teacher. I had done my practice teaching with fourth graders, so I had a rough—very rough—idea of what to look for. Pete grumbled when I asked him to answer a few questions, but complied; we ran through some math problems and discussed dinosaurs and Pilgrims and George Washington, and read from the cat book. He was deficient in math, but up to grade level on most other subjects. He admitted he had liked history. His mother had read to him every night; he was familiar with most of the children's classics. And he knew one hell of a lot about football.

The rain continued to dribble depressingly, so I had to refuse his invitation to practice kicking. I had a whole bagful of tricks for rainy days, culled from pedagogical journals, but in fact none of them worked well for children over the age of five. Even Joe copped out on us. "Kittens need lots of sleep," I said after Joe had refused an invitation to chase the string. "I have an idea. Why don't we explore? Maybe we can find someplace where we can play ball or hide-and-seek or something."

He agreed, rather listlessly. There were endless rooms, some locked, some open; some furnished, some filled with discarded odds and ends. The unfurnished rooms were too small for strenuous games, the furnished rooms had too many breakables. I was looking for something like a ballroom or a grand gallery. Surely houses of this stature had to have a ballroom? I couldn't find it, and Pete said he didn't know. He was bored and had no hesitation in showing it.

"Maybe it's in this part of the house," I said. We were in the corridor where Francesca's room was located; I indicated the door, now closed, that led to the empty wing.

Pete shrank back. "No. We cannot go there."

"Is it really dangerous? It's broad daylight; we can see if there are holes in the floor, or—"

"I don't like it there," Pete whispered. "Please, signora—don't make me go."

I took his hand. "You're freezing cold," I said, and then, quickly, "So am I. Let's run, okay? I bet I can beat you to the stairs."

So, in the end, we went looking for David. He was at work, mumbling and swearing, but we extracted him for a quick run around the grounds. By that time I had decided I preferred rain to boredom—not to mention whatever it was in the empty wing that had so frightened the child.

The run took quite a bit of time—not the running itself, but the assumption of outdoor garb and the removal of same, the drying of hair and the changing of clothes. Joe was awake and cooperative when we got back, so all three of us entertained him for an hour, and then it was almost time for supper.

David left, with self-righteous remarks about people who had to work while others frittered away their time. I had finally come up with an idea; Pete was sprawled on the hearth rug drawing a picture of Joe. There was no fire, and we could have used one that bleak evening, but even without it the room was cozier than Francesca's immaculate sitting room, and I didn't feel like dining alone with Emilia eyeing my flat stomach and freezing me with her silent criticism of my table manners.

"How about my having supper with you?" I asked.

"Will you?" He beamed with pleasure.

"I'll go ask Rosa. Be back in a minute."

Rosa and I communicated very well. She had three words of English and I had ten words of Italian, but both of us were great at gestures. She thought it would be fine if I ate with Pete. "Tell Emilia?" I suggested. She grinned and made a rude remark—it looked like a rude remark from the gesture that accompanied it. I left it at that. The cook was the one who was chiefly inconvenienced by changes in meals.

When Rosa brought the food she was accompanied by the *tuttofare*, both carrying trays. The covered dishes filled the entire surface of the table. There was milk for Pete and a bottle of wine for me.

"Let's have a toast," I said when we were alone.

"Good. I will have wine," Pete announced, reaching for the bottle.

"No, you will not. You've got to learn to eat American style if you..." I stopped just in time. I didn't want to tell him what was in store; according to Francesca, matters were virtually settled, but if the deal fell through, the disappointment would be crushing. "When you're as old as I am you can poison yourself as much as you like," I went on. "Right now it's wine for me and milk for you."

"It is not fair," Pete said. His lower lip went out.

"Life is not fair," I agreed. "Grin and bear it."

"I hate milk. Especially the Italian milk. It is too hot, never cold like American milk. Sometimes when they don't see me, I throw it away."

"Joe doesn't agree with you," I said as the kitten leaped onto the table, his whiskers twitching. "Grab him, Pete, he's heading for the chicken."

Pete thought it was funny. He sat there chuckling, and I reached for Joe. Joe eluded me and bore down on Pete's glass of milk. He didn't get more than a slurp or two before I collared him.

"Well, that gets you off the hook with the milk," I said, trying to sound stern. "Lord knows I'm not fussy, but that cat probably still has several varieties of unsanitary germs."

"I can throw it away?"

"Yes, you had better. But don't get any ideas about using Joe as an excuse, at least not while I'm around. I'm on to that one now."

Pete came back from the bathroom with a glass of water, so I gathered my lecture on American eating habits had had the proper effect. It was a pretty fiction, but I saw no reason to admit that alcoholism among American teenagers was rising like a rocket. Who should know better than a teacher?

The only way we could keep Joe off the table was by sneaking him tidbits. He particularly relished the chicken, which he gobbled up like a glutton.

It may have saved his life. We were barely finished with dinner when he let out a low moaning mew and began gagging. Saliva drooled from his open mouth.

"Leave him alone," I said to Pete, who was trying to get out of his chair. "He ate too fast. He's just..."

The chicken came out, as Pete would have said. That was

221

just the beginning. The cat's back arched in a spasm. He collapsed onto his side, kicking. Pete got to him before I could intervene, and pulled back a hand streaming with blood. Joe jumped high in the air and began racing around the room, ricocheting off the walls, falling and picking himself up again, crashing into the furniture.

I grabbed a blanket from the bed and pounced. The warm bundle under my hands writhed and howled; it felt like a tiger, not a small kitten. I fended Pete off with my elbow. Tears were streaming down his face.

"He'll be all right, Pete. It's okay. Leave it to me."

I hoped I wasn't lying. Fits can be caused by a number of things, from worms to epilepsy. If I had given the child a pet suffering from some fatal disease... The contorted lump finally went limp and I cautiously extracted it from the blanket, wrapping it in a fold of the fabric for safety's sake.

He wasn't dead. Not yet, anyway. His half-closed eyes were an uncanny white, the extra eyelid that shows when an animal is sick or comatose. The minuscule pulse was beating wildly and erratically. All I could do was hold him and try to reassure his hysterical owner. By the time we got him to a vet the attack would be over—one way or the other.

I had almost decided we had better make the attempt, at least, when the heartbeat started to steady. Joe opened one eye. He must not have liked what he saw, because he closed it again; but a faint purr began to vibrate through his body. A short time later, still glassy-eyed but seemingly recovered, he was curled up in Pete's arms ready to take a nap.

"What was it? What hurt him?" Pete's face was still sticky with tears.

"Nothing serious. It happens sometimes." What the hell could it have been? I ran over the symptoms in my mind. Vomiting, uneven heartbeat, muscular spasms—like the ones Pete had had that awful night...

And then I knew.

I wondered how I could have been so blind. The kitten was the final clue, but I ought to have known before. I had seen it before—in my own classroom, right in the middle of a quiz on the Louisiana Purchase. I remembered how I had paced the floor that night, raging, telling Bart about it, cursing the people who sold the stuff to children.

The balance of that evening reminded me, in retrospect, of a home movie some of my kids had produced for extra credit. One of the characters was the ghost of Abigail Adams. It's an easy special-effects technique and the kids loved doing it. Abigail lay recumbent on her deathbed, while a shadowy similacrum rose from her body and strolled hither and yon, then returned to blend into the original form again. That's how it was with me. I sat on the floor holding Joe, in dumb horror, while my shadow double finished dinner, chatted with Pete, watched the cat play with the remainder of the food, thanked Rosa when she came to take the trays, tucked Pete into bed....

It was the shadow me who kissed Pete good night and closed and locked his door; the shadow who undressed and put on robe and slippers; who stood by the door until she heard Francesca pass down the corridor and enter her room; who continued to wait, counting off the minutes, until the house was quiet; who tiptoed up the stairs and into Pete's room; who locked the door—on the inside.

Not until I lowered myself into a chair did the two parts of me click back together. One of us must have been thinking, because I could see the whole thing now, in all its deadly completeness.

Lysergic acid diethylamide. It could have been one of the other hallucinogenic drugs, mescaline, DMT, morning-glory seeds—but it was probaby LSD, a small fleck of which can produce all the symptoms I had seen. There must have been more than a speck in that glass of milk. The cat had only absorbed a minute quantity, but its body weight was so small it had been violently if briefly affected.

Why hadn't I recognized it in the child? That was easy. For the same reasons Sebastiano had never thought of drug abuse as the explanation for Pete's illness. By the time he saw the boy, the physical symptoms had passed. He might jeer at Francesca's melodramatic diagnosis of hereditary madness, but he had only substituted the conventional theories of his own specialty—"infantile death wishes," "transitory manic-depressive state characteristic of mourning," "breaking through of the unconscious at night." Pete's history fit that diagnosis. It didn't fit the pattern of drug abuse. The child had no access to drugs. He was isolated from his peers, from the outside world.

Besides, the symptoms of LSD vary widely, depending on a number of factors—dosage, individual tolerance, psychological strengths and weaknesses. The most common effect of the drug, the one sought by habitual users, is an intensification of sensory impressions. Colors blaze out, textures are magnified, sounds take on a richer meaning. Often there is a phenomenon called synesthesia, the confusion of one sense with another. Users *see* music, *feel* color, *hear* light. During the course of a single episode, extreme mood swings can occur, from ecstasy to terror. Also suspicion and hostility...

I had done my homework on drugs; a teacher who doesn't is neglecting part of her job these days. You have to know the facts. The kids can tell when you fake it, and the truth is never quite as bad as the things you imagine. To call LSD a hallucinogen isn't strictly accurate, because the users rarely have genuine hallucinations. They see and feel the real world. They just don't see it in the usual way. They can even control the effects to some extent, if they are fully aware of what is happening. The so-called bad trips are much more likely to occur if the person is anxiety-prone or emotionally disturbed to begin with, or if he doesn't know what to expect.

Pete hadn't known. He was not even aware he had taken a drug. I thought of him waking in the middle of the night with his heart pounding and shudders shaking his body, to see his familiar room transformed into a crazy house—the red chair humming in a low baritone, the rain shooting rays of bright light through the barred window, his pajamas rubbing his skin like sandpaper. I had read of one case in which the user looked in a mirror and saw his face sag and run, like melting wax. What had Pete seen in his mirror before he smashed it? What ghastly transformation had altered my face when he covered his eyes and refused to look at me?

I had to clench my jaws to keep my teeth from chattering. My thin cotton robe wasn't much protection against the April chill, but it was not cold that made me shiver. My first impulse, an impulse I was still fighting, had been to grab the child and run. Some remnant of common sense had warned me that might be disastrous. There were too many unknowns, and I was too vulnerable—in a foreign country, with no legal right to act for the boy, opposing an adversary who had all the clout and influence I lacked. Many of the options I would have sought if I had been at home were closed to me here. For once in my life I had to stop and think before I acted.

Think. Think. Try to figure out their next move. How many more days? She had talked about the weekend. Wouldn't she prefer to wait until after I had gone—until David was no longer on the premises? Why commit such a vile act with witnesses present, when she could easily rid herself of them?

I wanted to believe that. It would have given me more time. But every scrap of evidence confirmed the probability that Friday was the day. The ambiguous hints that had perplexed me took on a new and dreadful meaning. She had said the final decision as to Pete's future would be made on Friday—"late Friday, perhaps." She had suggested I wait until Saturday before calling home. By that time I would be in a position to tell my parents of my plans. Naturally I would want to stay over for the funeral. . . .

If she had entered the room at that moment I would have gone for her throat. I no longer doubted her intention, even though I did not understand her motive or her reasons for not waiting until I was out of the picture. It would be Friday night. And since she was so certain of the result, the next attempt wouldn't be like the others. It would be brutal and direct.

Don't imagine it was easy for me to believe that Francesca was planning the murder of her own grandson. I kept turning the bits and pieces of evidence over in my mind, trying to find another explanation. One possibility, that Pete was taking the stuff himself, just didn't make sense. The only person from whom he could obtain illegal drugs was Alberto; and in addition to the inherent unlikeliness of such an alliance, I felt sure Alberto wouldn't dare do such a thing without Francesca's approval. Nor was it likely that the boy could have brought a supply of drugs with him. She had made him discard his clothes, his books, his toys; where could he hide the stuff?

I would love to have cast Alberto in the role of chief villain, but that wouldn't wash either. If he wanted to rid himself of an obstacle, he'd use a club or a gun. He and Emilia must be involved. It would have taken both of them to carry out the scheme with the kitten, and it was probably Emilia who drugged the boy's food. But neither was capable of inventing a scheme so diabolically subtle. They were only the tools; the brain directing them belonged to someone else.

Francesca wasn't the only candidate, though. There was another possibility.

David.

I knew nothing about him except what he had told me. Francesca had been satisfied with his credentials, but she wasn't omniscient. Surely it was a strange coincidence that he should turn up now, on a job that was, to say the least, rather unusual. David had taken pains to ingratiate himself with the cook. He couldn't always arrange to be hanging around the kitchen when the boy's food was prepared, but the drug had not been used every night. There had not been time for David to fetch the kitten from Pete's room, but if Joe had escaped by himself and David had spotted him outside, he might have been able to slip in and free the dog.

The most damning evidence against David was the drug connection. The night I saw him in the garden and mistook him for Bart he had been smoking pot. The smell was unmistakable.

I didn't believe it was David. I didn't want it to be David. I had not even thought of him initially. It wasn't until I sat huddled and shivering in the darkness, forcing myself to think before I acted, that the thought occurred to me. Which proved I had been wise not to take Pete and make a run for it. I probably would have run to David.

I had read a lot of books with plots like this. I had often wondered how any heroine could be dumb enough to mistake the villain for the hero. I had often thought contemptuously, Why doesn't the stupid wench go to the police? Now I knew why. I could see myself trying to convince a local cop that a member of one of the most distinguished families in Tuscany was planning to kill her grandson. "And who are you who make this accusation, signorina?" Oh, just a passerby, a stranger, a foreigner—a woman who is fresh out of a mental institution. I'd be lucky if they didn't lock me up.

The night should have dragged on interminably, but it was all too short. The window was a sickly square of cloud-shadowed dawn before I knew what I must do. Get the boy away. By myself, confiding in no one, because there was no one I was certain I could trust. I was not completely without resources. There were people who would testify to my character. I had no criminal record; I had been sick, but raging paranoia wasn't one of my problems. The boy's aunt and uncle might help. My father . . . He'd hop the first plane if he thought I was in trouble.

Given time, I could marshal those allies and put up a fight, especially if I held the trump card—Pete. The only question remaining was where to hide him. I couldn't get him out of the country without a passport. I think I would have risked a charge of kidnapping with hardly a qualm if I had had that essential document; but after I had considered the pros and cons I realized it wouldn't work. The flight took too long. By the time the plane landed, they would know Pete and I were aboard, and we'd be met by a platoon of assorted law-enforcement agents. Besides, Francesca probably had his passport, and my chances of finding it were slim to nil, with Emilia watching every move I made.

There was only one place I could take him. It had the advantage of being so illogical only an idiot would have thought of it.

Chapter Ten

I STILL have nightmares occasionally—not about Bart, but about that last, awful day. I'm carrying the child and trying to run through some dark viscous substance that sucks at my feet. Far ahead I can see the gray light of morning, but there is darkness all around me and behind, where the dog is close on our trail. The jingling of its broken chain gets louder and louder. Dim forms lunge at us from the side of the path as we struggle forward—Alberto, aiming his rifle, Francesca, reaching out with arms that stretch like rubber and end in taloned hands. I pass them in a desperate burst of speed. I'm gaining on the dog; the sounds behind grow fainter. The path ahead is clear. And then *he* is there, blocking the way, laughing, lank greasy hair covering his face. Almost all his face.

That was the mood of that final day—frustrated desperation, desperate frustration; I wanted to act, and I could not. The only thing in my favor was that the weather continued to be cloudy. For once in my life I was praying for rain. We'd have a better chance of getting away if we waited until night-time—darkness veiling our movements, hours elapsing before our absence was discovered. It was the best plan, but it was susceptible to change, depending on the circumstances. I dared not assume Pete was safe until Friday night. I had to be ready to make a break for it if he was threatened, or if an unexpected opportunity presented itself.

I dreaded seeing Francesca that morning. I was afraid I wouldn't be able to hide my knowledge, that she'd see my feelings written on my face. It wasn't easy, but I managed it. You can manage anything when you have to. She was distracted too, and that helped. When we sat down to breakfast she had a list in her hand, and the first thing she said was, "You haven't forgotten that you have a fitting today?"

I had forgotten. I was trying to think how to get out of it—for I had no intention of leaving Pete unwatched for that length of time—when Francesca went on, "Unfortunately I will not be able to accompany you. You don't mind going alone, do you?"

"Maybe I'll take Pietro with me," I said. "We could pick up a few things for the trip—games, comic books."

"If you like." The only emotion she displayed was the usual poorly concealed incredulity that I could possibly enjoy the boy's company. So far so good, I thought. I went on, "We'll have lunch in Florence."

She nodded, studying her list. I couldn't believe it. I said casually, "There's no need for Alberto to drive us. I'll take my car."

I might have known it wouldn't be that easy. Francesca looked up, frowning. "That would be foolish," she said sharply. "It is raining and you don't know your way. I won't be needing Alberto this afternoon. I have a great deal to do here."

I was afraid to press the point. I felt as if I were balancing on a tightrope; the wrong word, the wrong look could betray me. She continued to inspect me with a new keenness. "You don't seem your usual self, Kathleen. Did you sleep well last night?"

I was prepared for that one. "I didn't, as a matter of fact. I was worried about Pietro. It seemed to me he was a little high-strung last night. When I went up to look in on him he was awfully restless. I guess it was just overfatigue, but I didn't like to leave him, and . . . Well, I fell asleep in the chair and didn't wake till daybreak."

Stop there, I told myself. Don't explain too much. I had to have some sort of explanation, in case they had discovered I had spent the night in Pete's room. It would have been wiser to avoid that change in routine—the only thing I had going for me was the fact that they believed I was unwitting—but I had simply been unable to face the alternative.

Francesca appeared to buy my excuse. "I admire your conscientiousness. But you mustn't wear yourself out. Your health is important."

I assured her I felt fine, top-notch, in the pink; but I knew I had better get out of that room. There were limits as to how long I could play the game.

So much for the hope of getting him away before nightfall. If I could keep from cracking under the strain, the trip to Florence would give me a chance to make a few essential preparations and throw Francesca off guard.

Pete graciously accepted my invitation. "Will we go to a movie?" he asked hopefully. "I have not gone to a movie since I came here. I like movies about murderers and robbers."

"We'll see."

231

Pete had a good time, at any rate. I must have put on an adequate performance; he didn't seem to notice anything odd in my behavior. He was bored at the couturier's, but I cut that as short as I could by telling the astonished fitter that everything was fine the way it was. I don't suppose she had ever had such an easy time of it with any customer, especially with Francesca or her kin.

I did derive some satisfaction out of running Alberto ragged. I made him drive all over town looking for the things I wanted, and I dismissed him as cavalierly as Francesca would have done while Pete and I ate lunch and sat through a long movie about bank robbers. I would never have permitted a child to see such a film under ordinary circumstances—when the "hero" wasn't shooting guards or massacring witnesses, he was making love to his girlfriend—but I decided this was no time to cavil at minor moral issues. The important thing was to stay out of the house as long as possible. In the course of the day I managed to complete all my errands—stocking up on games and reading material for Pete, buying a carrier for Joe, and cashing my traveler's checks. I had a little over seven hundred dollars, and I figured I might need it. I also bought Pete a coat and a cap and had the store wrap them. It wasn't much of a disguise, but it was better than nothing.

My last move was to take Pete to a trattoria and stuff him with every filling item on the menu. It was getting late by then and Alberto was obviously resentful of the delay, but I didn't think he was suspicious. He was not smart enough to figure out why I wanted Pete so full he couldn't eat his supper. Pete was big-eyed with delight at the idea of choosing anything he wanted, and I watched benevolently as he finished off his meal with ice cream and an assortment of pastries.

Twilight was closing in when we returned to the villa, and my spirits began to revive. The interminable day was almost over. I would only have to face Francesca one more time, kill a few more hours, and then we would be on our way. The nasty encounters that were sure to follow didn't worry me. There was only one thing that did worry me, and once Pete was safe, I could handle abuse, accusations, and anything else.

Pete went rushing up to show Joe his carrier. I doubted that Joe would share his enthusiasm, and cautioned him about introducing it gradually and tactfully. If Joe started howling when we carried him out, we were in trouble. I took the parcel containing the coat and cap with me and locked it in my suitcase.

My next stop was the kitchen, where I told Rosa Pete had already had his supper and cautioned her not to give him anything more to eat or drink. I was ninety-nine percent sure of Rosa, but she couldn't help me; she was too much in awe of Francesca.

After I had returned to my room I sat down and went over my plans again. Was there anything I had neglected, anything else I could do, any emergency I hadn't anticipated? The answer to the last question was a resounding, depressing yes. The definition of an emergency is something you have not anticipated. But I'd done everything I could and I was now at the point where my thoughts ran around in circles like a hamster on a wheel.

I walked into the *salone* without knocking. Francesca was at her desk. My unannounced appearance startled her so that her pen made an ugly jagged line across the page on which she was writing.

"I'm so sorry," I said.

Slowly and deliberately Francesca crumpled the paper and dropped it into a wastebasket. She was edgy, no question about it, and her nervousness lessened mine. For in spite of all my logic a doubt lingered in my mind. Was I committing the same error of which I had been accused so often and so justly—misinterpreting facts, building fantastic theories on inadequate foundations? I knew myself well enough to know it was possible. The very monstrousness of the plot made it hard to believe. It was not the first time I had faced that possibility, but the answer was simple and incontrovertible. Right or wrong, sane or demented, I had to carry out my plan. I could not take the chance of being... right. So I met Francesca's frown with a bland smile, and when she asked if I had completed my errands, I said glibly, "Yes, we had a great time. I cashed a few traveler's checks and bought a carrier for the kitten. I almost forgot that."

"The cat?" Her eyebrows arched. "It can be left with Rosa. She will stay on as caretaker."

"Pietro is very attached to it. You know when a child is facing a big upheaval in his life it helps him to have some familiar object to cling to. The cat won't be any trouble. I thought I would take it to the vet tomorrow and get the necessary papers."

"I see." She shrugged, dismissing the subject. "Was the fitting satisfactory?"

"Oh yes. They said they'd have everything ready by Saturday afternoon."

She nodded. Of course they would have everything ready. Her pen hovered over a fresh sheet of paper, and I said, "I can see you're busy. Please go on with whatever you were doing. Can I help in any way?"

"Thank you, no. Unless you will be good enough to ring for Emilia. I must just finish this note and then I will join you."

Emilia responded to my touch on the bell, and as she arranged glasses and carafe on the table, I thought how seductive it must be to have such power at one's disposal. A little pressure of a single finger, the contraction of a few small muscles, could produce an industrious bustle of activity. It would be fatally easy to become accustomed to controlling other people's lives with one push of a button.

When Francesca sat down beside me she again apologized for her distraction. "There is always so much to do when one travels."

"I've been trying to get organized too," I said. "Maybe I should return that rental car tomorrow, instead of waiting till Sunday. Would it be possible for Alberto to drive me back?"

"Of course." Her smile was warmer. She approved of that idea. (Don't ask why, don't try to find double entendres and hidden meanings—you're far beyond that now. Just stick to your plan.)

She had left the businesswoman at her desk and was now the charming hostess, but there was a change in her manner—not so much nervousness as suppressed excitement and anticipation. If I hadn't known better, I would have supposed she was looking forward to her trip. (*Il principe, monsieur le comte*, waiting in a secluded chalet in the Swiss Alps.) Her moments of dreamy abstraction and her veiled glances at me—glances that seemed to hold a greedy pleasure—began to wear on my nerves. I wondered if I could get through the evening after all.

Unwittingly, Francesca provided a distraction. "I have asked Professor Brown to join us for dinner. I felt I owed him that, since he will be leaving soon."

I had been careful to avoid David. Guilty or innocent, Francesca's accomplice or independent villain, he was not a factor in my plans, only an obstacle to be avoided at all costs. I was not happy at the prospect of spending an evening in his company.

Francesca saw my reaction and appeared to be amused by it. "I hope you won't be too bored, Kathleen."

"He does tend to go on and on about subjects I find somewhat tedious," I said. "But one last evening won't kill me."

At least I hoped not.

David was wearing a proper shirt, for once, with a relatively respectable jacket over it—probably a concession to the chilly weather rather than a mark of respect for his hostess. He was carrying a brown cardboard box.

"These are the Coptic fabrics you wanted to see," he explained, dropping the box at Francesca's feet.

She studied it with disgust. It was far from clean, and there were cobwebs clinging to its sides. Unaware of his faux pas, David beamed at her. I was reminded of a dog who has just presented his owner with a particularly smelly dead rat.

"Mind if I move this stuff?" David went on, shifting the decanter and wineglasses. "I'll lay the pieces out here. I'm afraid some of them are a little damp."

They were damp, and they smelled of wet fabric, chemicals, and sheer musty age. However, they aroused Francesca's interest; she actually touched one or two, commenting intelligently about the type of embroidery used and questioning David about the age and history of the specimens.

Finally she said, "It is most interesting, Professor. I am grateful to you for rescuing the collection. If you would be good enough to instruct me as to how they should be preserved?"

"Well, see, the problem is they aren't dry," David said. "What they need is a temperature- and humidity-controlled, sealed glass case, but if you put 'em in that environment now, while they're still wet, they will be ruined. I calculate three or four more days—"

"I don't have four days," Francesca said curtly. "Why can't we use heat lamps?"

"That's risky. I don't have the proper equipment—"

"You will have to do the best you can. The house will be closed early next week, perhaps before then. If you can arrange to leave Saturday or Sunday..."

"Whatever you say, of course."

It was not a pleasant meal. David was sulky and ill at ease,

Francesca abstracted. I need not describe my state of mind. On the surface the interview was precisely what I would have expected: the grande dame dismissing the now inconvenient hireling, but expecting him to accomplish the impossible before she threw him out, and the hireling resenting the whole business. If there were hidden nuances I had missed, then I had missed them, and that was that. I was exhausted by surmises.

Finally the uncomfortable dinner drew to a close. David withdrew, his carton under his arm, presumably to spend the rest of the evening drying his scraps. I sat with Francesca for another hour, massacring my embroidery. My hands were quite steady, but my mind was not on my work.

When the clock chimed ten I got to my feet. It was the usual procedure; she was an early riser, and usually went to her room at ten-thirty. As I stood there saying good night, a strange feeling came over me. Everything in the room—furniture, fireplace, the woman sitting poised and groomed on the couch, her needle in her white hand—went flat and two-dimensional, like a painting. Frozen for all time, but unreal, dead. I suppose she spoke to me, returned my "good night." I didn't hear her. Painted faces cannot speak.

I wasn't nervous or afraid. One good result of that long, agonizing day was that I had used up all those emotions. There was nothing left except a flat calm. I took off my jacket and skirt and put on my robe. I filled the pockets of my raincoat with the things I needed—passport and money, keys and wallet. They were big patch pockets; I stuffed one or two odds and ends of clothing in on top of the other things, to make sure they didn't fall out.

I opened the door and left it ajar. I sat down and picked up a book at random. When I saw it was Browning's *Poems* I almost tossed it away, but it didn't matter; I was incapable of reading print, much less absorbing the content. I sat with the book open, turning pages; now and then a line caught my eye. "Then all smiles stopped together." The Duke, remembering his last Duchess, who had been too indiscriminate in her affections. "Childe Roland to the Dark Tower came." The stuff of nightmares, the dying sunset kindled ahead, the hills crowding in on the quarry at bay.... "Grow old along with me! The best is yet to be...." I hope so, Robert; I certainly hope so.

I stopped even pretending to read. My watch held the slow time back. The minute hand stayed fixed for eons, then suddenly jumped and stopped again. At a quarter to eleven Francesca came upstairs. Her heels clicked past my door, not pausing; then came the sound of her door opening and closing. Half an hour later it opened again. A brief murmur of voices—Emilia, bidding her mistress *buona notte*. Her heavy footsteps, thudding away. She'd take the back stairs, the servant's path to her room.

I closed the book. Stood up. Turned out the light. Blackness closed over me. The night was clouded, utterly dark. I didn't need light or want it. I took off my robe, put on slacks and jacket, picked up my shoes and the parcel with Pete's clothes. I took my coat out of the closet. I stood by the door waiting. Waiting can be an all-consuming activity, requiring every ounce of concentration. I waited.

At twelve-thirty I opened the door. One light shone at the end of the hall near Francesca's room. Another lit the head of the stairs. I went up into the dark, feeling for each step. The key was in the lock. I turned it and went in.

The dim lamp in the corner of Pete's room made me blink; it seemed bright after the Stygian darkness of the hall. The kitten, curled in the bend of Pete's knees, raised its head with a soft inquiring mew. The light reflecting from its eyes made them glow phosphorescent green.

This was the first hurdle. How do you tell a boy of ten that someone wants to kill him? How do you convince him he

238

must come away with you, a stranger, known for only a few days?

Joe helped me awaken him, pouncing and purring, happy to find an intelligent person who was willing to play with a cat in the middle of the night. When the boy stirred sleepily I spoke. "Pete. Wake up. It's me, Kathy. Don't make a noise."

His hand went out, reaching for the cat. "Signora? Is it morning?"

"Not yet. I have to talk to you, honey. It's important. A secret, just between the two of us—and Joe, of course."

He sat up, rubbing the sleep from his eyes. He looked even younger than ten; his hair stood up in little tufts, and the bones of his arms were as fragile as twigs. I hated what I had to do. I had rehearsed the speech so often that it came out flat and unconvincing. I didn't believe it myself.

"You've got to listen to me, Pete. Listen carefully. Someone is trying to hurt you. You aren't sick. The attacks—the bad times you had—came because they put a drug in your food. You've heard of drugs. They can make people do strange, dangerous things. I want you to come with me—now—to someplace where you'll be safe. You and Joe. I know you find this hard to believe, but you have to...."

Then came the first surprise of the night—the only pleasant surprise. He was nodding his head. His pupils were dilated; his eyes looked like little jet marbles rimmed with blazing silver.

"You believe it," I said, gulping.

"I know it. This drug—I don't know that—but I know I am not sick. I am afraid. Always afraid. Only no one would believe me. Where will we go, signora?"

My icy calm quivered under a burst of relief and thankfulness. Over the first hurdle and still running—and he was a marvel, a miracle, cool and unafraid.

"I know a place, Pete. First get dressed. Something warm and comfortable.... Here." I pulled slacks and shirt, sweater

239

and socks from the dresser drawer.

He moved instantly to obey, stripping off his pajamas and reaching for the clothes I handed him. His thin little body quivered, but not, I thought with fear.

"We must take Joe."

"Of course. That's why I got the carrier today. And this coat and hat for you. No one has seen them; if they start looking for you—"

"I know. Like the movie. You were clever to think of it, signora."

Bless him, he was cool as a cucumber—a lot cooler than I was. I watched him entice Joe into the carrier and put his favorite game—the one I had bought him—in his coat pocket. After a moment's thought he stuffed a few of the comic books in the other pocket. "I have not read them," he said. "Now, signora, I am ready."

He stood straight and fearless, the unbecoming cap pulled low over his forehead, hiding his hair. The coat was too big; it hung below his knees and covered his hands to the knuckles. I knelt beside him and turned back the cuffs. My hands lingered, but I didn't hug him. We were brave adventurers, partners in a daring escape. This was no time for sentiment.

"Okay," I said. "This is the plan. We're going down the back stairs, through the kitchen, to the garage. To my car. Get in the back seat with Joe and crouch down. I hope we can get away without being seen, but just in case—"

"I know. Now, signora, I will lead the way. I know it better than you in the dark."

"Yes, sir!"

He gave me an aloof kindly smile, like a general encouraging a loyal subordinate.

I locked the door and took the key. Anything to prolong discovery. He let me carry Joe. Joe was shifting around and murmuring. I hoped he wouldn't decide to yell, but the carrier had a flap that snapped over the grille at the open end. I had chosen it for that reason. It was our only piece of luggage. We were traveling light, not even my purse to get in the way.

The second hurdle was behind us when we got out of the house without being seen. I had not expected much difficulty there, but the next jump wouldn't be so easy. There was no way I could get the car out of the garage without starting the engine. The stableyard was perfectly level. Alberto and Emilia slept in the house, so David was the only one I had to worry about. He might waken when he heard the car start, but it was not his job to care who came and went. I hoped, and assumed, he would not interfere. But there were so many things that could go wrong....

I swore under my breath when I saw there was a light in David's window. After a moment's indecision I decided not to wait for it to go out. He might decide to work all night.

Pete put the carrier into the back seat. Then he turned to me. "Signora," he whispered, "will we break the Mercedes?"

I could have kicked myself for not thinking of it. The trouble was, I didn't know how to break the Mercedes. I had no idea how to open the hood. There's one thing any vehicle needs, though, and that's a set of intact tires. I inspected the rack of tools hanging on the wall; there was just enough light from the open door of my car to enable me to select an awl, sharp-pointed and heavy-handled.

"I'll break it," I murmured. "Get in the car and crouch down."

Puncturing the tires wasn't as easy as I had thought it would be. Mine always seemed to go flat when they ran over a pin, but I had to pound and jab before I heard air start to hiss out. I had dealt with the two back tires when a flashlight beam caught me full on.

The shock stopped my heart for a second. I had not heard

241

a sound of warning, and believe me, I had been listening.

"Turn off that light," I said. My voice was ragged with anger and terror.

He turned the light away, but he didn't switch it off. Holding the awl behind me, I edged toward my car.

"What are you doing?" David said. I could hear him now, coming down the stairs.

"I left something in the car."

"Something you need desperately at one in the morning?"

"What business is it of yours?"

"I'm making it my business. Why do I get the strange impression that you are doing a moonlit flit—without the moonlight? Flitting is easier in the dark, I admit."

I said, "If I want to leave, that's my affair. What do you care?"

"I don't. I don't give a good hearty damn whether you stay or go straight to hell, so long as you are alone. I'll just have a look in the back, and if you have no passenger—"

"Stay away from that car, David. I swear I'll run you down if you get in my way."

He made a soft ambiguous sound that might have been a smothered curse or a jeering laugh. My first miscalculation— and possibly my last. How I had patted myself on the back for having the intelligence and the courage to admit that David might be involved. But I had not really believed it, not in my blood and my bones, my heart and my soul. If I had believed it, I would have known that lighted window raised the odds against us a thousand to one. I'd have thought of some other plan. Too late now. Too late for anything except... My fingers tightened around the heavy wooden handle of the awl. Could I use it? I had to. I had to prevent him from stopping us, from giving the alarm. The path to the gates was clear, but the gates would be locked, they always were; by the time I got them open, he'd have caught up with us. And there was his motorcycle. Even if a miracle occurred and we got out of the gates, he could follow.

"Kathy," he said, in a different, softer voice. "Think what you're doing. There is still a way out of this. Maybe you don't realize..." He was moving as he spoke. I could tell from the soft sounds his feet made on the stairs. Then I saw him in the open doorway, a featureless shadow against the lighter stones of the courtyard.

He spoke again. "Kathy, please listen to me."

I almost dropped in my tracks. His voice came from the dark at the foot of the stairs. He was still inside the garage.

From the hulking shadow in the doorway came a hoarse laugh. "No, signora. Eccola—la carabina. Capisce?"

He wanted to make certain I understood. A switch clicked and lights blazed out. Alberto stood there, his heavy lips parted in a grin, the rifle cradled in his arms.

Every ounce of feeling in me vanished under an overwhelming surge of frigid rage. "God damn you all," I said. "You're not going to touch him. You'll have to shoot me to get at him. At least you may have a hard time convincing the police it was an accident this time."

I wrenched the door open and got into the car. The keys were in my hand. The headlights went on, sending Alberto's shadow darting blackly across the stones. I could hear the child gasping, like a runner after a sprint. We didn't have the ghost of a chance, but I wasn't going to give up until they dragged me kicking and biting out of the car.

I turned the key. At the first cough of the motor Alberto jumped back, moving with the light-footed agility of a boxer. He held the rifle loosely, carelessly. There was no hurry. One shot would do it.

David came out of the garage, across the glare of the lights. I knew who it must be, but I wouldn't have recognized him; he was only a blur of movement, a streak of speed. He tackled

Alberto low, knocking him backward. The rifle hit the ground. David made a dive for it, but Alberto was up again, quick as a cat. His booted foot crashed down on David's hand. David's face was a white oval in the glare; his mouth opened in a cry I heard even through the closed window. With his other hand he grabbed Alberto's ankle and pulled. The two bodies closed, writhing in a monstrous tangle of limbs. I slammed my foot down on the gas.

I brushed the gatepost as I turned, felt the car shudder and heard the scream of tortured metal. The car rocked and skidded as it swung around the house and onto the drive. Branches reached out black arms that raked at the windows and clawed at the windshield. The gates loomed up ahead. I hit the brakes, fought the sideways slither of the wheels, and got out, leaving the door open. The key was there, on the nail inside the lodge door. When I ran to the gate I saw Pete was out of the car and started to yell at him; then I shut up. He already had the bar off its supports. After I had turned the key he pulled one section of the gates back while I opened the other. He was crying. His face glistened in the headlights, but he didn't utter a sound.

When we got back in the car I could see the glow of light from behind the villa—not one light but a whole battery of them, all around the stable area. The car splashed through puddles as I sent it down the steep road at a speed I'd never have dared attempt in daylight. We hit a pothole with a jar that jammed my teeth together, and I let up on the gas. I couldn't risk a broken axle or a flat tire.

We had passed through the sleeping village and reached the main road before I could speak. "Okay back there, Pete?"

"O-kay," said a very, very small voice.

"I think we made it. Remind me to tell you someday that you are my number-one draft pick."

His breath caught. "You are the same for me, signora. Joe does not like to ride in a car."

"I noticed that." Joe's protests were piercing and heartfelt. "Most cats hate cars."

"Will I come in the front with you, signora?"

I started to tell him no, it wasn't safe, before I realized he needed to be closer to me. And I needed him closer, too. I was operating in the deceptive calm that follows a shattering shock—or a series of them, in quick succession. I said, "Come up. Be careful."

He tumbled over the seat and rearranged himself. His tears had been dealt with in manly privacy. His face was streaked and grimy, but quite dry.

"Signora?"

"Yes, Pete."

"We will not go to Dr. Manetti?"

"Do you want to go to him?"

"No! He will send me back."

"That's the way I figured," I said. "Pete, did you ever tell Dr. Manetti someone was trying to hurt you?"

"No. He will not believe me."

It made me sick to think of the quiet terror in which the boy had lived for so many weeks. He had only one advantage—a child's fatalistic acceptance of the illogical. He knew they hated him and wanted him dead. He didn't have to know why. The adult world was incomprehensible anyway. This was only another manifestation of its innate senselessness. And with the cunning of all small, hunted animals, he had learned not to trust any of the hunters.

"We aren't going to Dr. Manetti," I said. "For a start, we're going to telephone your aunt and uncle in Philadelphia."

"Maybe they don't want me," Pete said. "I write them letters, but they don't answer."

His voice was flat and unemotional, but I knew that had been another hurt, and not the least of the ones he had endured. I said quickly, "I'll bet they did answer, Pete. Letters don't always reach the people to whom they are addressed.

245

Can you remember what happened after you heard about the plane crash? You were with your aunt and uncle then; did they tell you you were going to live with your grandmother, or did she come and get you, or what?"

He didn't understand the implications of the story he told me, but it confirmed my worst suspicions, and my fondest hopes. No, no one had told him he was to leave until he found Aunt Vera packing his suitcase. She cried all the time she was packing it, though she tried not to let him see. Uncle Ben had been angry, very angry; his face was red and he talked in a deep, growling voice. He had had to leave a lot of his things behind. They could only take one suitcase on the plane, Uncle Bart said.

"You mean Uncle Ben," I corrected. The lights of Florence were a puddle of brightness in the valley below. We were almost there.

"No, Uncle Bart. He said to call him that. He was like a brother to my father, and so—" Pete stopped with a gulp. "Oh," he said. "Oh. I forgot. They made me promise. . . . To say his name will make you sad."

Somehow I managed to get the car off the road and onto the shoulder without hitting anything. There was not much traffic.

"I forgot," Pete whispered. "I made you feel bad."

"No. No. You could never make me feel bad. You've made me better. In fact," I said, "I think I'm completely better now."

Chapter Eleven

NGELO WAS at the desk. I had assumed he would
be; he always was. He was no more surprised to see
me stroll in at two in the morning, accompanied by
a child and a cat, than I was to see him. A British
Butler's demeanor would have been wildly emotional compared to the imperturbability of Angelo.

Yes, of course, he had a room. Had he not said there would
always be a room for me? He didn't ask who Pete was, he
only nodded affably and admired his tastes in reading materials. He spoke with equal affability to Joe and produced
an ingenious makeshift set of sanitary arrangements without
batting an eye.

The child was about to drop with exhaustion and even Joe
looked a little wilted; he had worn himself out howling for

thirty miles. I put them both to bed. Pete was drowsily pleased at being allowed to sleep in his underwear. He had always considered it a frightful waste of time to keep changing clothes. They were both asleep before I closed the door.

I had explained to Pete what he must do in case I didn't come back. Of course I would come back; but just in case . . . When I went downstairs Angelo was back behind the desk. Yes, he knew of an all-night coffee bar. (I felt sure he would.) I took over the desk and a sheet of hotel stationery while he went to get the coffee.

I had almost finished the letter by the time he got back. It was a long letter, but I didn't have to stop to think as I wrote; it was all very clear in my mind. The coffee was strong and black, like the best espresso. I knew I might need an extra jolt of caffeine before morning, although I felt abnormally alert and clearheaded.

I finished writing, put the note in an envelope, and sealed it. "You see," I said. "Another secret letter."

"Ah," said Angelo.

From my pocket I took what was left of my money. I had given most of it to Pete. The remainder came to over a hundred dollars. I handed it to Angelo, along with the letter; and for the first and last time saw his jaw drop in astonished disbelief.

"The money is for you," I said. "The only thing you'll have to pay for is a telephone call to the States. The boy knows the name and the address. If I'm not back here by morning, help him make the call. Keep trying until he gets through. Then take the secret letter to your brother—the policeman."

"Ah," said Angelo.

"It could mean a promotion for him, Angelo. This is a very serious matter—a matter of life and death."

"And the peace of the entire world?"

"Right. I forgot that. Can I trust you?"

Angelo folded the letter and put it in his shirt pocket. He

dropped the wad of lira notes onto the counter and delicately, with a flick of his fingertips, pushed it away. It was the most superbly theatrical gesture I have ever seen in my life.

ii

I DROVE steadily, without haste. The rain had stopped; the clouds were blowing eastward. A star shone bright through a rift in the hills ahead. I wished I could regard it as an omen.

I had known I would go back even before Pete's revelation had torn my world apart as the wind was shredding the storm clouds. David had made the same error about me that I had made about him, and knowing what I now knew, I could understand why he had been so ready to suspect the worst of me. As I reviewed the conversations I had had with him, I realized we had been at cross-purposes from the start, misunderstanding each other's motives, misinterpreting actions and words in the light of our own false preconceptions. It was no coincidence that David was at the villa at this time. He had come for a purpose. He couldn't confide in me because he didn't trust me, and he didn't trust me because I had not told him the one fact that might have changed his mind. How could I tell a stranger what I had tried to hide even from myself?

And now the picture was complete to the last detail. It wasn't like a jigsaw puzzle, made up of fragments meaningless in themselves; it was more like the inlaid roses on the floor of the hall in the villa. Each part was complete—a rose, a leaf, a petal. But the central motif had been missing, the stem to which all the elements were attached. Once I had that, the other pieces formed a perfect pattern. Every ambiguity was resolved, every question answered, even the motive that had eluded me.

The gates were still open, as I had left them. I drove past without slackening speed and pulled off the road at the top of the hill, in the same place where I had parked before. The rain-soaked ground let me pass with little noise as I plodded along the weedy track and climbed the broken wall.

The lights in the stableyard still burned, and as I crept closer I heard the clang of metal on metal. Someone was working in the garage—Alberto, mending the tires of the Mercedes, I assumed. David's window was dark. I didn't expect they'd have taken him to his room but I had planned to have a look. No chance of that now, with Alberto nearby.

I turned and went the long way around, through one garden after another, toward the front of the house.

I'm describing what I did, not how I felt while I was doing it. There are no words for that. The fact that I lost my way is no indication of my state of mind, because I might have done that anyway. The desolation of the abandoned gardens was even worse at night. The boughs moaned as the wind stirred them; the white marble of an armless statue glimmered amid a shroud of strangling vines. Brambles caught at my feet, my hair, my hands. And the walls—walls everywhere, casting shadows deep enough to conceal a dozen enemies, shutting out the normal world, barring the way I had to go. Finally I blundered into a more open space and saw the fallen columns of the little antique temple shining pale in the starlight.

I had to sit down for a few minutes to catch my breath. I tried not to think of the confrontation that lay ahead. I was afraid that if I did, I would turn and run. A soft small voice, the voice of common sense and cowardice, insinuated slyly: You could go back. Go to the police; get help. With what you know now—and other facts, easily obtainable—you can convince them. They'll believe you now. Go. You can slip out the way you came.

Yes, I could probably convince the police—eventually.

Eventually was too far away, eventually was too long. They wouldn't harm David if they thought they could use him as a means of retrieving the child; but once the police cars rolled up to the gate, once they knew for certain that Pete was out of their grasp, David was as good as dead. They had no reason to leave a witness alive. A body could lie hidden in the acres of woodland and rough pasture for months, years, forever.

I got stiffly to my feet. Through the delicate grillework of the final gate I saw the front lawn, a sea of silver-gray streaked with shadows. The fountain was a black mass of monstrous shapes, the pitted metal too rough to catch the starlight. The shrouded windows of the formal reception rooms made the place look abandoned, but the lanterns at the front door shone bright, as if awaiting the return of a belated traveler.

I wondered how they would react if I walked boldly up to the door and knocked. I might come to that in the end. Even if I could get into the house without being seen, my chances of finding David were slim. He could be anywhere, in the villa or out of it. But I wasn't ready to face that door and what lay beyond it. Not yet.

The windows of the villa weren't all dark. One section of the terrace was illumined by a glow of light. It came from Francesca's sitting room. Of course. That's where they would be. Planning their next move, trying to find a way out of the dilemma I had created for them.

I had to cross most of the front of the villa to reach that room, for I was at the wrong end. It was a long walk. I kept to the shadows and tried to move quietly, but my feet made little crunching noises on the gravel.

I went up the stairs and crossed the terrace. The windows were closed. The draperies had been pulled back. Though thin curtains blurred the scene inside, I had no difficulty in recognizing Francesca. She was wearing a long, flowing robe and she sat on the love seat, facing the windows. She was talking to someone. Her hands moved in quick gestures. I

251

couldn't see the other person, only a black-clad arm and a hand, resting on Francesca's shoulder.

She stopped speaking. After a moment she rose, gathering the folds of her robe more closely around her. She moved toward the door, her steps slow and dragging, her shoulders bowed.

The figure of a man came into view. He stood with his back to me, watching Francesca. I had not meant to move but I did, step by slow step, drawn by fascinated horror. I may have made a sound. He may have caught the flicker of movement out of the corner of his eyes. He spun around. I stood full in the light, staring, unable to move.

He came to the doors and threw them open.

"I knew you'd be back, Kathy."

Marveling at the steadiness of my voice, I said, "Hello, Bart."

iii

HE HADN'T changed. Slim as a panther in black slacks and turtleneck, silver eyes gleaming, he was tanned and fit and as incredibly handsome as ever.

I walked into the room. He closed the window behind me. "You don't look surprised, *cara*. I thought you'd swoon with astonishment and joy."

"I never really believed you were dead. Somehow I always knew."

His eyes narrowed with laughter. "Yes, that was your trouble, wasn't it? When I think of those stupid shrinks trying to cure you of your neurotic obsession... Well, I'm sorry about that, darling. I simply couldn't risk telling you the truth."

"Of course you couldn't risk it. What was my sanity compared to your... your what, Bart? Your life? Your freedom? What were you running away from?"

He didn't like my choice of words. His level dark brows drew together. Instead of defending himself, he hit back. "Maybe it was you, Kathy. Did you ever think of that?"

"Often."

It was a simple admission of fact, but to Bart it was something more—an admission of ignorance. He thought I had accepted his devastating, hurting excuse, that I had no suspicion of any other motives. His frown cleared and he said magnanimously, "I might have acted differently if I had known. Why didn't you tell me you were pregnant?"

It was a good thing he had reminded me. That little matter had slipped my mind—and yet it was probably the strongest card in my hand. I said, "I didn't know..." and without willing the movement, stepped back as he started toward me.

He smiled. "You're still afraid of me, aren't you, Kathy? You always were."

"I always was," I said. "You enjoyed that, didn't you?"

"Of course. And so did you. Don't pretend you didn't."

He took me in his arms. A shudder ran through me, and Bart laughed softly. He turned my face up toward his; his fingers were hard, painful. As his mouth covered mine I wondered why it had taken me so long to realize that for Bart a kiss was a demonstration of mastery, not of love.

He let me go with a quick, careless movement that sent me staggering, one hand to my bruised mouth. "That will have to wait," he said. "You've made a pretty mess of things, as usual. Where's the boy?"

"Really, Bart." I pouted prettily. "You make me so mad, you really do. I guess I did go off half-cocked, but damn it. It's your fault. You've been here all along, haven't you? Playing your little tricks, getting me all worked up—"

"I couldn't resist. You're so susceptible, *cara*. Did you like the lingerie?" His smile broadened. "The time you caught me, down by the gate, I almost whisked off my wig and my hump and confronted you. But I wasn't quite ready for that."

"You—you were—"

"The imbecile, yes. You never suspected, did you?"

I ought to have suspected, though. What had Sebastiano said? Lon Chaney, the *Hunchback of Notre Dame*? Bart's roles were always derivative. He was an excellent mimic, but a rotten actor.

I said, "No, I didn't. That was quite a performance."

"Too good a performance," Bart said complacently. "Was it the imbecile you were fleeing tonight? What the hell possessed you to pull a stupid stunt like that?"

"I was running away from Alberto." I let some of my rage and disgust spill out. "Damn you, Bart, I'm not as stupid as you think. That so-called accident of Pete's was pretty clumsy. Alberto shot the dog because I got in the way."

"Alberto? That clod couldn't hit the side of a barn. It was your loving husband who saved your life—and that of his unborn son."

"Thanks," I said.

"Don't be sarcastic, Kathy. It doesn't suit you. So you thought Alberto wanted the kid out of the way?"

"I thought it was Francesca," I admitted.

Bart threw his head back and shouted with laughter. "Francesca? You really have slipped a few cogs, sweetie. Francesca doesn't like the brat; he's too much like his father. I was always the golden boy around here. But she wouldn't... No one would hurt the kid. Where is he?"

"Where is David?"

As soon as I spoke I knew I had blundered. Bart was a wholehearted supporter of the double standard. It was all right for him to have other women, I was expected to tolerate that. But I couldn't even smile warmly at another man without arousing a storm of rage—filthy accusations, even physical violence—but in the latter case, only against the poor devil who had been decent to me. Bart had never struck me.

He didn't have to. He could hurt me a lot worse in other ways.

I had to convince him that I didn't care about David, and pray he didn't know David was anything more than an innocent bystander. Slowly and deliberately I seated myself, leaned back, crossed my legs. He watched me with narrowed eyes. I said casually, "Bart, you always were too impetuous. What was that poor wimp supposed to think when he saw Alberto waving a gun at me? He jumped in, playing hero, and now I suppose you've got him locked up somewhere, bleeding all over the carpet. If you don't explain and apologize and get him out of here before he has time to brood about his bruises, he'll slap an assault charge on you."

"Wimp?" Bart repeated. "How unkind, darling. I thought you had taken a fancy to the man."

I laughed. "He reads Browning," I said.

Bart's head turned. He was looking at himself in the mirror. Smiling at his reflection.

"That might be the best solution," he said. "But I'll let you do the apologizing."

"I'll be damned if I will. You always expect me to—"

"While I fetch my poor little cousin home. Where is he?"

"With the carnival."

"What carnival?"

"The one at Fiesole. I thought it was rather a clever idea," I said defensively. "David knew one of the people—the man who runs the carousel. We were there the other day and Pete loved it. So I left him with . . . what is the man's name? Bartelli, or something like that."

"Clever? It was crazy, my poor demented girl. I do believe you need a few more sessions with the head doctors. As usual, it's my job to clear up the mess. I'll go get the kid and you explain to your boyfriend that his heroics weren't needed. He'll feel a bit of a fool when you tell him the truth, I expect."

"Oh, all right. Where is he?"

"In the storeroom with the rest of his junk." Bart added casually, "He may be in need of repairs. There's some first-aid stuff in the butler's pantry."

"Then get it," I said shortly. "I haven't any idea where to look." My hands were shaking. I jammed them in my pockets.

"You've changed," Bart said, giving me a speculative look. "The little mouse has grown sharp teeth. You know, I think I like you better when you fight back."

"That will have to wait," I said. I knew if he tried to kiss me again I'd do something foolish. "Hurry up, Bart, and let's get this nonsense over with. I want to go to bed."

"So do I, *cara*."

After we had found the first-aid materials, Bart said he'd go up with me and explain the situation to Alberto. "I left him guarding the door," he explained glibly. "Lover boy was frothing at the mouth. I thought we had a crazy man on our hands; had to lock him up."

The story was developing nicely. By now, I thought, Bart probably believes it himself.

Alberto sat on the top step, the rifle beside him, smoking a cigarette. When he saw Bart he snapped to attention, his brutal face doglike in its devotion. Bart spoke to him in Italian; then, turning to me, he said, "I don't suppose you understood. You never were any good at languages. I told him you'd patch up the chap's wounds and explain matters to him. I'll be back in an hour or so, and add my bit, and then we'll get rid of him."

"Why wait? I'll tell him—"

"He can't leave till I get back. I'm taking his bike."

"Why?"

"Because you did the job on those tires, my helpful little

darling. They can't be patched. Now get the hell in there. And be convincing."

They had had the decency to leave him a light, the same battery-operated lamp he used for his work. The light wasn't very bright; the batteries must be running low. In the pallid glow I saw him, lying unmoving on the floor. Bart hadn't bothered to mention that he had decided it was necessary to tie the madman up. For a heart-wrenching moment I thought there might be one other minor detail Bart hadn't bothered to mention, but when I bent over David, he opened one eye and inspected me briefly before closing it again. Only one eye was functional. The other was swollen shut, and the lower part of his face looked lopsided.

I began working on the knots that held his wrists behind his back. The only thing I succeeded in doing was breaking a nail. After a time he said, "Have you come to gloat, or to share my captivity? Not that it's any of my business, but I like to get these things clear in my mind."

"It's more complicated than that." Another nail bent painfully back, and I swore. "But we're on the same side. Pete is okay. They won't find him."

"Then what the hell are you doing here?"

"That's complicated too. You were one of the considerations, however."

"Is that right? I don't know that it makes me feel any better."

The knots were too tight. I went to the door. "Give me your knife," I said to Alberto. "Don't tell me you don't have one, you filthy clot. Knife. Give me—"

"The word," said David, "is *coltello*."

Alberto finally got it through his thick skull. He wasn't thick enough to hand me the knife; he cut the ropes himself, and went out.

257

When I reached for him, David let out a bleat of distress and flapped his hands feebly. "Don't touch me!"

"I can't carry out the plan I had in mind without touching you."

He rolled over and sat up, his back against a steamer trunk. "If you mean what I hope you mean," he mumbled, "go ahead. I'll clench my jaws like a true hero and stifle my groans."

It was an inauspicious occasion for our first embrace. But I needed it, the way an invalid needs medicine. David's lips wiped away the last lingering memory of Bart's kisses and made me whole again. It wasn't until I tasted blood and knew it was his that I pulled away. "It's my fault," I whispered. "If I had confided in you—I wanted to, David, but I was afraid—"

"It wasn't your fault, or mine. It was what somebody once called the general cussedness of things. If I had...What are you looking at me that way for?"

"You have no idea how nice it is to hear someone tell me it isn't my fault."

"Maybe I do. Kathy, I know how lousy this is for you—having to choose between your husband and the child—"

"Lousy? Wait a minute," I said. "Let's get a few things straight. Until about two hours ago I thought Bart was dead. I identified—not his body, there wasn't enough left of it to.... But I saw his wristwatch, melted and blackened, a ring I had given him. When I made a run for it with Pete, I thought Francesca was the one who had tried to kill him."

"How did you...Never mind, it doesn't matter." His one open eye was steady and pitying in the grotesque mask of his face. "You found out he was alive, so you came back. You still—"

"Love him?" Laughter bubbled in my mouth, wild, sick laughter. And then it died. "I hated him. I was glad when

258

he died. That's why I fell apart after the accident, because I was glad, because I had prayed to be rid of him."

iv

THERE WERE other women, right from the beginning. There were his insane fits of rage about other men—not jealousy, but possessiveness. The final blow came when I found out he was dealing drugs. In a way it would have been easier to take if he had used the stuff himself. I could have viewed addiction as a sickness and tried to help him. But he never touched it, except for marijuana now and then. He despised the people who did. He used them, without mercy or compunction.

The night before the accident he was with one of his women. He didn't call, he didn't tell me he wouldn't be home. He came in next morning looking like a cartoon caricature of a cheating husband, even to the lipstick on his collar, and stinking of pot. I blew up. He knew I would. He threw a few things into a suitcase and stormed out of the house. The last thing he said to me was, "You'll be sorry. It's your fault. You never understood me, never tried. . . ."

He was always picking up hitchhikers. It was a way of taking chances, flexing his muscles, playing macho. The body they found, burned beyond recognition, must have been that of some vagrant he had picked up, deliberately choosing someone about his age and size. He must have planned it well in advance and waited for the right weather conditions—it wouldn't take long, not in January in Massachusetts. The storm had been forecast the day before. The schools were closed, there were few cars on the road.

And now I knew why he had done it. I assumed he'd be in trouble sooner or later, with the police or some of his business associates; he'd have no qualms about cheating them if he thought he could get away with it. But that wasn't why he faked his death. A few weeks earlier he had read of the plane crash and he knew that only a small child stood between him and the dignities he had always wanted and had falsely claimed. Il conte Bartolommeo, master of the Morandini estates. They must be worth more than I had supposed. The land itself had considerable value.

When Pete told me that it was Bart who took him from his aunt and uncle, it was like a lightning bolt that illumines a dark landscape. Suddenly I realized that everything could be explained by one simple assumption: that Bart wasn't dead. He stood to profit from Pete's death. He had access to the drugs Pete had been given. It wasn't a ghostly memory that had tormented me, it was Bart himself. He'd been here all along. That assumption even explained Francesca's peculiar behavior. When she equivocated about the child's future, she didn't know herself what Bart planned to do. He'd have brushed her questions aside: "Leave it to me. I'll make the arrangements." She didn't care enough to persist. She didn't suspect him. People believe what they want to believe.

My unexpected arrival forced Bart into premature action. He had been in no hurry before that, he could take his time. Six months, a year, building up the picture of a child tormented into recklessness, driven by grief and "hereditary madness." Sooner or later one of Pete's escapades would have ended fatally, and after a proper period of mourning the new Count Morandini would have assumed his title. There would be no problem with the police, even if his activities in the States had aroused suspicions. His presumed death had closed that file; five thousand miles away and a year later, who would make the connection? At least that's how Bart would reason. He shared that happy human faculty of believing only what he wanted to believe.

He had been prepared to close the file on me, too. When my letters arrived he had probably told Francesca I had no claim—that he had never married me. Even when I showed up at the door she tried to get rid of me, until she got the idea that I was carrying Bart's child. Unconsciously she had already written Pete off. Sickly, psychotic, accident-prone— he would never live to carry on the name. In her mind Bart was already *il conte Morandini*, and the imaginary embryo was the next heir.

What a deadly, disproportionate effect that one seemingly harmless lie had had on everyone involved! Francesca must have been nagging Bart for days to tell me the truth; he must have had a hard time fending her off, thinking up excuses why he couldn't. Matters came to a head when I told Francesca I was going home. "But it would be different if Bart were here," she had said. My decision had forced Bart's hand. He couldn't put Francesca off any longer.

That was what she looked forward to seeing on Friday— the great revelation, the joyful reunion of two lovers. Off we would go for a second honeymoon—with, of course, a proper wardrobe for the signora so she wouldn't disgrace her new family and her elegant husband; and before long the inconvenient holder of the title would disappear. The world is full of dangers—speeding cars, wild animals, poisonous plants. Sometimes unhappy children run away from home. Sometimes they are never found.

v

IT DIDN'T take long to tell. David kept up a monotonous undercurrent of groans and curses as I tended to him, but he listened intently. Finally he said, "That should do it. Don't tell me any more, Kathy, it just makes me mad, and I haven't got time for that. We'd better get the hell out of here before your homicidal husband comes back."

"It's all right. He's going to let you go."

"Say what? He may not be very bright, but—"

"He's bright enough in some ways, but his vanity is so enormous, it leads him to underestimate other people. He thinks I'm still under his spell. I'm supposed to be explaining to you that this has been an embarrassing misunderstanding. You don't know anything about the danger to Pete. You jumped Alberto because you thought he was going to attack me. I have now set you straight on that and told you your services aren't wanted. As soon as Bart gets back..."

My voice trailed off. David was shaking his head, slowly, monotonously. "My dear girl," he said. "My poor, dear, innocent girl."

I covered my face with my hands. "I'm the one who isn't very bright."

"Most people would be in state of catatonic shock after what you've been through tonight. And it isn't easy to accept the fact that someone you once...Gets back from where? Where has he gone?"

"To Fiesole," I said listlessly. "I told him I'd taken Pete there, to one of the carnival people. David, I'm scared. I thought I was so clever, and yet I overlooked so many things I ought to have anticipated. When he gets back, without Pete, he'll be raging. He'll know I lied."

"But it was a brilliant idea, Kathy. Better than you realized. The carnival is moving on tonight; Lucca is their next stop. It will take him hours to track them down and discover Pete isn't with them. That means the only one we have to worry about is Alberto."

I said hopefully, "Didn't they teach you karate or kung fu, or something, in the Secret Service—or Interpol, or whatever organization it is you're with?"

I think the expression on his face was surprise. It was hard to tell. "The only organization I'm with is the University of Colorado. Somebody probably teaches karate, but it isn't obligatory for junior faculty."

"The University of... Aren't you a policeman? Didn't you come here looking for Bart because of his drug dealings?"

David started to laugh, then stopped, touching his lip tenderly. "Talk about a Comedy of Errors," he muttered. "It would be funny if it weren't so catastrophic. I'm not a cop, honey. I wish I were. I'm Uncle Don. The baseball *star*," he added.

"Pete's uncle?" I gasped. "But what—how... I'm sorry, I think my brain has finally given way. David—Don—"

"David is my middle name. And my last name really is Brown. I couldn't change that, because I had to have genuine credentials to show the contessa. I figured she wouldn't remember my sister's maiden name. It's a common name, after all."

"Then Pete's mother was your sister!"

"Yes." His face hardened. "I knew Guido pretty well, too. The last time Pete saw me he was about five, and I had a beard then. He couldn't possibly remember what I looked like. I was in Europe last year, on a grant—I'm on the tail end of it now—when Guido and Amy left Pete with Vera. I met them, for the last time as it turned out, in London later in the fall. I was still in England when I heard about the plane crash. I didn't know Amy and Guido were on the plane till Vera finally tracked me down, and by the time I got home Bart had already gone off with Pete. You can imagine the state Vera was in. She had lost two people she loved—Guido was as close as a brother—and then to have the boy snatched away too, when she was hoping they could keep him... They weren't even allowed to correspond with him. The contessa told them Pete's doctor had recommended a complete break with the past.

"I had gone back to England but I was in touch with Vera, and I didn't like the sound of things. Guido had mentioned his cousin—not that he anticipated trouble from Bart, the subject just happened to come up. He said Bart was a bad

263

lot, mentioned a few unsavory episodes... Well, when I heard it was Bart who had come for Pete I started to wonder, and the more I thought about the situation, the more uneasy I became. So I figured I'd go to Italy and have a look. It took me a while to arrange the necessary references. I really am looking for old diaries, and I had even talked to Guido about looking through his family papers, but I knew that wouldn't cut any ice with the contessa, and I decided, just to be on the safe side, that I wouldn't tell her who I was. She was never particularly fond of the Brown family.

"Even before you arrived and I finally got to see Pete I knew the arrangement wasn't right for him, but I hadn't seen any signs of cruelty or mistreatment that would give me an excuse to intervene. It wasn't until the incident with the dog that I started getting funny ideas. I talked to Rosa, and she told me about the other 'accidents.' And then I really got cold chills."

As he spoke he was rummaging in the boxes. He didn't have to explain what he was looking for.

"And you assumed I was one of the bad guys," I said. That rankled, even though I had made the same error about him.

"Well, you see I knew one fact you didn't know." David lifted a cracked marble lamp base, shook his head, and put it aside. "I knew Bart was alive. In fact, I didn't know he was supposed to be dead. Car fatalities are only too common; the story didn't make the national news. I figured he'd be here, and I even saw him a few times—always at night, driving out in the Mercedes or walking in the garden. I didn't understand why he was keeping a low profile, but I was afraid to ask questions for fear of blowing my cover.

"Then you turned up, and Rosa told me the romantic story of the pregnant, brokenhearted young widow, as it was told to her. It was the first I'd heard of Bart's 'death.' I asked Rosa about the man I had seen; she told me there was nobody else here except Alberto's half-witted assistant. What was I to think? Obviously that your husband had staged his death and that, after a decent interval, you had joined him here. From Guido's caustic comments I gathered Bart might have excellent reasons for wanting to be thought dead. When I realized someone might be planning a fatal accident for Pete, I had no doubt as to who that someone might be."

"But you saw me with Pete. You should have known I—"

He sat back on his haunches. "I didn't want to believe it, Kathy. I didn't think you were actively involved. But I thought you were still in love with your husband, and people in love don't always have good judgment. If you cared that much about him you might follow his instructions blindly, without letting nasty suspicions enter your mind. I knew things were coming to a head when the contessa gave me the bum's rush, and when I found you in the garage I was afraid the final accident was in progress—that you were taking the kid to Bart. It wasn't until Alberto appeared and you cussed us both out that the light dawned. Forgive me?"

"I guess I'll have to, since you're nobly overlooking my refusal to trust you. What are you doing?"

He had amassed a collection of small heavy articles, ranging from a brass doorknob to a miniature marble bust of some bearded dignitary. "Defensive weapons," he said, loading up his pockets.

"I thought you were looking for something you could use as a club or a—"

"Club? Honey, if I found a saber I wouldn't use it. I don't intend to get within arm's reach of that gorilla. He has already beaten the you-know-what out of me once tonight. And don't suggest any clever little schemes like luring him in and bashing him over the head. It would take a two-by-four to even stagger him. I know; I tried it."

"Then what—"

David pulled himself to his feet, leaning heavily on the table. I could see he had delayed this move as long as possible. "We are going to move furniture," he said. "I don't think he'll bother us unless we try to open the door, but let's keep it quiet, okay?"

It was impossible to be quiet. We had to push some of the larger objects, such as a massive mahogany sideboard, and they made loud screeches on the rough floor. If I had been Alberto, I'd have been curious. Luckily he lacked that characteristic. Dull obedience and a few flashes of innovative sadism were his whole repertoire. When we finished it would have taken a stronger man than Alberto to force the door open. A ten-foot-high barrier of furniture and heavy boxes barred the way.

"That should do it," David said, holding his heaving sides. "Let's go. Pray it didn't occur to them to lock the other door."

Crossing the room was an exercise in mountaineering—over boxes, under tables, between barrels and trunks. Alberto must have landed a few blows above and below the belt; David kept catching his breath and emitting eloquent nineteenth-century curses. Commiseration would have been a waste of time. He would certainly be in worse shape if Bart got hold of him again.

The door wasn't locked. Instead of opening it David held up the lamp, which he had brought with him, and studied me with sober concern. "Are you all right, Kathy?"

"Whatever happens," I said, "it's been worth it."

"Don't get mushy." He smiled, and brushed my tangled hair back from my forehead, his fingers lingering. "We'd better figure out where we're going before we rush out into the night. I don't know what is outside that door; I never came this way. What's the quickest route out of here?"

"There isn't any quick way out. I only hope I can remember how I came before. It's either the kitchen door or the front entrance, David. I'm not sure where the other exits are, and

266

if they're locked we could find ourselves in a blind alley. Alberto's not the only one we have to worry about. Emilia is around somewhere, and so is Francesca; Rosa and the *tuttofare* have probably been told you're a desperate criminal; if either spots us, she might sound the alarm. The front door may be our best bet. At least I know how to unlock it."

"Okay. Then into the gardens—we can play hide and seek there indefinitely if we have to—"

"Only if we have to. I left my car off the road at the top of the hill. If we can reach it, we're home free."

"Good." His hand closed gently over my shoulder. "One heroic rescue per night is all I'm entitled to, Kathy. If we're separated, don't wait for me. Get out."

Darkening bruises and shadows made a caricature of his face, which had never been much to look at even at its best. At that moment it seemed more beautiful to me than the classic features of Michelangelo's masterpiece.

"The same goes for you," I said.

"Right. 'Neck by neck, stride by stride, never changing our pace.... Not a word to each other....'" He switched off the lamp.

We stood in darkness till our eyes adjusted. Gradually the shapes of the windows became visible, half hidden by piled-up boxes, and lighter than I would have liked. It was pitch-dark where we stood and I heard, rather than saw, David open the door.

"Stairs," I whispered.

"How many?"

"Damned if I know."

He let out a soft breath of laughter.

I sympathized with his decision not to use the lamp, but as we blundered through the warren of rooms and passage-ways I wondered if any prisoners in fact or fiction had ever carried out such a farcical escape. We barked our shins on sharp edges of furniture and tripped over chairs; ran into

267

door frames and groped for openings. Even in daylight I had been bewildered by the absence of any coherent plan in this part of the house.

After David had fallen headlong across a low iron bed in one of the maids' rooms, producing a hideous howl of rusted springs, he switched on the lamp. He was grinning like an idiot, and if he was crazy, so was I; I wanted to laugh too. This wasn't James Bond or Jane Eyre, it was the Marx Brothers.

I knew why I felt so ridiculously lighthearted. It was David. Maybe Browning had a word for him. The only ones that came to my mind were totally inadequate.

"I'm afraid to get up," he said in a low voice. "Do you think there's something alive under here? Where the hell are we?"

I looked around the room. It was exactly like a dozen others on that corridor, but at least I knew which corridor it was. "I picked the wrong door. The one we want must be farther along. It leads to another storeroom, and that opens into a big room with windows overlooking the front, and from there you go into the corridor where Pete's room is. And from that—"

"I've got it." He heaved himself off the bed, amid another screech of rusted metal. "We'll have to use the lamp. I don't mind telling people I've been beaten and tortured, but I'll be damned if I want to admit I broke a leg tripping over a chamber pot."

It was easier with the light. David switched it off again when we reached the passageway stretching along the front of the house. From there the route was known to both of us.

As we passed the door of Pete's room David reached for my hand and squeezed it, and I knew he was thinking the same thing I was. Whatever became of us, the boy would never be locked in that room again. I had accomplished that much, at any rate. If I didn't return to the Grande Albergo, my letter would go to the police, and my disappearance would confirm the accusations I had made. From what David had told me, I felt certain Pete's aunt and uncle would hurry to be with him. He would be all right now. I only hoped the same could be said of us.

Down the stairs to the second floor, to lighted corridors at last. Not a sound broke the stillness. Francesca must have gone to bed. David gave me the lamp. His right hand went to the pocket of his jeans, where his "defensive weapons" made unseemly lumps. Down, farther down, to the wide landing. David stopped and looked over the balustrade. The bulbs in the chandelier shone on the polished marble of the floor of the hall, and reflected in the polished brass of door handle, bolt and chain.

"The door is unlocked, David! We can—"

"Sssh." His finger touched my lips.

Then I heard it too—a far-off rumble that rose to a roar and ended in a crash and a crunch of stone. David abandoned his favorite poets for a more emphatic comment. "Son of a bitch! He's back. I'd know the sound of that motor anywhere. I wonder what—"

Of course Bart would use the front door. Only tradesmen and servants went to the back. I heard the furious thud of his feet crossing the terrace; then the heavy oak panel exploded open. We had barely time to retreat a few steps, out of the light, but if he had looked up he would have seen us. David had taken the brass doorknob from his pocket. His fingers curled around it and I thought insanely, "Fast ball."

Bart didn't look up or pause. He was in a towering rage. Without stopping to close the door, he ran across the hall and disappeared from sight under the stairs. Another door crashed open.

"Run for it," David said, taking my hand.

We didn't have much time. Bart would be up the back stairs like a bullet, and when he found the door was blocked he would really blow up. He wouldn't waste time forcing it, he was smart enough to know what we had done. He must know every inch of the house, every door, every room.

Illogical though it was, I almost hated to leave the house. The front terrace and stairs were so open, so well lighted; and it was such a long way to the car. Then I saw the motorcycle lying on its side at the bottom of the stairs.

We made a bad mistake then. But the temptation was almost irresistible—fast transportation, practically at our feet. If I knew Bart, he had left the gates open. And there was no other functioning vehicle in the place.

David righted the bike and mounted. I jumped on behind, wrapping my arms around his waist. His foot hit the pedal; the still-warm engine caught instantly. The roar was loud enough to alert everyone for miles around.

We hadn't gone ten feet when I felt the machine lurch and slide. There was something wrong with the steering. Either it had been damaged when Bart threw it down or the furious pace he had set along the rutted road had done the job. We took the turn too wide, branches battering our heads, and narrowly missed the trunk of a tree. I missed it; David's knee didn't and the jar threw him even farther off balance. We slid off the drive at an angle, straight at the trees. At the last second David did the only thing possible—he let himself fall sideways, pulling me with him. We hit the ground, the bike hit a tree trunk and landed on top of us. By the time we had untangled ourselves I knew it was too late. A flashlight beam cut through the branches over our heads, and when David tried to stand, his knee gave way. He dropped down onto his side. "Run," he gasped.

I suppose I might have tried. The shrubs were thick and the shadows were dark. But they could have tracked me by the sounds I made, and it was a long way to the gate. The crack of a rifle and the whistle of a bullet through the boughs made up my mind for me. Twigs and pine needles showered down onto my head.

"All right, you've had your little run," Bart said. "I hope you enjoyed the exercise." He clamped a hand over my arm and yanked me to my feet.

The rifle was in his other hand. Alberto held the flashlight. In the same cool, pleased voice Bart went on, "You little bitch. I know you have the tastes of a peasant, but I didn't think you were that low. You must have been desperate to shack up with him."

I looked at David, blinking foolishly at the light shining in his eyes. It would have been hard to find a more disreputable specimen of manhood. "You're right," I said. "You are absolutely right, Bart. I was desperate."

He wasn't quite sure how to take that. The irony eluded him, but he must have sensed some undercurrent. His fingers tightened till I had to bite my lip to keep from crying out.

We started back to the villa. Bart kept jerking and shaking me, like a child venting his anger on a stuffed toy. It was stupid, and it hurt. But I was more concerned about David, stumbling behind us. Once I heard a slither and a gasp, and knew he had fallen. Alberto laughed.

When we reached the open space in front of the fountain Bart stopped. I had expected he would take us inside, but as he began arranging his tableau, pushing me down to kneel at his feet, ordering David and Alberto to take up a position nearby, I understood. Setting: a villa near Florence. I wondered how Bart had cast himself, as hero or villain. He wouldn't care, so long as he had the leading role.

I tried to get up. He pushed me down. "Where's the boy?"

"I told you. With the carnival."

"You rotten little liar, I looked for him there."

"Then you didn't look hard enough or ask the right people. I didn't exactly advertise his presence."

The faintest shadow of uncertainty crossed his face. That was why he had returned earlier than we had expected. He hadn't looked hard enough. Patience was never one of his virtues, and his arrogant manners wouldn't go over too well with the independent carnival people. No doubt he had started giving orders and they had told him what he could do with them.

"That won't wash, Kathy," he said. "How can I trust you when you were ready to betray me? How long have you known this—this scarecrow?"

"I never met him until I came here. That's the truth, Bart."

"But you preferred him to your husband. What lies have you told him about me? What *were* you doing, if you weren't running off with your lover?"

Unfortunately, that was the difficulty. Either I was running off with a lover or trying to escape a killer. I couldn't deny one accusation without admitting the other. I tried to think of a third possibility, but there wasn't an idea left in my head.

David cleared his throat. "I'd like to say something."

"The only information I want is the location of the boy."

"I don't know where he is. If I did know, I wouldn't tell you."

This time I made it to my feet, shaking my head frantically at David. Neither he nor Bart paid the slightest attention to me.

"Why not?" Bart asked softly.

"Let's not fool around, okay? You're a sensible man; you know when it's time to retreat and regroup. The police have been informed that you're here. They know all about your background and they know what you were trying to do to the child. They could arrive at any minute. If you make tracks right now, you stand a good chance of getting away."

It was a sensible, reasonable speech. If he had been dealing with a sensible, reasonable man, it might have had the desired effect. Bart's reaction was to swing the rifle to his shoulder.

David's eyes widened, more in surprise than in fear; it had never occurred to him that Bart would do anything so stupid as commit deliberate murder in front of two witnesses. I wasn't surprised. David's speech had threatened Bart's most cherished images of himself: the great lover, the brilliant schemer. As Bart's finger tightened on the trigger I grabbed the barrel of the rifle. The bullet hit the ground. The recoil sent me sprawling, my ears ringing with the blast of the explosion.

When I got my eyes back in focus I saw that Bart was standing quite still, the rifle in one hand. Alberto had David in a wrestler's grip. All three were looking up, toward the top of the staircase.

The light behind her left her face in shadow and outlined her slender, erect form. The sweeping folds of her robe and the fur-trimmed neckline and the flowing sleeves gave her the look of a character in some dark Renaissance melodrama—the duchess pronouncing sentence on the traitors, the princess awaiting the return of her lover from the war. Emilia, all in black, hovering, might have played the malevolent duenna or housekeeper, or a witch crying doom on the ancient manor.

"Go back inside, Francesca," Bart said. He spoke English. I suppose his adopted language came easier and more naturally by now. Or perhaps he wanted me to know he was still in command.

"You have lost your senses," she said in the same language. "No matter what she has done, you must not risk your child."

"How do I know it's mine?" demanded my devoted husband. "She's had the scarecrow and the shrink since she arrived; the latest of a long list, I'm sure."

"You are obscene," Francesca said frostily.

273

Before she could continue, Emilia sidled forward and tugged at her sleeve. I didn't understand the hissing, hostile speech, but Bart did; a slow, unpleasant smile lifted the corners of his mouth. "Well, well. Who would have thought it? Guess what, my honorable little wife. Emilia says you aren't pregnant after all. What do you say?"

"Oh, what difference does it make?" I said impatiently.

Francesca started. "Is it a lie?" Her voice was not as steady as usual.

"You see, it does make a difference," Bart said, showing his teeth. "You don't suppose Francesca tolerated you for your own sweet sake, do you? She—"

"She'll stand by and watch you commit two murders?" I cut in. "What lie did you tell her to explain why I took Pete away tonight? She doesn't know you want him dead, that you tried—"

He reached for me. I had expected a blow, and tried to duck; instead of striking he caught me and pulled me against him, his hand spreading over my mouth and throat in a grip so agonizingly painful I couldn't move. David, who had stood meek and limp in Alberto's grip, brought his head sharply back. The chauffeur let out a yell and released his hold, clasping both hands over his nose. David started toward us.

"Stop right there," Bart said. "I'll snap her neck if you take one more step."

Francesca stood unmoving, aloof as a spectator at a play she found faintly disgusting. "Go back inside," Bart said. "I'll deal with this. It's my right—my honor that has been sullied." Still she didn't move. Bart's voice took on a softer, wheedling note. "She lied to you, *carissima*. You wouldn't take the word of a liar, a stranger, against mine?"

He knew he had won. His caressing voice poorly veiled the note of confident triumph. His hand tightened; fingers and thumb had settled into points of pressure against nerves

274

and arteries. They contracted and relaxed, rhythmically, sensuously, and spots danced in front of my eyes.

Francesca straightened. She spoke slowly, articulating every word with such precision that even I understood.

"Alberto. The rifle. Take it from him. Bring it to me."

The chauffeur's heavy body swayed, forward and back, as if invisible hands were tugging at him from two different directions. Emilia let out a long, keening cry. That was the only sign of emotion—I almost said of humanity—either gave. Emilia was suddenly silent. Alberto started walking toward Bart.

Bart was even slower to react. He cried out to Alberto in Italian, stumbling over the words. His voice was high with disbelief. Alberto kept walking. Bart backed away. I was an impediment now; he tossed me aside, carelessly, without malice for once, as he might have brushed an object out of his way. Again I measured my full length on the gravel. I didn't even notice the pain, I was too stupefied. David raised me to my feet and we clung together, like children seeing monsters in the dark.

Bart's voice had lost all its trained beauty. It was a hoarse, breathless monotone. He appealed to Francesca, who stood like a marble statue, to Alberto, who plodded steadily forward, to Emilia... astonishingly, horribly, to me. "Kathy, tell her you lied, goddamn you, tell her, you got me into this, it's all your fault...."

It was fitting that those were the last words I heard him speak. He had reached the steps and was backing up them, stumbling, his eyes fixed on Alberto. The chauffeur started up after him. His hand went out.

Bart raised the weapon. The muzzle could not have been more than a foot from Alberto's chest when he pulled the trigger.

Dark liquid spattered against the balustrade. The impact

275

flung Alberto back, then forward, as his body rebounded from the stone railing. He fell, his arm still extended. Only the stiffened hand touched Bart, but it was enough to make him lose his footing. If he had dropped the gun and caught the balustrade he might have saved himself. Still clutching it, he toppled backward, and his sleek black head struck the sharp edge of one of the stone steps.

The dull, soggy sound seemed to go on echoing for hours. It was the only sound, the only movement; we were all characters in some unbelievable black farce, frozen in the final tableau as the curtain fell. The only figure of genuine tragedy was the woman who stood silent and motionless at the head of the stairs. She was a little more, and a little less, than human at that moment—the personification of some cold abstraction such as Justice or Retribution. For a moment she stood looking down. Then she turned and walked steadily into the house.

It was Emilia who crawled down the stairs, her face slobbered with tears, to raise, not her husband, but mine, into her arms, and cradle his head against her breast. His eyes were open. They were tarnished and muddy, like pools of stagnant water.

I've often wondered if Francesca knew what would happen when she gave her servant his final order. She must have realized Bart would never endure such a challenge to his authority, especially in the house where he had always been master. I wonder, too, what intangible evidence tipped the scales in my favor. I'd like to think it had something to do with her feelings for me. Not love or liking or fondness, but something more important, at least to me. What was it she said? "I respect those qualities, if I do not admire them."

I will never know. I never saw her again. She never answered my letters. All I can do for her is respect her wish to be left alone.

* * *

David and I limped down the drive toward the gate. He was hobbling like a rheumatic old man and I was so exhausted every step was a supreme effort. Neither of us spoke. As David said later, it would have been impossible to invent dialogue that wouldn't have sounded banal and anticlimactic.

The gates were open, as Bart had left them. I said, "Why don't you wait here? I'll get the car."

"I accept," David said promptly. "Old baseball injury," he added, indicating the wounded knee.

I smiled feebly. But as I started forward he caught my hand. "Kathy," he said. "Don't be long."

The mountaintops were black against the dawn. I said, "'There's the grey beginning....I know my own way back. Don't fear me!'"

I heard his laughter, so different from that other laughter, as I started up the hill toward the sunrise.

BESTSELLING BOOKS FROM TOR

☐ 58725-1   *Gardens of Stone* by Nicholas Proffitt $3.95
  58726-X   Canada $4.50

☐ 51650-8   *Incarnate* by Ramsey Campbell $3.95
  51651-6   Canada $4.50

☐ 51050-X   *Kahawa* by Donald E. Westlake $3.95
  51051-8   Canada $4.50

☐ 52750-X   *A Manhattan Ghost Story* by T.M. Wright
                                                    $3.95
  52751-8   Canada $4.50

☐ 52191-9   *Ikon* by Graham Masterton $3.95
  52192-7   Canada $4.50

☐ 54550-8   *Prince Ombra* by Roderick MacLeish $3.50
  54551-6   Canada $3.95

☐ 50284-1   *The Vietnam Legacy* by Brian Freemantle
                                                    $3.50
  50285-X   Canada $3.95

☐ 50487-9   *Siskiyou* by Richard Hoyt $3.50
  50488-7   Canada $3.95

Buy them at your local bookstore or use this handy coupon:
Clip and mail this page with your order

TOR BOOKS—Reader Service Dept.
P.O. Box 690, Rockville Centre, N.Y. 11571

Please send me the book(s) I have checked above. I am enclosing
$_____ (please add $1.00 to cover postage and handling).
Send check or money order only—no cash or C.O.D.'s.

Mr./Mrs./Miss _____

Address _____.

City _____ State/Zip _____

Please allow six weeks for delivery. Prices subject to change without
notice.

MORE BESTSELLERS FROM TOR

☐ 58827-4 *Cry Havoc* by Barry Sadler $3.50
    58828-2   Canada $3.95

☐ 51025-9 *Designated Hitter* by Walter Wager $3.50
    51026-7   Canada $3.95

☐ 51600-1 *The Inheritor* by Marion Zimmer Bradley $3.50
    51601-X   Canada $3.95

☐ 50282-5 *The Kremlin Connection* by Jonathan Evans $3.95
    50283-3   Canada $4.50

☐ 58250-0 *The Lost American* by Brian Freemantle $3.50
    58251-9   Canada $3.95

☐ 58825-8 *Phu Nham* by Barry Sadler $3.50
    58826-6   Canada $3.95

☐ 58552-6 *Wake in Darkness* by Donald E. McQuinn $3.95
    58553-4   Canada $4.50

☐ 50279-5 *The Solitary Man* by Jonathan Evans $3.95
    50280-9   Canada $4.50

☐ 51858-6 *Shadoweyes* by Kathryn Ptacek $3.50
    51859-4   Canada $3.95

☐ 52543-4 *Cast a Cold Eye* by Alan Ryan $3.95
    52544-2   Canada $4.50

☐ 52193-5 *The Pariah* by Graham Masterton $3.50
    52194-3   Canada $3.95

Buy them at your local bookstore or use this handy coupon:
Clip and mail this page with your order

TOR BOOKS—Reader Service Dept.
P.O. Box 690, Rockville Centre, N.Y. 11571

**Please send me the book(s) I have checked above. I am enclosing
$_____ (please add $1.00 to cover postage and handling).
Send check or money order only—no cash or C.O.D.'s.**

Mr./Mrs./Miss _____

Address _____

City _____ State/Zip _____

**Please allow six weeks for delivery. Prices subject to change without
notice.**